SYLVIE HATED THE COUNTDOWN TO A NEW YEAR. ESPECIALLY IN A CROWD OF COUPLES.

Everybody would be kissing in nine seconds and she was standing there with her third glass of champagne. Glancing around the room, Sylvie locked eyes with the only other guy who looked as though he wanted to be anywhere but there.

Nine!

That man is fine! she thought as she set her empty glass on the edge of a table. Maybe she was tipsy and that's why she started walking toward Mr. Sex Appeal.

Eight!

Sylvie heard the voice of reason telling her to stop, pump her breaks, and don't head over to this stranger. It wasn't as if she had a right to expect a midnight kiss from him. But her feet wouldn't stop, especially when their eyes met.

His golden-brown eyes reminded her of warm honey, and his slow once-over heated her body like a rocket ready to explode. Maybe he wanted this kiss as much as she needed it.

Also by Cheris Hodges

Just Can't Get Enough
Let's Get It On
More Than He Can Handle
Betting on Love
No Other Lover Will Do
His Sexy Bad Habit
Too Hot for TV
Recipe for Desire
Forces of Nature
Love After War
Rumor Has It
I Heard a Rumor
Deadly Rumors
Strategic Seduction

Published by Kensington Publishing Corp.

Tempted at Midnight

CHERIS HODGES

Kensington Publishing Corp.

www.kensingtonbooks.com

DAFINA BOOKS are published by

Kensington Publishing Corp.
119 West 40th Street
New York, NY 10018

All Kensington Titles, Imprints, and Distributed Lines are available at special quantity discounts for bulk purchases for sales promotions, premiums, fund-raising, and educational or institutional use. Special book excerpts or customized printings can also be created to fit specific needs. For details, write or phone the office of the Kensington special sales manager: Kensington Publishing Corp., 119 West 40th Street, New York, NY 10018, Attn: Special Sales Department, Phone: 1-800-221-2647.

Dafina and the Dafina logo Reg. U.S. Pat. & TM Off.

ISBN-13: 978-1-4967-2382-6
ISBN-10: 1-4967-2382-1
First Kensington Mass Market Edition: October 2019

ISBN-13: 978-1-4967-2383-3 (ebook)
ISBN-10: 1-4967-2383-X (ebook)

10 9 8 7 6 5 4 3 2 1

Printed in the United States of America

Acknowledgments

Writing can be a lonely gig, and I wouldn't be anywhere without my family and my tribe of sister friend writers who have always had my back. So, to my Mom and Dad, my big sister, Adrienne, and my big brother, Timothy, thank you for believing in a little girl's dream.

To my tribe of sister writer friends—Farrah Rochon, KD King, Carla Fredd, Adrienne Mishel, Sharina Harris, Synithia Williams, Piper G. Huguley, Seressia Glass, K.M. Jackson, Kaia Danielle, Jamie Wesley, Vanessa Riley, Jacki C. Kelly, Phyllis Bourne, Deborah Fletcher Mello, Carolyn Hector Hall, LaShon Hill, Sharon C. Cooper, Kianna Alexander—thank you for the love, the support, and kicks in the butt when needed!

To all the readers who continue to read my books and allow me a little time in their lives, thank you. Without you, there is no me.

Prologue

Sylvia Elaine Gates knew two things for sure. She had a thriving design business and enough money in her account to pay for the forty thousand dollars' worth of Christmas decorations she needed to create a winter wonderland at Ella Kaye's house. The local actress had commissioned SG Designs to decorate her house for the holidays. Despite the argument she and her partner, Amanda West, had had about all of the holiday jobs they'd committed to, Sylvie had added this one because she loved Ella Kaye's style. The fact that her favorite actress noticed her work and wanted her to design her holiday theme left her beyond proud.

Amanda had called her selfish and told her that overextending the company with all of these decorating jobs was more about ego than the company's expansion.

And expanding the company had been another argument the women were having on a daily basis. With their headquarters now in Atlanta, Sylvie wanted to open an office in New Orleans, her hometown, and dedicate it to the memory of her father. She knew of a couple of designers in the Big Easy who would be happy to work for her. Amanda thought the move was so that she could show people who doubted her how successful she was.

Standing in the middle of a shop, holding a declined bank card, made her feel like anything but a success.

"Can you try it again?" she whispered to the clerk.

"Sure. We have been having issues with the system today." The clerk smiled and Sylvie felt as if she had said that just to spare her feelings.

Sylvie held her breath, hoping the card would go through this time. But when her phone vibrated in her pocket, she'd gotten her answer as to why she was having these issues.

Pulling the phone out, she read Amanda's text message.

I've decided to end our partnership and I've taken my investment from the corporate account. Good luck in your future endeavors.

"Fucking bitch!" Sylvie exclaimed, then placed her hand over her mouth when the clerk eyed her with extra attitude. Sylvie held up her hand. "That was not directed at you." She reached into her purse and pulled out her personal credit card. "Just put it on here."

"Is it going to work?"

Now Sylvie could understand little sister getting tired of running a card with no money on it, but could she put a little bit of respect out there? "Yes, it will." Of course, once this purchase went through, she was going to be in more debt than she wanted to think about. Closing her eyes, she imagined wrapping her hands around Amanda's throat and squeezing until she lost her breath for about three minutes. She didn't want to kill her, just make her as uncomfortable as she felt right now.

"Thank you, Miss Gates," the clerk said as she handed Sylvie her credit card back.

Sylvie nodded and waited for a couple of workers to load her items in the SGD van. She put on a brave face as she drove to Ella's, but in the back of her mind, all she could think about were the fifteen projects that she and Amanda had on the schedule.

It was way too late to call people and cancel. She would be ruined. In Atlanta, reputation is everything. And the way people love to spill tea, the first time Sylvie canceled a job, everyone would know.

Then there was her career-making project, the remodel of Jordan Industries—the premier African American cosmetics company. The business was going to be featured in a few national magazines, and the owners wanted to update the company's image. When she'd gotten the call from the CEO's assistant, she was floored. Growing up, Saturday mornings meant going to the mall and getting the latest Yvonne red lipstick. According to her mother, every woman should have the perfect tube of red lipstick. Obviously, her father agreed. Because when her mother painted her lips with a Jordan cosmetics product, her father always smiled. And later on in the evening, Sylvie always heard what she called kissy noises.

Working for JI would give her a chance to find out something she'd been wondering about for years. What happened to the Yvonne red lipstick?

Erik Jordan wished he could hide out in the lab down on the bottom floor of Jordan Industries; instead he was walking into a meeting with the board of directors, tasked with explaining the unexplainable—the arrest of his father, the founder of the company. Simon Jordan had been stealing from the company for years. Had he not been pushing the sale of Jordan Industries so hard, Erik may have never discovered his dad's wrongdoing. The last thing Erik wanted was to see someone else run the company. It had always been a source of pride to be a member of the family who made women of color look more beautiful. When he found out the chemistry that went into creating makeup, he dove in feetfirst.

Though he wasn't an artist like his little brother, Logan, Erik knew he created masterpieces.

Times had changed and there were now multiple companies catering to black women when it came to makeup. Many times Erik and Simon bumped heads about Jordan Industries being behind the times. His father felt as if the company could just rest on its history, but Erik knew enough about marketing and social media to know that wasn't going to work. People were beginning call their cosmetics "grandma makeup."

Last year, though, Erik designed a line that brought the company into the twenty-first century. It had been one of the most profitable lines in recent history. When he'd approached his father about doing another line similar to that one, as well as some skin-care products, Simon said the money wasn't there. Erik didn't believe it, and as a board member, he started looking into the financial health of the company.

When he found two sets of books and unexplained losses, he took the information to the board. Once the investigation started, Simon called his son a traitor and told him they'd never be able to prove a thing. Erik had been smart enough to install cameras in his father's office and caught him trying to destroy evidence two nights ago.

By the grace of God, Simon's arrest hadn't made headlines yet, but it was only a matter of time before the scandal was picked up by the media.

Heading into the building, Erik ignored the whispers about his father's arrest. When the receptionist stopped him, Erik sighed. "Yes, Diane?"

"The board is in the main conference room." She flipped her blond weave. "Now, I have a question."

He eyed her and counted to five in his head. "What is it?"

"Are we going to shut down now that Mr. Jordan is in jail?"

"Tell everybody to calm down. We're not shutting down, because one person doesn't make this company."

"Why do you think I'm—"

"Let's not go there, okay."

Diane grinned. Her reputation as an office gossip was well earned. Erik winked and smiled at her, then headed to the conference room, ready to pay for the sins of his father.

Standing outside the room, he gripped the door handle and counted to ten. He was going to miss working for JI. But he was sure the last thing the board wanted was a Jordan anywhere near the company.

The board actually applauded when Erik walked in to the conference room.

Chairman of the board Jack Taylor stood up and walked over to Erik. "Took some balls to stand up against your father and do the right thing."

Erik shrugged. "I did what was right for the company. This is bigger than my father and my family." He pointed around the room. "All of you and our stockholders deserve better."

Louise Parker cleared her throat. "What you did had to have been hard. Even if it was the proper thing to do. But we need people in leadership positions who will make hard choices when those are the only choices to make. We're going to be in that position real soon."

"And people we can trust to restore our financial health." Jack held up a copy of the true financial state of the company. "We don't want to sell, but if we can't turn things around, then we won't have much of a choice."

Erik gritted his teeth. Despite all their praise for him turning Simon in, he knew the next thing was probably going to be these people asking for his resignation. "When we start our national search for a new CEO, we need to make sure our new CEO is financially responsible and—"

"And we know *you* will be." Jack smiled. "Erik, you have what it takes to save this company."

"I make the products. I'm not—"

Graham Shaw raised his hand. "Jordans built this company, and to keep up appearances, we need a Jordan at the helm or our only choice will be to sell. Erik, I'm not trying to pressure you, but when the truth comes out about your father, we're going to need some good PR."

Erik knew Shaw was right. But he hadn't

wanted to be the man in charge. All he wanted to do was save the company and keep creating products that women loved. CEO? But if he had to do it to keep the company from being sold, then he would.

"We'll make the announcement on the second of January. New Year, new direction," Jack said with a nod.

"We haven't voted yet or officially removed our current CEO." Erik folded his arms across his broad chest.

"Erik, if we have any chance of saving this company, you are going to have to spearhead the charge. We took a straw vote and you're in." Jack leaned back on his heels. "Think about a new future, a new era for Jordan Industries."

Erik sighed. He'd expected that he'd be giving his resignation, but he'd been promoted. Now he just had to figure out how he was going to save the company and his family.

Over the next two weeks, Erik realized that his PR team was underpaid. There had only been one news brief about Simon's arrest. Granted, it was the holiday season and good news ruled the airwaves.

But there would be no merry Christmas for the Jordan family. When Erik finally spoke to his mother, she told him in no uncertain terms that neither he nor Logan were welcome in the house for the holiday.

"You've betrayed your father for a taste of power."

"Dad brought this on himself."

"You always thought you knew everything, son. I hope you know this little coup of yours won't stand." And with that she ended the call.

Seconds later, Logan called. "You talked to our mother?"

"Yeah. I'm a bastard and not welcome for Christmas."

"Good, come to Paris. I have a show and Olivia's coming . . ."

"Not a third wheel. Besides, this banishment will give me a chance to figure out how to bring the company back from the brink of destruction."

"Ah, you're going to be that guy."

"What guy is that?"

"Mr. All Work, All the Time."

"I don't think so, but I can't ignore the fucked-up situation Dad left the company in."

"Rome wasn't built on Christmas Day."

"Well, this ain't Rome."

"All right, I'll give you Christmas, but I'm hosting a New Year's Eve gala in Atlanta and you have to be there or I'm going to kick your workaholic ass."

Erik sighed. "First of all, you got one more time to threaten me. What's up with all the parties, though?"

"Because life is a celebration. And I'm going to ask Olivia to marry me."

Erik grunted. He hadn't been a party boy for years. There was a time when he'd been photographed with some of the most beautiful women in the world and hunted supermodels for sport. Of course, it was all in fun and consensual. Erik loved photo shoots where he'd get to see his products on the most beautiful women in the world.

Some of them ended up smearing their makeup all over his thousand-thread-count Egyptian-cotton sheets.

For the most part, Erik had been satisfied with loving them and leaving them. No hurt feelings, no stalker chicks in the background. He even had a girl call him the real MVP once—most valuable penis. Not that he was looking to settle down and get married anytime soon; Erik was starting to enjoy the quiet life and the booty call on his terms.

Logan, on the other hand, was head over heels in love with this girlfriend and muse, Olivia Brown. Erik wasn't big on romance, but Olivia and Logan were the kind of couple who inspired rom-com movies. If anyone had a soul mate, it was Logan. He and Olivia fit perfectly.

Erik didn't see himself connecting with someone on that level. Love was more work than he planned to put in for something that might not last. "I'll be there, only because you're surprising Liv."

"I guess I'll accept that. And maybe Mom will come around when she realizes how wrong Dad is."

Erik didn't want to say it out loud, but what if their mother was involved too? "Maybe," he said after a beat.

Logan muttered something in French and then told Erik he had to go. Closing his eyes, Erik knew things would get a whole lot worse before they got better.

Chapter 1

Ten!

Sylvie hated the countdown to a New Year. Especially in a crowd of couples. Everybody would be kissing in nine seconds and she was standing there with her third glass of champagne. Sylvie didn't even like champagne, but as the room celebrated the engagement of her best friend, Olivia Brown, and her man, LJ, she had to drink the swill. The ballroom was buzzing with excitement, though. Everyone wanted a look at Olivia's ring and the portrait LJ, a renowned artist who'd just finished a family portrait for the former first family, had painted of his future wife. It was beautiful. The night was romantic. Sylvie was bored.

Glancing around the room, she locked eyes with the only other guy who looked as though he wanted to be anywhere but there.

Nine!

That man is fine! she thought as she set her empty glass on the edge of a table. Maybe she was tipsy and that's why she started walking toward Mr. Sex Appeal.

Eight!

Sylvie heard the voice of reason telling her to stop, pump her breaks, and don't head over to this stranger. It wasn't as if she had a right to expect a midnight kiss from him. But her feet wouldn't stop, especially when their eyes met.

His golden-brown eyes reminded her of warm honey, and his slow once-over heated her body like a rocket ready to explode. Maybe he wanted this kiss as much as she needed it.

Seven!

His lips were delectable looking. Full. Thick. Hopefully they were as soft as they looked from across the room. But he wasn't across the room anymore. She was just a few more steps away from him. She grabbed another glass of champagne from a waiter's tray and kept walking.

Six!

It was now or never. She could turn back or take two more steps. Sylvie thought about the year she'd had. Her business partner had left her high and dry, forcing Sylvie to have to finish fifteen decorating jobs alone. Though she'd gotten the work done, made a great name for herself and lined up some exclusive clients, including Jordan Industries, one of the largest cosmetic companies in the Southeast, she was tired and needed a release.

Five!

At least she could pretend she was there to

share a toast with him if the kiss thing didn't work out.

Four!

She was standing in front of him. "Hi."

"Hello, beautiful," he replied. His voice was just as sexy as he was. Deep. Low. Hypnotic.

"Happy New Year." Sylvie held out the glass of champagne to him. Their fingers touched as he took the glass from her hand.

"Thanks for the drink. Maybe I should've thought of bringing you one earlier."

"Well, it seems as if we're the only people who came without dates tonight."

"And that's a good thing. Stealing you away from another man wouldn't have been a great way to start the New Year."

"Trust and believe, I can't be stolen."

"Is that so?"

She slapped her hand on her shapely hip. "Do I look like a piece of property?"

Three!

"You look beautiful, actually. The prettiest woman in the room."

Sylvie's cheeks heated, but she reminded herself to be cool. "Where's your date tonight?"

"I just met her. I'm Erik, by the way."

"Sylvie."

Two!

Erik's eyes drank in the curvaceous Sylvie. Long legs, thick thighs that he wanted wrapped around his waist. Then his stare fell on her lips. Full. Kissable and painted his favorite color—

red. She ran her tongue across her bottom lip and his dick stood at attention.

Erik noticed Sylvie when she'd walked into the ballroom. His plan had been to skip the party, but Logan, his younger brother, told him about his plan to propose to his lovely girlfriend. As much as Erik wanted Logan to be a part of the company as more than just a board member, he supported and applauded this brother's artistic endeavors. Logan made a name for himself with his murals and gallery shows. Erik knew Logan was going to Paris after the board meeting. He knew his brother was going to be just fine; he wasn't so sure about the company.

Happy New Year!

Balloons fell around Sylvie and Erik as the chords of "Auld Lang Syne" began playing. Sylvie took one step closer to Erik and brought her hand to his cheek. Their lips touched gently, then Sylvie went in for a real kiss.

Erik was taken aback by the sweet forcefulness of her kiss. He wrapped his arms around her waist, pulling her closer to his body. Her tongue danced with his, tango, lambada, and disco. She stroked the back of his neck. Erik moaned as she pressed her body against his and their kiss deepened.

His body responded to her sensual kiss, his erection pressed against her thighs, and she didn't seem to mind at all. Did she just thrust her hips into his?

Yes. She. Did. Erik cupped her behind and it

was soft. Very soft. Squeezing her cheeks, he thought about holding her ass tight while they were naked.

Their lips parted and her bright red lipstick was smeared across her beautiful mouth. "Want to get out of here?"

Sylvie nodded. He wrapped his arm around her waist and led her to his Maserati.

Sylvie watched this man with a lustful gaze. He moved with the confidence of a panther, stalking his prey. His tailored shirt didn't hide his broad shoulders and muscular arms. In fact, that white shirt seemed to make him look more appealing. Like a meal from a fine restaurant that she wanted to slowly devour. Sylvia licked her bottom lip. What in the hell was she doing? She didn't know this man from Adam's alley cat. But good lord, those lips. She'd heard of being kissed senseless, but she'd never felt it until now. And maybe that was why she'd climbed into this Gran Turismo with a man whose last name she didn't even know.

She watched him as he slid into the driver's seat. This car seemed to mold to his body. She wanted to be embraced by his amazing body, lips pressed against his and him buried deep inside her love-starved body. But wait. Would it be worth it? Suppose he was all talk and very little action?

Sylvie turned her head away from Erik.

"Second thoughts?"

"Not at all." She faced him as she nibbled on her bottom lip. He placed his hot hand on her thigh, stroking her gently. Then he shifted the car into gear and took off like a bullet. The way he handled the car, she wondered if he would ride her curves the same way. This clearly wasn't going to be a waste of time.

Tonight, she could be wild and free because tomorrow she'd never see him again.

Erik parked his car and struggled to keep his hormones under control as he looked at Sylvie's thighs. Her dress had risen above her knees as they pulled into the parking deck. He wanted to drive between those thighs, wanted to see if she was as sweet down there as her mouth was.

"What?" she asked when they locked eyes. "Are you having second thoughts?"

"Just wondering how sweet you are all over."

He leaned over and popped the seat back. "And I have no patience. I need to know now."

"Really?"

Erik's answer was to slide her dress up and slip his hands between her thighs. She was wearing thigh-high stockings with the lace tops that he loved. And she wasn't wearing any panties.

"Damn," he whispered as he stroked her wet slit. "Beautiful yoni."

"Mmm," she moaned as he continued to stroke her. Sylvie's hips followed his rhythm as he pressed in and out of her. Pulling his finger from her honey pot, Erik licked his finger. She was so sweet.

"Just as delicious as I thought you would be."

"Your hands are magical, but I need more."

"Let me give you what you need and get everything I want."

"And what about what I want?"

"You're going to get everything you want." Smiling, Erik opened the driver's-side door and crossed over to Sylvie's side of the car. "Before we go inside, I need another sample." He opened the door and spread her legs. Erik silently thanked the universe again for her being panty-less as his tongue lashed her throbbing pearl. Sylvie cried out in pleasure as he licked and sucked. Her thighs trembled as she felt herself about to come. And just when he saw she was about to explode, Erik stopped.

"Really?" she purred. "You're just going to crank me up and leave me like this?"

Erik winked at her. "Sorry, not sorry."

Sylvia took his hand and got out of the car. Soft. Her hands were smooth like silk. Erik wanted her hands roaming his body, finding his hot spots and giving him pleasure.

She pressed her body against his as they stood in the parking lot. "I'm going to make you pay." She brushed her lips against his, as Erik gripped her hips.

"You're making it hard for me to move."

"Payback is a mother."

He scooped her up in his arms. "Let's go." Erik nearly ran up to the elevator and pressed the button with vigor. Sylvie licked the side of his neck as the doors to the elevator opened. Shivering, he nearly dropped her because of the tingles running through his body.

"Stop, stop," he moaned.

"I told you I was going to get you back."

"The night is still young and I can give as good as I get."

"We'll see. My mother always said talk is cheap." Sylvie winked at him.

Once they arrived at the suite, Erik made short work of opening the door and pressing Sylvie against the wall.

"What was that about talk being cheap?" Erik captured her mouth in a hot, wet kiss. Sylvie moaned in delight as the kiss deepened and he slid the straps of her dress down her shoulders. She pressed her hand against his chest.

"Slow down, cowboy, we have all night."

"Is that so?"

She ran her tongue across his bottom lip. "All night long."

Erik took her hand and placed it on his waistband. Sylvie made short work of unbuttoning and unzipping his slacks. She pulled his pants down his thighs. His boxer briefs did little to hide his growing desire and Sylvie was happy to see that he was every inch of what she'd hoped he'd be—maybe even more.

She stroked him, making him moan with pleasure. Sylvie tugged at his boxer briefs, pulling them down, and marveled at the sight of his perfect erection. Her mouth watered as she inched closer to his crotch. Licking her lips, Sylvie ran her finger down the length of his dick. In a flash, she covered his hardness with her hot, wet mouth. Erik threw his head back as she took him deeper into her mouth. Suck. Lick. Deeper.

Erik's knees were weak as she licked the length of him, and then when she sucked the head of his erection, he was about to explode. Pulling back from her, he expelled a satisfied sigh. "That mouth of yours is magical."

"And that was just a small taste." She rose to her feet and smiled. "Then again, there wasn't nothing small about what was in my mouth."

Erik winked at her, then took her into his arms. "My turn to taste you again." Laying her on the bed, he spread her thighs and smiled at those stockings. Erik stripped her dress off as he stroked her wetness. "You're too sexy for words."

She thrust her hips forward. "Then stop talking."

He dove between her legs, his mouth watering as he slipped a finger inside her wetness. Sylvie moaned, reminding Erik of a sexy saxophone solo. Pressing deeper, he watched her face contort in pleasure as he found her erogenous spots.

Erik quickly replaced his finger with his tongue. Licking her until she exploded and his face was wet with her desire. He rose from the bed and crossed over to the door, where his pants had been discarded. Sylvie watched his every move, ogling his wonderful ass.

After he slid the condom over his erection, he crossed over to Sylvie. She reached up, propped up on her knees, and wrapped her arms around his waist. With one hand, she rubbed his dick, making him toss his head back in delight. Erik had never been known for his patience, so he grabbed her hand and pushed her back on the bed. He lifted her legs and spread them. Sylvie's lips curled into a smile as he rubbed the tip of his dick against her pulsating lips. "Such a tease," she moaned as he continued to rub against her.

"Trust me, you're going to get it real good." Then he thrust deep into her, taking Sylvie's breath away. She closed her eyes and moaned, then matched him hard, stroke for stroke. Gripping his shoulders, Sylvie pulled him closer in a silent plea for him to go deeper. Erik heard what she was saying and went deeper.

"Harder," she moaned as she arched her back. "Harder."

Never one to disappointed a beautiful woman, he pounded harder and she wrapped her legs around his waist and gripped him tighter.

"Yessss." The word came out like a hiss before

she used her lower body strength to flip him over. On top of him, Sylvie bucked and rode him like he was a wild mustang in the desert. Erik relished the delight as her hotness enveloped him. He wrapped his arms around her waist, slowing her down so he could hold back on his climax. Sylvie leaned forward and licked his bottom lip. Then she took his lip between her teeth as she ground against him. Erik pumped in and out of her until she fell against his chest and howled in delight.

Erik knew he could finally come and he did, exploding as Sylvie bounced her ass up and down against his dick. He stroked her sweaty back and closed his eyes.

"Wow."

Sylvie sighed and wiggled out of his embrace. "Those were some real fireworks." She turned over on her side and ran her hand across his chest. "That's the way to ring in the New Year."

"We're not done, Miss Lady." Erik grabbed her wrist and flipped her on her back. "I think we have some more fireworks to pop off."

Erik's soft snore woke Sylvie, reminding her that the last few hours weren't a sensual dream. But reality was nibbling at her conscience. She had work to do. She had to finish the designs for Jordan Industries. She'd come up with an idea she hoped they would go along with: a small museum showcasing the history of the company and her favorite lipstick.

She always wondered why the company stopped making the Yvonne shade of lipstick. It was a bright red that her mother loved. On Saturdays, when the new shades would come out, she and Lydia would be at the mall. They'd spend the day trying on lipsticks, lip glosses, and moisturizers.

Lydia would leave with five shades of red lipstick and something lacy. When her father would come home from work or fishing, Sylvie would be ushered out of the house for a couple hours. It wasn't until she was older that she noticed her mother's lipstick would be smeared and her father would have lipstick on his neck.

Kissing was always important to Lydia. That's why she told Sylvia that the right shade of lipstick was key to life.

And her life was about to be taken over by this project. No matter how good it felt lying in this man's strong arms. She. Had. To. Go. Glancing at his sleeping frame, she drank in every inch of his ebony skin, his strong chin and curly eyelashes. Then those lips. Full and soft as pillows. She started to lean in and kiss him, but if he woke up there was no way she'd leave. Her eyes traveled down to his thick thighs. Obviously this man didn't skip leg day. Nor did he neglect his abs. Arms either. He reminded her of a superhero. He'd probably been Chadwick Boseman's stand-in during the filming of *Black Panther*.

As questions about who this man really was started to dance in her head, Sylvie knew she had to go. They shared a New Year's kiss, some great sex, and all she had to do was leave and move on with her life. She inched out of the bed, grabbed her purse and dress. Creeping into the bathroom, she dressed quickly and quietly.

And because she had a flair for the dramatic, Sylvie dug a tube of drugstore lipstick out of her purse and wrote a message on the mirror. With her shoes in her hand, she crept out of the room, leaving Erik sleeping like a baby.

Chapter 2

Erik woke up to an empty bed. He figured his succulent date was in the bathroom. It was five after six and he was ready to make his exit. The last thing he wanted was for anyone to get confused about what was going to happen next. He had to go. The holidays were officially over and the real work was about to begin. Swinging his long legs over the edge of the bed, Erik stroked the sheets, remembering every erotic move he and Sylvie had made. Work could wait. He needed another taste of that sexy woman.

Heading for the bathroom, he was taken aback when he didn't hear the shower going. But the minute he saw a note scribbled on the mirror in red lipstick, Erik was floored.

Thank you for a funky time. Happy New Year.

"You have got to be kidding me." Who did Sylvie think she was? He was the one who reminded folks that checkout was at noon, while he was on his way out the door. Shit like this didn't happen to Erik Jordan.

Chuckling, he realized that he was upset about a one-night stand that had only been meaningless fun. But there was something about Sylvie No-Last-Name-Shared. He couldn't remember the last time he'd been so instantly attracted to a woman. A woman who was effortlessly beautiful, sexy without trying, and obviously didn't know who he was. Stroking his chin, he wiped away the embarrassing note on the mirror with a plush washcloth. The whole world didn't need to know he took an L.

A few hours and a shower later, Erik was sitting alone in the CEO office of Jordan Industries. His desk, which he was still trying to reconcile was his now, was covered with plans for the coming year, including a press release for him to approve about the change in leadership and the new direction of the company. He'd been giving it a glance when his cell phone rang.

"This is Erik."

"You know you messed up last night," Logan said with a laugh.

"What are you talking about?"

"I saw you leave the party early, but I didn't see which model you took with you when you left."

"The way you and Olivia were tonguing each other down and showing off that bling, I'm surprised you noticed I was there. That portrait was amazing, by the way. I don't understand why you and Dad didn't work something out so that—"

"Let me stop you there and remind you that you said the key word, *Dad*. I've done everything in the world to distance myself from all that is the superficial beauty of Jordan Industries, and that man was still calling me a painter three months ago."

Erik knew the history of his father's *disappointment* in Logan's artsy side. For Simon, if a Jordan didn't work at the company, he wasn't worth his weight. Though Erik had taken to the science of the cosmetics side of the business, he'd never paid attention to the numbers and day-to-day operations of the company.

It was a fucking headache.

"Erik, are you listening to me?" Logan's voice forced him to look up from his papers and focus on the phone call.

"Sorry, I was catching up on some reading. What did you say?"

"Man, you're already letting it consume you." Erik could hear the judgment in his brother's voice. "Maybe allowing some of those French investors to come in and take the pressure off would be a good thing."

"What do you know about that? Having even one percent of this company owned by someone who doesn't care about this community or the history of this company is unacceptable."

"Now you're starting to sound like Simon. How much do you think he worried about the community and family legacy when he was stealing from JI? Maybe it's time do things a new way. You have the power to make that change."

"And I have the power to prove Simon wrong, but keep a legacy for our future kids—your future kids."

"What's that *our* about?" Logan chuckled. "I know damn well you didn't fall in love with that model and now you're thinking about a family. Or did you find out that you have a teenager in California or something?"

"Hell no. You're the one who's getting married, and despite what Dad did, this is our legacy."

Logan scoffed. "Some legacy. It's time for you to get your own legacy and stop trying to make Dad's dreams fit your feet."

"As much as I know you hate Jordan Industries, I don't hate what it represents to so many women who have been told they're not beautiful or that they have to conform to someone else's idea of beauty." Sylvie flashed in his mind. She'd been wearing the faintest amount of foundation because she wasn't trying to hide. It wasn't as if there had been many flaws for her to cover up.

Wait. Why was he thinking about this woman? A woman who obviously had no problem forgetting him. She didn't even give him the "Darling Nikki" treatment, because she didn't leave a number at all. Thank you for a funky time, indeed.

"Olivia and I are having a small dinner tonight with her family, and you have to represent the sane side of the Jordan clan, so get your shit together and meet us at Modele's by seven. Be ready to get hugged to death by Mrs. B."

"As long as there isn't going to be one of Olivia's cousins sitting there thinking I'm her date for the evening."

Logan snorted. "We've given up matchmaking. You're a hopeless case, and it seems you're about to be married to your job anyway."

"And if you want to see me at seven, you better let me get something done in the next few hours."

"Don't be late. Mrs. B is already feeling some kind of way about our family issues as it is."

Erik sighed but didn't tell Logan about his attempt to reach out to their mother earlier in the afternoon, only to be sent straight to voicemail. He knew she'd been screening her calls, but he didn't know if it was because she wanted to keep the peace with their father or if she was actually on Simon's side.

"I'll be there." After hanging up with his brother, Erik dove back into the reports. Then he found himself thinking about New Year's Eve again and that kiss. That woman's mouth was magical. And that tongue. The way she licked him like a lollypop made his knees quake just thinking about it. Too bad he'd never see her again. Now, he just needed to get his dick to realize that.

His electronic calendar chimed, alerting him to a meeting. Erik grabbed his phone and sighed.

That stupid redesign. He tossed his phone across his desk and dug out the cost report on his father's vanity project.

If he had his way, he'd cancel it. The last thing they needed right now was attention. But there was going to be a spread in a national magazine about the *family* company. JI's amazing PR division had told him the article could be his coming-out party as the CEO of Jordan Industries, and they could use the interview as a chance to control the narrative about Simon's arrest and why Erik was going to be the savior of the company.

Rising to his feet and crossing the room, Erik still wasn't sure he wanted to take this mantle. But he didn't have much of a choice.

Olivia shook her head as she sipped her coffee and listened to Sylvia tell her story about the man she'd left the party with.

"You are too much," Liv said as she set her coffee mug on the table in Sylvie's makeshift home office. "First of all, you just decided that you were going to kiss a stranger. Then you went to his hotel room and had sex with him."

Sylvie nodded and glanced at her sketch. "I was caught up in the moment."

"But you left him a note on the mirror in lipstick? Why?"

She shrugged. "The moment passed. You know what these last few months have been like for me. I needed a release and he was just what the doctor ordered and more."

"Then why didn't you exchange phone numbers? Get to know him and . . ."

Sylvie threw her hand up. "Slow down. We all don't get to find Prince Charming and travel the world with him."

Liv glanced down at her five-carat diamond and sapphire engagement ring. "He is charming, sweet and . . ."

"The last of his kind," Sylvie muttered as she drew a line on her sketch of the Jordan Industries lobby. "Do you think LJ would donate a painting to my new project?"

Olivia shook her head furiously. "Nope. He wouldn't even sell you one."

"Why?"

Liv sighed. "Ask him."

Sylvie shook her head. "Sounds like drama, and you know I'm drama-averse. But I think it would make my stock shoot up like a bamboo tree!"

Liv shook her head. "You're really close to being someone who uses people. Logan doesn't want anything to do with those people and I'm not mad at him."

Sylvie looked up from her sketchbook. "Is there something I should know about these people before I cash my check and commit the next six weeks of my life to them?"

Liv sighed and took a sip of her coffee. "Logan's last name is Jordan."

Sylvie shrugged, and then the realization of what her friend said hit her like a ton of bricks. "As in, he's a part of the Jordan dynasty? How could you not tell me this?"

"Have you noticed that Logan doesn't have anything to do with his family or his last name? There's a lot of bad blood there, and I haven't even met his parents. It wasn't something that I thought was important to mention."

Sylvie raised her right eyebrow. "And you're cool with that?"

Olivia nodded. "From the way he talks about his father, I think I'm dodging a bullet."

"Then I guess you don't know what's going on with the company, then?"

Olivia shook her head, then picked up her coffee mug. "Logan is on the board, but he allows his brother to make all of the decisions. I meant to introduce you two last night, but I guess both of you decided to leave early. Workaholics."

"Technically, I wasn't working, I was working it." Sylvie gyrated her hips as if she were a video vixen.

"Please tell me those were not the moves you put on Mr. Midnight. That man was probably happy to wake up alone."

Sylvie tossed a pencil at her friend. "Don't be jealous of my boogie."

Olivia rolled her eyes. "Honey, I got my own moves. Logan is totally satisfied." She glanced at her watch. "Speaking of Logan, we're having dinner with my family. You should come."

Sylvie shook her head. "As much as I love Mama B's collard greens and black-eyed peas, I have to make sure my proposal and designs are on point for my meeting next week."

"Have I told you how proud of you I am? You're really doing the damn thing, despite everything your old partner put you through."

"Please, don't remind me. I wish I had three days to sleep." Sylvie dropped down in her leather desk chair.

"Now, don't kill yourself trying to write your name in history." Olivia walked over to her friend's desk and closed Sylvie's sketchbook. "You can take a break."

"This is a make-or-break moment for me. Failure isn't an option."

"And dying to prove the world wrong isn't an option either. Get some rest and call your mother."

"She and Vernon are spending the rest of the holidays in Alaska on a cruise. Who does that?" Sylvia laughed. "When I think of a cruise, I want sun and sandy beaches. She and Stepdad are out looking for polar bears and icebergs."

"Your mom and mine are the last of a special breed. I wonder what she'd think about how you rang in the New Year?"

"Get out!" Sylvie quipped. "Because if she finds out, I'm wearing a hot-pink pantsuit to your wedding."

Olivia rolled her eyes and headed to the door. Pink was one of her least favorite colors and if anyone knew that, it was Sylvie—even if she'd tried to incorporate pink into the redesign of her townhouse.

Once she was alone, Sylvia glanced out of the window, thinking about the enormity of this Jordan Industries project. What if she failed? What if people hated what she designed and her company went down in flames?

Suppose Amanda was right and SGD was too much about Sylvia and not enough about the clients, and she was destined to fail? Nah. Amanda was just a small-minded hater, and this project was going to prove her wrong. Sleep could wait.

She opened her sketch pad and started drawing again.

Chapter 3

The only thing Erik realized he missed about the holidays was a plate full of steaming collard greens. *Thank God for Mrs. B and her cooking.* He dug into his third plate of greens and cornbread as everyone around him chattered and talked about the upcoming wedding.

Erik had told Logan all he needed to do was tell him where he needed to be on his wedding day and he'd be there. All of this other talk about venues, colors, and the like just went over his head. Not that he was against marriage or didn't share in Olivia and Logan's happiness; his mind was just on work. When he'd finally read all of the financial reports, he knew that Jordan Industries was in more trouble than anyone knew. There had been two sets of books and both of them were in the red.

When the stockholders found out the truth, heads were going to roll. Erik knew he'd have to share all of the evidence the SEC had against Simon and answer a lot of uncomfortable questions. The stockholders had a lot of money invested in the company and would be justified in any anger they displayed.

He also needed to call a meeting with his legal team to see how they could make sure that this investigation focused solely on his father.

Then he wanted to see if he could get an outside agency to do a parallel investigation to make sure his father was the only one involved in stealing from the company. Specifically, he wanted to make sure his mother wouldn't end up in a women's prison somewhere. She couldn't be in on her husband's scheme.

"Erik, are you okay?" Mrs. B asked when she noticed the pensive look in his eyes and that he'd stopped eating.

"Oh, yes, ma'am. I think I may have overdone it on dinner." He wiped his mouth, then smiled at the older woman. He could see where Olivia got her beauty and heart. Mrs. B was like an angel who could give Bobby Flay and Devon Harris a run for their money in a kitchen, on or off the Food Network. She greeted everyone with a hug or a kiss on the cheek. After not seeing his mother over the holidays, Erik was surprised by how touched he was by Mrs. B's kindness today. He and his mother had a close relationship that he often took for granted. She'd been the one who took the brunt of his father's anger whenever Erik did something that pissed the old man off.

Back in the day, it could've been something as simple as breathing. Luckily, Erik had brought in a lot of money with his creativity in the lab. He thought his dad had finally learned to respect him. Clearly, he was wrong.

She patted the back of his hand and smiled. "Are you ready to be the man at Jordan Industries now? I hope you'll bring my favorite lipstick back."

Why did she have to say *lipstick*? Erik smiled despite himself. "I'll see what I can do."

She gave him a warm smile. "You can always take some greens home with you. I know you don't have a lot of time to cook some good food."

"Mrs. B, I don't cook at all. You are a lifesaver."

Logan tossed a napkin at his brother. "You're going to act like you don't have a cook?"

Erik rolled his eyes at his brother. "Had a cook. She got the idea that we were starring in a romantic comedy that would end up with us getting married."

The table went silent and everyone looked at Erik, silently begging him to tell them more. Logan knew the whole story and watched his brother squirm.

"Well, Erik, you're just going to have to stop being so charming and settle down," Mrs. B said with a low chuckle.

He took a quick sip of his iced tea and wished it were whiskey. *Here it goes*, he thought. "Mrs. B, that isn't an option for me right now. I'm about to settle into this job right now."

Logan rolled his eyes at his brother. "He's a

lost cause. I'm just hopeful that he doesn't let Jordan Industries consume his life."

"How about we change the subject to that cake over there?" Erik nodded toward Mrs. B's famous sour cream pound cake.

Olivia winked at her future brother-in-law. "Good save!"

After a few more hours of good conversation and even better food, Erik reluctantly headed back to the office to see what he had on his plate for Monday morning. When he saw the first thing on his list was a meeting with the interior decorator, he immediately palmed it off to his assistant—well, his father's assistant. Hell, he was still trying to wrap his mind around being the CEO of Jordan Industries.

One thing he wasn't going to get too involved in was this redesign. Sure, he'd do the article, but he wasn't going to be involved in picking out samples and colors for the wall.

He was about to send an email when the office phone rang. Who knew he was there and why were they calling the office and not his cell?

Erik started to ignore the phone, but then noticed the call was from his parents' home.

"Erik Jordan."

"Should've known your backstabbing ass would be sitting in my office as if you belong there."

Erik gritted his teeth. "To what do I owe the pleasure of this phone call?"

"I'll be damned if I allow you to call yourself taking my company. I'll burn it to the ground before I let you or the board force me out."

"Dad, you did this to yourself. If you loved the company so much, why were you robbing it blind?"

"Boy! You aren't so grown that you can question me about what I do. I built this company and—"

"What you did was illegal. And why?"

The dial tone sounded in his ear. Erik closed his eyes and squeezed the bridge of his nose. His mind went back to the last time he walked into this office late at night.

The whirl of the paper shredder filled the air in the empty offices of Jordan Industries.

Simon Jordan knew his misdeeds were going to be the topic of discussion at the board meeting, but he'd like to see those smug bastards prove anything without evidence.

"All they have to do is agree to the sale," he muttered as he loaded more financial documents into the shredder. Suddenly, the door swung open with a violent force. Erik Jordan glared at his father.

"What in the hell are you doing, Dad?"

Simon returned his son's hard stare. "This is none of your concern. You just walk out that door and go home."

Erik crossed over to the documents lining his father's desk. "What are you trying to hide?" He picked up a stack of tax records.

"You're my son, you should—"

"I'm also a board member, and if I haven't learned anything else from you, I've learned this company comes first."

Simon snatched the files from Erik. "You selfish son of a bitch. I built this company, gave you a sandlot to play in. You need to get the board to agree to this sale and—"

"I need to call the SEC." Erik walked over to the shredder and shut it off. "This is fraud and you're not going to get away with this."

"Who's going to stop me? You?" Simon laughed.

Two police officers walked in and Erik nodded toward his father.

"Simon Jordan," the taller officer said. "You're under arrest."

Erik had no warm feelings watching his father being cuffed and led out of the office. Part of him had hoped he'd been wrong about his father. He would've rather found his father having a torrid affair or anything but the financial malfeasance the board had suspected him of.

When Erik hired a forensic accountant to see if there had been any wrongdoing, he had been disheartened to find proof of his father's embezzlement. Erik made sure there were no media trucks around when his father was arrested. He didn't want the media storm to start immediately. But it wouldn't be long before Jordan Industries made headlines for all the wrong reasons.

There was no doubt in his mind that the time for reckoning was upon them.

* * *

Sylvie woke up with a start, thinking that she was late for her meeting. It would've served her right since she'd spent her nap dreaming of Erik and that kiss. And everything that happened after that kiss. Why was she acting as if she hadn't been horny before? And the sex had been amazing, but she couldn't lose focus on her main goal, growing her business.

It wouldn't be a lie to say that Sylvie wanted to fall in love, but she stopped believing fairy tales were her thing when she realized that Cinderella was really a story about the right shoes changing a woman's attitude. Prince Charming was totally overrated.

But that didn't make her want one any less. For now, she'd settle for a thriving business and veggie burger. Glancing at the clock on her computer, she saw that it was just a few minutes after ten. She could calm down and get something to eat, and then obsess over her meeting at Jordan Industries.

As overconfident as people thought Sylvie was, the truth of the matter was, this project scared her.

It wasn't as if she hadn't designed for businesses before. Her first client, the Sweet Spot, was a Brooklyn bakery. Her redesign of the space became just as popular as the succulent desserts the bakery sold.

Every month Sylvie received a basket of goodies from the bakery.

Padding into the kitchen, Sylvie made a snack and decided to veg out in front of the TV for a while. Maybe if she thought about something else she could lower her anxiety about tomorrow's meeting. Of course her mind floated right back to New Year's Eve.

Erik.

Sylvie wasn't one for regrets, having learned a long time ago that it was such a useless emotion, but she wished that she hadn't left that saucy note on the mirror. What if Erik's was that magic New Year's kiss she'd been dreaming of her whole life?

Stop it. That man was a good lay and that's it. No need to worry about things you can't control. Sylvie grabbed a cup of yogurt and a spoon. Why did it even matter what he had going on when she'd never see this man again in her life? She dipped her spoon in her peach yogurt and sighed. Tomorrow was shaping up to be the biggest day of her career, and she was thinking about a hot one-night stand?

Focus on what's important. Jordan Industries. Plopping down on the sofa, she polished off her yogurt while watching the evening news. When she heard the anchor mention Jordan Industries, she reached for the remote to turn up the volume. But before she could focus on the story, her cell phone rang. Sylvie rushed to her bedroom to grab the phone. When she saw her mother's face on the screen, she smiled.

"Hey, Ma!"

"Just wanted to give you a call and let you know that I'm back in Charleston."

"How was the cruise?"

The satisfied sigh that chimed in Sylvie's ear told her everything she needed to know. Her mother had had a great time.

"It was so beautiful, Sylvia. The snow-covered ice caps and the polar bears. But when we got to Juneau and took that tram, I realized that I was in love."

"Ma, you better not move to Alaska!"

"Excuse me? You're forgetting who the mama is here, young lady. Luckily, I wouldn't be able to function in a place where it's dark for sixty-seven days straight. But the fireworks show Vernon and I saw was magical. I think we fell in love all over again when the sky lit up blue and red. Enough about me. Please tell me you did something exciting to ring in the New Year."

Sylvie closed her eyes and Erik's naked body flashed in her mind. "Oh, not really. Went to Olivia's party. She got engaged."

"Good for her. But what did you do?"

"Drank some champagne, ate some sushi, and prepared for my new project." Sylvie bit her bottom lip as if she was trying not to tell her mother how she really rang in the New Year.

"You need a life that expands beyond work, Sylvia. When is the last time you had fun?"

"Fun is overrated."

"Little girl, I'm going to tell you like Billy Dee told Diana, *success is nothing without someone to share it with*. And you need to settle down and stop trying to be Superwoman."

"Ma!"

"Well, you're not getting any younger. And the older you get, the harder it is to find a decent man."

"That's a nice thing to say." Sylvie sighed and wondered why her mother was worrying about her settling down all of a sudden.

"I'm getting too old to worry about being nice, but no pressure." Peals of laughter filled Sylvie's ear. "And despite what Vernon says, I'm not going to start introducing you to the new guys at the church when you come visit. And when do you plan on visiting?"

Sylvie groaned inwardly. Her mother was being extremely extra tonight. "Ma, what's going on with you?"

"What do you mean? I want my only child to be happy and have a family. Why does something have to be wrong?"

"Who said having a family would make me happy?"

"Who said it wouldn't? Sylvia, I'm not telling you how to live your life, but just live a little."

"All right. I promise I'll take a vacation as soon as I finish this project. But I'll be going somewhere tropical, no matter how beautiful Alaska is."

"Just like your dad, you love the sun."

Sylvie smiled at the thought of playing on the shores of Grande Isle with her dad. "Yeah. I do."

"And you know something else that you have in common with your father?"

Here we go. You don't know how to relax. Sylvie and her mother had had this conversation so many times in the last three years.

"You don't know how to relax. He was so determined to provide for us that he worked himself into an early grave. Broke my heart to lose him. I am not going to watch you do the same thing."

"I'm not going to do that, Ma. But I have to get this business off the ground. Especially after what Amanda did to me."

Her mother sighed. "Didn't you work your ass off over the holidays to make up for that filthy heffa skipping out on you?"

"And it all leads to this. Ma, I'm going to be fine, have a good life and a successful business. I just want to make you and Dada proud."

"Honey, I'm proud, and Dada is smiling on you from heaven. You don't owe anyone a damned thing."

Just myself, she thought as her mother talked.

"Hey, Ma. I have to go. I love you, but . . ."

"You have to get ready for your meeting. Go ahead."

After hanging up with her mother, Sylvie headed back to her office. Booting up her laptop, she was determined to make sure her proposal for the new CEO of Jordan Industries was perfect.

It was well after midnight before Sylvie headed to bed. All she could do now was pray that she made the right impression in the morning.

Erik walked into the office with a cup of black coffee clenched in his fist. It was his third cup and he still felt as if he was sleepwalking. He'd spent the night going over financial reports—again. Somehow, he needed to find money to save jobs and rebrand the cosmetics line.

"Mr. Jordan," Linda said as he walked into his office enclave. "Ms. Gates is here, and since you said that I could take charge of this project, I let her into your office."

"You did what?" He struggled to keep his voice even. The last thing he needed was to have this decorator in his office when he had real work to do. "Y'all need to move this party someplace else, because I have a meeting with the executive staff." He glanced at his smart watch. "In an hour."

"Well, I did have your computer moved into the conference room. And—"

Erik held his hand up. "Linda, thank you. I'm

sorry if I was a little gruff, but I didn't get much sleep last night and I didn't expect Ms. Gates to start her project so soon."

Linda handed him a file showing the drawings Sylvia had gone over with her. "She is super talented."

Erik gave the drawings a brief glance and nodded. "I'm going into the conference room."

"Don't you want to meet her? She's really lovely."

Erik waved his hand and took off down the hall. Didn't matter how *lovely* this woman was, he had business to take care of that didn't include looking at color swatches.

Once he entered the conference room and sat down at the table, Erik realized one thing was for sure—he needed his chair. The foam seats of the faux leather chairs surrounding the table were beyond uncomfortable. Whether it was in the budget or not, Erik was buying new chairs. No one deserved his or her ass to be this sore.

Heading down the hall, Erik was stopped by one of the security guards he'd hired from a new company.

"Mr. Jordan, I wanted to let you know that the new security cameras have been installed and we've removed the access codes from the old system so that no one can access the system."

Nodding, he thanked the man. Knowing that Simon had always had access to everything at JI, Erik knew he needed to make changes to the building and the business's security. Tomorrow, he'd have a new IT team come in and sweep the network for any backdoor access to the servers and files. He knew his father had something up his sleeve and he was going to do whatever he could to stop him. Walking into his office, Erik was about to cross over to his desk and grab his chair. Then he stopped short when he saw a shapely ass covered by a pair of skintight jeans wiggling in the air. He took a lingering glance, and then cleared his throat. He was at work, and no matter how amazing that ass looked, he had work to do and this woman was . . . Sylvie.

Measurements, that's why she'd been on the floor, and thank God for being on her knees, because when she locked eyes with Erik, she would've passed out. What was he doing here?

"Sylvie?"

Stand up. You can do this. Her legs wouldn't cooperate. Nodding, she reached for the edge of the desk and pulled herself up. "Erik. Wow. What a surprise."

"That's one word for it." He drank in her casual image; formfitting jeans, low-heeled black boots, and a long-sleeved white shirt with her company's logo on the front. Right across her breasts. Clearing his throat, he smiled. "Didn't know you were Sylvia Gates."

She chewed her bottom lip as an uncomfortable beat passed. "How is this going to work?"

"Just fine, I suppose. We have a contract with your company and looks like you've already jumped in."

"Have you seen my portfolio? I'm damned good at what I do and—"

"Oh, I know you're good."

She speared him with a frown. "I had no idea who you were that night." Her voice was low, but there wasn't a sign of regret.

Erik threw his hand up. "That night was a *funky good time*. But we're adults and you can get this project done."

"You're damn right I can, and I don't think I like your attitude."

He shrugged. "You can quit if you'd like. Of course, we'd need our money back and then you're going to have to explain why you walked away from this. And here I was looking forward to seeing your vision."

Sylvie slapped her hand on her hip. "I don't quit, and if you have a problem with me being here, then fire me. That way I can keep the money."

Erik licked his lips. "Why would I do that when you have so many talents?"

She rolled her eyes and reached for her tape measure, which was on the edge of Erik's desk, and snapped it open. "Let me get back to work, unless you have notes for me."

He closed the space between them and smiled at her. "No notes. I came for something a little more important." Stopping in front of her, he glanced at her lips. When they locked eyes, Erik could almost feel her yearning for him to kiss her. But he rounded her and grabbed his chair. "Make sure you follow your designs. They looked good and I can't wait to see what you do with this place." And with that, Erik rolled his chair out of the office and down the hall.

Sylvie smirked as she watched Erik walk away. She deserved that. But who knew Erik, her midnight snack, was the CEO of Jordan Industries? *This changes nothing. Do your job and don't think about that man. That man who holds your future in his hands.*

Returning to measuring the area around his desk, Sylvie's mind flashed back to his naked body pressed against hers and his lips devouring her own. She'd thought he was going to kiss her. Scratch that. She wanted him to kiss her. Wanted his lips against her as if it was midnight on New Year's Eve again. But he seemed to make it clear that he was over it. Fine, she could be over it too.

A few hours later, Sylvie had finished her measurements in the executive offices and was ready to move on to the lobby, which she considered to be her calling card. She glanced at her sketchpad and realized that her ideas for the lobby weren't good enough.

Sylvie needed something that would celebrate the company's history and nod toward the future.

Erik. He was the future as the new CEO. A

portrait would be easy, but Sylvie wondered if she could push the boundaries with him. After all, she'd already seen him naked.

Looking up at a picture of what she assumed was the company founder and his wife, she couldn't help but wonder what kind of woman Erik would take a picture with and show the world. She'd been studying the portrait so intently that the sound of Erik's voice made her yelp.

"Didn't mean to startle you."

"I was deep in thought." She pointed to the black-and-white portrait. "The founders?"

Erik smiled sardonically. "Aka, my parents, Simon and Yvonne."

Sylvie stretched her eyes and pointed to the woman in the picture. "*The* Yvonne? The inspiration for the best line of red lipstick in the history of makeup?"

Erik rolled his eyes. "I should've known you were a fan. Red lipstick is your thing, huh?"

She narrowed her eyes at him. "Mr. Jordan, I'm sure you've walked out on a sleeping beauty once or twice."

He cleared his throat and ran his hand across his five o'clock shadow. "Actually, I planned to let you have the suite for the day."

"In other words, I beat you to the punch and you're salty? Wow."

Erik released a low chuckle. "You know I'm far from salty."

She turned away from him as heat flooded her cheeks. "Anyway. With all of the changes that have gone on here, I think your lobby should reflect that."

"Do what you want to do." He shrugged. "You're the expert."

Sylvie smiled. "Glad you think so. I need you to do something for me."

Chapter 4

Erik shifted his stance as his dick jumped at the thought of Sylvie needing him to do something to her. Or did she say *for* her? All day he'd been extra focused on work, to keep his mind off her in his office. Now, standing inches from her, he had to remind himself to look but don't touch.

"What do you need?"

"A portrait of you. But not like that." She pointed up at the picture of his parents. "Something edgy and artsy."

"As long as I keep my clothes on, I'm down. Guess it's time for me to put my mark on the place. What do you have in mind?"

Sylvie offered him a huge smile. "You wearing some of the best makeup you guys sell. Sort of like an abstract painting."

"Are you out of your mind?" Erik shook his head. "You got the wrong brother. I'm not the artist here."

She shrugged. "This really isn't about you being artistic, it's about showing the new direction."

"We're going to do that without me getting a facial."

Sylvie folded her arms across her chest and Erik was harder than marble. Looking away from her breasts, he tried to listen to the voice telling him to go home. Instead, he turned to Sylvie. "Why don't we go have a drink and discuss your ideas?"

"I'm still working and you've already shot down one of my best ideas. I don't need that kind of negativity mixed with vodka."

Erik shook his head and started for the exit. "Miss Gates, don't forget I'm the boss here."

She stuck her tongue out at him and Erik was taken back to their night in the suite. Her tongue was magical. Just as he was about to walk over to her, his phone vibrated in his pocket. Pulling it out, he saw it was his mother calling. What could she possibly want now?

"Ma?" Erik walked outside at a quick pace.

"Hope you're happy with yourself. Your father is in the hospital and I know it's because of your betrayal. Why, Erik? Why did you want power so bad that you just said screw the family?"

"Ma, you seem to forget that Dad committed a crime. He was stealing from the company and wanted to hide it by selling out. I find it hard to see how this is my fault."

"Simon built that company to give you ungrateful boys a legacy. He sacrificed everything for us and you . . ."

"Why are you defending him? Dad put you through a lot of hell. And—"

"Don't talk about my marriage. That isn't your business and I'm not going to allow you to try and break that up as well. Erik, if you are concerned about me, then you're going to tell the board and the police you made a mistake."

He sighed and bit back a caustic comment about how he wasn't the lying Jordan. "If you want to have blind loyalties toward Simon Jordan, then I feel sorry for you."

"I'm not blind. Your father is going to come after you, and this family isn't going to recover from a war. End it, Erik. End it."

He was about to respond when he noticed that she'd ended the call. Erik knew he'd started a civil war when he had his father arrested and went to the board about Simon's crimes. Just because the man had founded Jordan Industries, it didn't give him the right to rob the place blind.

Erik's internal investigation had discovered that his father had been embezzling money from the company for years, reporting false profit earnings to stockholders and the board. Those falsified reports had been one of the reasons why the company had been put up for sale. Because of Simon, the company was in the red, when Jordan Industries should've been earning millions of dollars in profit.

Erik wondered how much his mother knew about this. Was she really concerned about the family being at war, or was there something else behind her need to keep Simon from paying for his crimes?

"Excuse me."

The voice came from behind him, reminding Erik that he hadn't moved since his mother hung up on him. Turning around, he smiled at Sylvie. "Sorry."

"I thought about your drink offer and if it's still on the table, I'd like to take you up on it."

"Sure thing. And I promise not to dilute your vodka with negativity." He winked at her and thought he heard her moan. Maybe it was his imagination, since the last time they were alone together there was a lot of moaning going on.

"Where are we going?"

Glancing at her attire, Erik figured the Canvas Club, a bar frequented by well-dressed executives, wasn't the best place for them to visit tonight. And while he wished he could take her to his penthouse and peel those jeans off her wonderful body, he had to be a good boss and stick to a single drink.

"There's a little hole-in-the-wall bar down the street that has the strongest martinis in town."

"Martinis? And here I was thinking that you're a single-malt-scotch guy."

"Got me pegged, huh?"

"You're a specific type, if I can be judgmental."

Erik tilted his head to the side. "I got to hear this."

Sylvia looked him in the eyes and smirked. "Well, here's my snap judgment: You're not used to hearing the word no. You like being in control and you drink expensive liquor."

He shook his head as he laughed. "Do I get to play?"

She shrugged. "Why not?"

Erik stroked his chin. "You're impulsive and have no trouble speaking your mind. But inside, you're a scared little girl trying to prove to everyone that you're not."

Sylvie bristled at his assessment. "That was rude."

"You eloquently called me an asshole with a drinking problem, but I'm rude? Let's go get this drink before one of us gets further offended."

They walked to the parking lot in a tense silence. Erik felt as if he should've apologized, but for what? Maybe it was the term *little girl* that offended her.

"Erik, I realized something," Sylvie said, breaking the silence around them. "I have an early morning and I don't think I should drink tonight."

"If I offended you, I'm sorry," he said. "That wasn't my intention." Closing the space between them, he wrapped his arm around her waist.

"I-I . . ." Sylvie tilted her head upward and Erik brought his mouth down on top of hers. The kiss was slow, deep, and hot.

She melted in his arms and he wanted nothing more than to load her into his car and have a replay of New Year's Eve. Pulling back, he ran his finger across her smooth cheek. "That was inappropriate. But I'd like to do it again."

"No." Sylvie sighed. "I have to finish this project without distractions and that's exactly what your lips are. Please don't kiss me again."

Erik nodded. "Whatever the lady wants."

She inhaled deeply and took a step back. "Umm, yeah. So, rain check on the drink, okay?"

Erik tipped his imaginary hat to her and watched her walk over to her car. It was fitting that she drove a classic Jaguar XKR convertible. And of course it was red. Fiery, just like the driver and her now forbidden kisses.

"She better not come in here with red lipstick on," he muttered as he crossed over to his car.

Sylvie drove straight to Olivia's place and hoped that her friend hadn't left the country with Logan yet. She needed her ear. When she saw the couple sitting on the front porch, she released a sigh of relief. Then she remembered that Erik and Logan were brothers. She really couldn't have the gritty conversation she needed to have with her BFF while he was sitting there.

Parking her car, she hopped out and dashed up the stairs. "Olivia. LJ. We need to talk."

The couple looked at her with questions dancing in their eyes. Sylvia folded her arms across her chest.

"What's going on?" Olivia asked.

"Do I need to let you two have a minute alone?"

LJ rose to his feet, then his phone rang. "Saved by the bell."

"What's wrong?" Olivia asked as Sylvia sat in LJ's seat.

"Remember how I told you that I'd spent the night with the single guy at your party?"

Olivia smiled. "You found him?"

Sylvia ran her hand across her face. "Sure did. He's Erik Jordan."

Olivia bit her bottom lip, then burst out laughing. "I can't believe it. Aren't you working for or with him now?"

"Shut up. He kissed me."

"According to you, he did a lot more than that."

Sylvie popped her friend on the arm. "He kissed me tonight. What in hell am I going to do?"

Olivia crossed her legs and picked up her glass of tea from the wrought-iron table. "I know you're not going to quit, because you've been looking forward to this for months. Maybe you should just do your job and move on?"

She closed her eyes and tossed her head back. "I liked it when he kissed me, though. I felt . . . alive."

"Or, you're just horny."

"Liv!"

"New Year's Eve was two weeks ago and—"

"Olivia!"

She took a sip of her tea and then smiled at Sylvia. "Why don't you just go with it?"

"Hello! He's the CEO of Jordan . . ."

LJ reappeared on the porch. "You met my

brother? I guess you're the woman who has him drinking scotch tonight." He crossed over to Olivia and kissed her on the forehead. "I've been summoned to have a similar conversation."

"No one is talking about your brother," Sylvie said. "Make sure you tell him that."

"If I do that, he's going to know you're talking about him." LJ gave Olivia another kiss, then headed down the steps.

Sylvie turned to Olivia, who was still laughing, and scowled at her. "I'm glad you think this is funny."

"It's ironic as hell. You and my future brother-in-law hook up at my engagement party and now you're remodeling his business. That's what you get for not vetting him first."

"What was I supposed to do? You were so busy showing off your ring and people fawning all over LJ's portrait of you. We'd already kissed and it was only downhill from there."

"Downhill? That's what you're calling it now?"

"Why don't you march your happy ass in the house and pour us a couple of adult beverages?" Sylvie snapped.

"Wine or whisky?"

"Definitely whisky."

Olivia clasped her hands together. "You know what, Logan brought a single-malt scotch back from Scotland and this is the proper time to bring it out."

Sylvie's cheeks heated as she thought about the conversation that led to the kiss. A kiss that shook her even more than the midnight smooch. How in the hell was she going to work around him, inhale him, and watch him move around knowing what he looks like naked?

If I want to make my company a powerhouse, I'm going to have to focus on the work and not working my hips with Erik.

Erik nursed a glass of scotch while he waited for Logan to show up. After his encounter with Sylvie, he hadn't gone home. He'd headed for the Canvas Club. When he'd called his brother, it had been to lament about Sylvie. Then the FBI called. There was going to be an indictment against Simon; the federal prosecutor was making the announcement first thing in the morning. Erik knew the stock was going to take a nose-dive and leave the company open to a hostile takeover by the buyers who Simon had been courting.

"This might be the shortest CEO tenure in history." He downed his scotch and gritted his teeth. No matter how good the PR department was, there wasn't a way to get around what was about to happen. Erik was about to order another drink when he felt a hand on his shoulder. Expecting it to be Logan, Erik didn't even turn around before saying, "We're going to need a bottle of the good stuff to get through this."

"And what are we getting through, Mr. Jordan?"

Erik turned around and locked eyes with the

last person he wanted to see tonight or any other night.

Lori Anne Parker.

She was a woman who couldn't take a hint or buy a clue. She had applied to work in his lab three years ago, but after he found out that her credentials were forged, Erik rescinded his job offer.

"Why are you here?"

She smiled. "Just trying to be a reminder of the biggest mistake you've ever made. Then again, maybe I dodged a bullet. What's going on at JI?"

"Since you dodged a bullet, then it's nothing for you to worry about. Why don't you go enjoy your evening?"

"Well, I'm here celebrating. Finally have my own lab and I'm coming for you." She smiled and sauntered away. The childish side of him wanted to throw his empty glass at her retreating figure, but he had bigger problems.

Logan finally arrived and took a seat beside his brother. "You don't look too good and I know this isn't just about Sylvia."

Erik shook his head and waved for the bartender. "Nope. I got bigger issues. In less than twelve hours, everything is going to blow the hell up. The federal indictment against Dad is going to announced. Guess they got the files from the legal department."

Logan's mouth dropped open. When the bartender walked over to the men, Erik signaled for him to leave the bottle and handed him his credit card.

"What are you going to do?" Logan finally asked after pouring himself a drink.

"Brace for impact, I guess. The board and I have kept things quiet since his arrest, but this is one of those things that ends up on a cable news program."

Logan ran his hand across his face and shook his head. "Why did he do it?"

"Greed. Because he could? I don't know. The last time I spoke to him, he threatened me. Then Mom said he's in the hospital."

"Have you checked on him?"

Erik poured himself another drink before shaking his head. "I have to clean up his mess and I can't bring myself to care if he's lying in a hospital bed or not. We could lose the company."

"You mean y'all. Because I'm not a part of this shit show."

Erik rolled his eyes. "How about this: Maybe it's time for you to get involved. I need help, and right now, the only other Jordan I can trust these days is you."

"How am I supposed to help? I don't know anything about this company and—"

"You're a celebrity. People love your art, and if you lend your name to a line of makeup, that might help the stock from becoming worthless, for the time being."

"And that might just put my art career in a downward spiral. I don't know about this. I've worked too hard to distance myself from—"

"Simon! Dad didn't believe in you, but I've always had your back. Now I need you to have mine." Erik slammed his hand against the bar. Immediately, he felt bad for pressuring his brother. But he was desperate.

Logan must have realized his brother's plight because he agreed. "You're going to have to create a hell of a line. And I'm not talking some palette of wild colors that are going to end up on YouTube making women look like clowns either."

Erik leaned over and hugged his brother around the shoulders. "You're the best. And I got this." Reaching for his phone, he sent a text to his PR director asking her to come to the office immediately. "We got to get this ball rolling."

"Wait, Olivia needs to know about this first. You know, she's my brand manager."

Erik groaned. While he liked Olivia as Logan's fiancée, he didn't want her in their business. She had successfully guided Logan's career, but this was Jordan Industries business.

"What?" Logan asked as he took note of the scowl on Erik's face.

"Nothing, tell your brand manager."

"Why do I get the feeling that you don't want her involved?"

Erik shrugged. "Because I don't, but I can't fault you for running your business the way you see fit. Hell, you're the successful one."

"I'll tell her before the news goes public. After

all, it's not often that the great Erik Jordan asks for help."

"We got to get to the office. And since I'm probably beyond the legal limit of sobriety, you're driving."

"Great, this will give me a chance to tell you all about Sylvia and how she's sitting on my front porch talking about you."

Erik paused. "Why is she on your front porch?"

Logan rose to his feet and smirked. "That's Olivia's besty."

Erik blinked rapidly before standing up. "What in the hell have I gotten myself into?"

"Meaning?"

"Until this moment, I never believed in six degrees of separation. But got-damn! Even if I can deal with working around that sexy woman, she's never going to disappear from my life."

"Guess you're going to have to treat her right. Not really your strong suit when it comes to women."

"That's not true, I just don't do that whole long-term-commitment thing that you love. I give what I get, I don't make promises, and everybody knows what the deal is."

The men headed for the exit. "And why are you this way, Mr. Playboy?"

"Shut up." Erik never considered himself a playboy—he just wasn't the marrying type. Relationships were more work than he ever wanted to do. Worrying about another person's happiness and needs had been something he'd watched his mother do for years with no reward of her own.

Granted, his dad was an asshole and he was certain that if he ever fell in love she wouldn't be an asshole. But at some point, Simon must have offered Yvonne something that resembled love.

Erik wasn't going to take that risk. No matter how strong the temptation of Sylvie was.

Chapter 5

Sylvie and Olivia learned something tonight. Neither of them could handle scotch. Saying they'd overdone it was the understatement of the year as they lay on the sofa and love seat in the living room.

"Is the room ever going to stop spinning?" Sylvie slurred.

"Shh! My head is throbbing."

Sylvie closed her eyes and she could've sworn she heard Erik call her name. She felt herself reach her arms up to wrap them around his neck. The next thing she knew, she was tumbling off the sofa. Olivia's laughter filled the air. "My God, we're going to die!"

"Olivia Brown, I hate you." Sylvie placed her hand on the edge of the sofa and attempted to pull herself up. It took three tries for her to get up on the sofa again. "You could've told me that Logan was a member of the Jordan family. Then I would've been on high alert at your party and would've kept my lips to myself."

"Listen, you've been working so hard these past few months, I wanted you to have a good time and not think about work. Who knew you were going to go all 'Darling Miki' on Erik?"

"Nikki. It's 'Darling Nikki.' And . . ." Sylvie paused as she felt her stomach lurch. "We need food or I'm going to . . ." She didn't have to say it because she threw up all over the floor.

"Eww!" Olivia exclaimed. "I'm not cleaning that up!"

Tears sprang to Sylvia's eyes. "But I can't!"

"Where's Logan?"

"Gone."

Olivia nodded. "Right." She stood up on wobbly legs and headed for the bathroom to grab towels.

Sylvie looked at the mess and decided that this was what her life had become. A hot, steaming mess. Seconds later, Olivia threw two bath towels at her friend and Sylvia mopped up her vomit.

"This isn't what I should be doing right now."

Olivia frowned at her. "Sorry, Queen Sylvie, but you made the mess, now you clean it up."

Looking up at her friend, Sylvie frowned. "That's not what I mean. I'm talking about this project and how seeing Erik drove me to drinking."

"Oh. Well, if it makes you feel better, just know you beat him at his own game and you're in the driver's seat. Just keep your thighs together and make the magic that you're known for. Then you're going to be beating off requests for bigger jobs with a bat."

"You're right and I'm glad you have hardwood floors in here." She piled the soiled towels on top of each other. "I need your mop."

"I'll get it after I order pizza and Chinese." She gingerly walked over to the love seat and dug her cell phone from in between the cushions. "What in hell?"

"What's wrong?"

"Logan sent me a text. Said he's going to help his family business and we'll talk about it when he gets home. Who jumps on the *Titanic* after it hit the iceberg already?"

"What do you know that you refuse to tell me? Because it seems as if I'm on the same ship."

Olivia sighed and dropped her phone on the end table next to the love seat. "Erik became the CEO because Simon Jordan was arrested for embezzling money from the company. This happened in December, and somehow no one released any information about it. The board knows, the stockholders don't. It's only a matter of time before it all comes out."

"And this is going to be nothing but bad PR, and if I'm linked to this . . ."

Olivia waved her hand. "You're going to be fine. You're not an employee or a family member. Now, Logan." She sighed. "His LJ brand isn't associated with the family because his father never respected his talent and to this day calls him a painter. Erik is a chemist by trade, and him working with their dad fit. But he never judged Logan, and in the beginning, he was the main backer of Logan's earlier shows when people just came for the cheese and wine."

Sylvie smiled because free cheese and wine had brought LJ and Olivia together. They had attended a show at a new gallery downtown and the rest was history. Sylvie wasn't naïve enough to believe lightning would strike twice and her business arrangement with Erik would turn into a lifetime love.

Wait. What? Where the hell did that thought come from? Had to be the scotch.

"Sylvie? Are you listening?"

"Huh?"

"Are you still pretending to be a vegetarian or can we get a pepperoni pizza?"

"Make it sausage and peppers. I'll go back to vegetarian when I'm sober."

Erik, Logan, and Ingrid Jacobs, the head of Jordan Industries' public relations department, sat in the conference room huddled over iPads and coffee.

They'd crafted a response to Simon's indictment and planned a video that Erik would distribute to the board and the staff. Now, Erik was trying to find the right line of makeup to attach LJ's name to. But his brother was being difficult.

"That looks like clown makeup!" Logan said for the fifteenth time when Erik showed him an image.

Closing his eyes and counting to ten, Erik sighed. How was it that talking about his father's malfeasance had been the easiest part of this little powwow?

"Do you have any suggestions?" He handed his brother his iPad and Apple pencil.

Logan looked down at the blank screen and smiled. About ten minutes later, Logan had drawn a woman's face made up with colors that highlighted the ebony brown skin he'd created. Bright blues, deep purples, and a nude lip that shined like a diamond. There was just one problem: Erik and his lab staff hadn't created any makeup that would fit the beauty of the drawing.

"Do you know how long this would take to create?" Erik asked.

Logan shrugged. "That's your job, but this is what I'll sign off on." Saving the image, he texted it to Olivia. "And I'm thinking this should be the logo. We can do it in all skin tones, with the palette of each product."

"That is a good idea," Ingrid said with a yawn. "Not only would the public love the colors, but now people could have a little piece of LJ's art."

"Wearable Art by LJ!" Erik exclaimed. "That's the name of the line."

Logan faked a yawn. "That's boring and expected. This name and these products should pop."

"I'll put marketing on it in the morning. Provided they don't jump ship."

Ingrid glanced at her watch. "It is morning,

Erik. It's one in the morning and we still don't have much to combat the bad news that's going to be dropping in a few hours."

"Olivia would be a great help right about now," Logan suggested as he leaned back in his chair.

"Fine," Erik lamented. "See if she'll come down here and help us with this."

Logan rose to his feet and headed out into the hallway. Once Ingrid and Erik were alone, she turned to him with a wide smile on her face.

"Can I say that it's good to see you and Logan working together. I never understood why Simon didn't want his artist son a part of the company."

"Obviously my father is an idiot."

She placed her hand on top of his. "Don't judge him too harshly."

"The court of public opinion will do that for us. Why are you defending him?" Erik narrowed his eyes at her.

"When your father hired me, I had a public relations internship under my belt and a bunch of ideas no one wanted to listen to."

"And you were cheap labor. Ingrid, please don't tell me you're involved in this or . . ."

She snatched her hand away from his. "No! I love this company as much as you do. You're right, I was cheap labor, but your dad helped me grow into the professional I am today. And, as you know, I'm well compensated for it."

"Yes. I just processed a raise for the entire department and I appreciate you being on call for me when I need you."

Ingrid leaned forward and smiled at him. "If you ever need anything more, you got my number."

"As tempting as that sounds, we'd better keep this relationship strictly business."

Ingrid leaned back in her seat. "I didn't . . . It's late and I was out of line. Sorry about that."

"No harm, no foul." Erik rose to his feet and headed for the door. "We'd better call it a night. The real work starts tomorrow."

"But I thought Logan's brand manager was coming to meet with us. I really want to have something to say about his line after the news about Simon breaks."

As if he heard his name, Logan walked into the room. "Liv isn't going to make it. She's a little drunk right now. But she said we're welcome to come by the house and go over a few things."

"I'm going home," Ingrid said. "If you need me for anything, Erik, my phone will be on. Right beside my bed." As she sauntered out of the conference room, Logan turned to his brother.

"What did I miss while I was on the phone?"

Erik shook his head. "Nothing. Are you sure meeting with a drunk Liv is going to be helpful at all?"

"Maybe. But if nothing else, you can take all of the scotch out of the house. I told that woman she needs to stick to wine and champagne."

Sylvie polished off the last slice of cold pizza and realized she and Olivia were way too old to drink and eat pizza this time of night. She knew that she was going to have heartburn and a bitching hangover. How was she going to focus on her work at Jordan Industries and ignore her want for Erik?

"You ate all of the pizza, huh?" Olivia asked as she handed Sylvia a laundry basket. "For your towels."

Sylvia gathered the soiled towels and stuffed them in the basket. Then she headed to the laundry room with Olivia on her heels. "I need to go home."

"Absolutely not. That wouldn't be safe. You can sleep it off and then get back to work. Logan's on his way home and we have some work to do." She shook her head. "If he's going to do this thing, then we got to make sure it's going to be done right."

"Hmm, maybe I can get that painting after all."

Olivia pointed toward the bathroom. "Go take a shower and go to bed."

Sylvie laughed. "That's the best idea you've had all night."

"Excuse you! You're the one who said pour some adult beverages. Don't blame me."

Shrugging, Sylvie headed toward the guest bathroom at the end of the hallway. "Here's hoping that you have some of my favorite French soap in there."

"Nope, just some Ivory." Olivia's laugh alerted Sylvie to the fact that her friend was lying. When she entered the bathroom, she saw her favorite rose-scented soap on the counter.

Sylvie loved hot showers and this one was needed. The water beat down on her and she felt her mind clearing. Her focus on work was coming back. But that also meant thoughts of Erik flooded her mind. That kiss—the one that drove her to drink scotch.

And this is why I don't like brown liquor. Sylvie lathered herself with the fragrant soap and tried to pretend she didn't have a problem. But she did. She liked kissing Erik. She wanted to do it again, and that was the problem.

After rinsing and lathering again, Sylvie inadvertently wet her hair. She screamed as the water dripped into her eyes. Shutting the water off, she hopped out of the shower and realized she hadn't grabbed a towel from the hall linen closet. Despite the fact that Olivia was going to kill her for dripping all over the floor, Sylvie had to dry off before the water went all the way cold.

"Well, damn."

Okay, Sylvie was hearing things again because there was no way she heard Erik's voice again. Blinking the dripping water away, she thought she was seeing things because there he was—five o'clock shadow and all. And. She. Was. Naked.

"E-Erik?"

"Had no idea that you were here and so wet." He opened the linen closet and handed her a towel. At this point, Sylvie didn't care about her wet hair, she just needed to cover her wet body and get out of Erik's presence.

"Umm, why are you here?"

"God's plan, I guess."

She wrapped the towel around her body and shook her head, flinging droplets of water across his chest. "Excuse me."

"Sylvie, it's not as if I haven't seen it all before. And it's just as amazing as I remembered."

"Go to hell," she hissed as she dashed into the bathroom. Slamming the door, Sylvie willed her heart to beat normally. She dried her body and her hair. Just as she was about to leave the bathroom, there was a knock at the door.

"Go away!"

"Sylvie, I actually have to use the bathroom," Erik said.

"Not my problem. And there is another bathroom upstairs."

"But I'm here now."

She opened the door and glared at him. "Have at it." Sylvie rushed out of the bathroom and tried not to think of how she would deal with this later. Right now, she just needed to go to sleep.

Erik didn't have to use the bathroom as much as he thought he did. Seeing Sylvie naked and dripping had been an unexpected treat. He was going to slap Logan for not warning him that temptation was in his house.

He left the bathroom, quietly wondering where Sylvie went, then headed back into the living room. Though he knew Logan and Olivia were the most PDA couple he knew, walking in on them being all kissy face when they had business to take care of annoyed him. Well, if he was honest, he was annoyed because he wasn't holding Sylvie. There was something about seeing her standing there bare. Wet. Sexy. And shy. Where was the woman who'd wished him a funky good time in red lipstick?

"So, this is how y'all get work done?" Erik said.

Olivia and Logan broke their embrace and looked up at him. "Personally," Olivia began, "this doesn't make good sense for the LJ brand. I know that your family is all about the cosmetics business and being down for the cause of black women feeling beautiful, but . . ."

"Babe, we're going to do this," Logan said.

Olivia sighed and rolled her eyes. "I do like the potential packaging. But I think you need to make the name of this line about the women who will wear the makeup. Something like the Yvonne line was."

"That was my father's attempt at an apology to my mother," Erik said. "It had nothing to do with—"

"While that may be true, the consumer doesn't know that, and I don't know too many women who didn't love that lipstick."

"So we're supposed to lean on nostalgia?"

Olivia snapped her fingers. "Yes! That's what you should do: classic beauty."

Logan nodded. "Take it back old-school, with a new take on skin care and that red lipstick."

Erik tugged at his ear. Red lipstick was going to be the death of him. Without even thinking, he looked down the hall, expecting to see Sylvie. He was a little disappointed when he didn't.

"I'll run it by marketing and get Ingrid and her crew to launch a campaign. First order of business will be to bring that fire-red lipstick back."

"Good. Now can y'all stop this business talk so that I can go to sleep?" Olivia said through a yawn.

"You guys about to remodel?" Erik asked as he started for the door.

"No," Logan said. "We're barely here and . . . Oh, you must have run into Sylvia."

"How? She was in the shower . . . Y'all are horrible!"

Erik held up his hand. "Calm down. She needed a towel and I was heading for the bathroom. Totally accidental."

Olivia shook her head and rose to her feet. "Sylvie is my friend and you need to respect her for the boss that she is."

"I totally respect her. Every inch of her." Erik looked over Olivia's shoulder and locked eyes with Sylvie. It was a sin for a woman to look that good in a tank top and a pair of boxer shorts.

"Y'all talking about me?" She walked into the room and crossed over to Erik. "Can we talk outside really quickly?"

"Sure." They headed out to the porch and Erik reminded himself that this was just a talk and he needed to keep his hands to himself.

A beat passed and Sylvie bit her bottom lip. "Erik, we have to address the elephant in the room."

"Sylvie."

She placed her hand on his chest, then dropped it as if she'd been burnt. "Erik, this project is important to me and I want to do a good job. I need to know that we can work together without *things* getting in the way."

"Define *things*." Erik folded his arms across his chest. Secretly, it was good to see her squirm a bit. As she bounced from left to right, Erik watched her breasts jiggle. Feeling like a lecher, he turned his eyes up to her face.

God, why did she have to be so beautiful? Her pecan-brown skin was flawless. She had the kind of skin that would put him out of business.

"We had sex and it was good. But we didn't know that things were going to turn out this way. I don't want you to judge me based on one night."

Erik nodded and placed his hand on Sylvie's shoulder. "Both of us are grown-ups. And I need you right now."

She furrowed her eyebrows. "You need me?"

"Listen, any positive publicity for the company right now is vital. People love a good makeover, and from the little I've seen of your work, this is going to be a good one. As a matter of fact, I'm going to get with my PR department and see if we can do some kind of tie-in with the rebranding of the company and your work."

Sylvie smiled and clasped her hands together. "That would be awesome. I think you should reconsider the CEO portrait, you know, since you're rebranding and everything."

Erik shook his head and dropped his hand from her silky shoulder. "Not a chance. See you in a couple of hours." He started down the steps, then looked back at her. "Good night, Sylvie."

"'Night, Erik."

Chapter 6

Sylvie didn't sleep at all after Erik left. It was something about the way he said he needed her that sparked something inside her. Of course he was talking business. He didn't need anything else. The man had everything.

She spent more time than she wanted to admit following his exploits on Google. The man loved models. Erik was also the man behind the makeup. She enjoyed reading a story about his work in the Jordan Industries lab. Her favorite quote from the article was, "I want to make every woman in the world feel beautiful."

Somehow, she believed that was his mission. By the time the sun came up, Sylvie was beyond tired, but thankfully, she didn't have a hangover.

Olivia, on the other hand, was suffering. The sound of her friend throwing up in the bathroom made Sylvie feel bad. She headed for the kitchen to make Olivia some tea, but Logan had beaten her to it.

"I made two cups because I thought both of y'all were going to be sick this morning," he said as he held a teacup out to Sylvie.

"I'm pretty sure we're done with scotch forever. Logan, why didn't you . . . Never mind."

He sighed and walked over to the one-cup coffeemaker to brew a mug. "You have questions about my family, right?"

"It's none of my business. But you could've been large a long time ago if people knew you were one of those Jordans."

Logan shook his head. "Sometimes I wish I wasn't one of those Jordans. But don't listen to me. I see you and my brother have this spark between y'all."

Sylvie laughed nervously. "That's just creative energy."

"If you say so. Word to the wise, Erik doesn't let much get to him. You got to him."

Sylvie was about to reply when a disheveled Olivia walked into the kitchen. "Sylvia, get out of my house. You did this to me."

Logan walked over to Liv and gave her a quick kiss on the cheek. "Don't blame her, you know you're a lightweight." Ushering her to a seat at the breakfast bar, Logan pushed her cup of tea over to her.

Sylvia looked at her watch. "I do have to go."

"Ugh, so do I," Logan said. "I bet if I turn the TV on I'll see more of my father today than I've seen in years."

Olivia patted the back of her man's hand. "It's okay, babe."

Sylvia felt as if she was in the middle of something intimate and wanted to leave without killing the vibe. When Logan and Liv looked up at her, she waved and eased out of the kitchen. Now, she was curious. What was really happening at Jordan Industries? The business side of Sylvie now regretted spending the night looking at pictures of Erik and not getting information about the company.

Erik was on his third cup of coffee and he still didn't feel awake yet. Despite all that talk of being an adult and not holding New Year's Eve against Sylvie, he'd spent his three hours of sleep haunted by her wet, naked body. In his dream he'd taken her against the wall while the *Purple Rain* soundtrack played in the background. She'd wrapped those thighs around his waist and just as he was about to explode—his alarm went off. Talk about anticlimactic. But he needed to stop thinking about sex with Sylvie and take a more active role in the renovations.

He was about to look up color swatches on the Internet when Ingrid burst into his office.

"The news is breaking," she panted. "Simon was arrested again. This time there were cameras there."

"They arrested him at the hospital? That's some cold shit."

"No, he was released yesterday. This happened at your parents' house. Now would be a good time to release a statement," Ingrid said. "But you look tired."

"Didn't get a lot of sleep last night."

"I can tell." Ingrid reached into her pocket and handed him a concealer stick.

He shot her a questioning look. "What am I supposed to do with this?"

"Hide the circles underneath your eyes. Come on, you create makeup, you should know how to use it."

"I don't need to know how to use it, because I'm not putting that on my face. Doesn't it make sense that I look a little out of sorts? My father was arrested and now I have to clean up his mess."

"You still want to present an air of confidence to the consumers and the board. Is Logan going to join you?"

Erik chuckled. "And you're worrying about how I look?"

"But he's an artist, people expect that. You are supposed to be the face of the company. Put the concealer on!"

Erik took the stick from her hand and grinned. "You will speak nothing of this."

"You're going to need a mirror." She exited the office and Erik shook his head. His sleepless night should've been because of the company's turmoil, but it had more to do with the woman he'd just seen walk down the hall. Sylvie filled out a pair of jeans like nobody's business. And he'd seen her dressed in her finest and in her birthday suit. Rising to his feet, he called her name.

Sylvie knew she wasn't hearing things this time because she looked Erik in the eye as he approached her. Was he really looking like a hearty snack this early in the morning?

"'Morning. I was going to grab some coffee before getting back to your office. But . . . Why do you have concealer in your hand?"

"Because I'm about to be on TV and my . . ."

"There you are." The woman with the silky voice and long legs looked as if she was happy to see Erik, until she caught a glimpse of Sylvie. "Who are you?"

"Ingrid," Erik said. "This is Sylvia Gates, the owner of SG Designs. She's the woman behind the redesign."

"Oh," Ingrid replied, then held up a mirror. "Erik, it's time to get you ready for your close-up. The press is circling outside." She turned to Sylvie and offered her the fakest smile. "Nice to meet you. I'm sure your work here will be amazing."

"Yes, it will," Sylvie replied and returned Ingrid's cool smile. "Erik, I'll be in your office soon."

He nodded at her and headed inside his office with Ingrid. Sylvie tried to act as if she didn't think the tall chick wasn't the second most annoying woman she'd ever met. That number-one spot would always belong to her former partner.

Not that she wished bad luck on anyone, but if a truck hit Amanda, Sylvie wouldn't shed a tear. But she'd send flowers to the service.

This Ingrid chick reminded her of the pretty girl from high school who stayed pretty while other people aged, and let them know she'd kept her girlish figure and could still wear her prom dress. The way she looked at Erik, Sylvie knew she wanted him to be her prom king. But whatever. She was here to do a job, and seeing this was just what she needed to put distance between Erik and her thighs. Heading down to the coffee nook, Sylvie couldn't help but get drawn into the office gossip swirling around.

"I can't believe Mr. Jordan got arrested," a woman said to her colleague as she loaded her mug with sugar.

The other woman shook her head, her face contorted. "Do you think Erik is really going to be able to run this company? They just snatched him out of the lab because his last name is Jordan. What does he really know?"

"How to sleep with the models, for one. Remember Madison Monroe? She was supposed to be the face of the new collection and he messed that up."

The other woman took a sip of her coffee and then grinned. "I thought it was because she had a drug problem."

"A drug named Erik's dick."

Sylvie fought her laughter and lost. The two women glanced in her direction, then gathered their coffee and pastries before exiting the room. *Poor Madison, I can totally understand how that addiction can start.*

She filled a paper cup with coffee and two packages of sugar. It was time to work and stop thinking about Erik and Ingrid. Still, she couldn't help but wonder what was going on at the company and if she was going to get the chance to show off her work or not.

Erik may have felt as if he had a ton of makeup on, but the quality of Jordan cosmetics had his face looking smooth and natural in front of the camera. Ingrid told him to smile but not show all of his teeth before starting his statement. He needed to present the air of a leader and a surprised son. Erik didn't realize he needed to be part Denzel Washington to be a good CEO.

"Ladies and gentlemen, the news about the arrest of former CEO Simon Jordan is a blow to the legacy of Jordan Industries, but we are going to weather this storm by continuing to produce quality products and restore faith in the minds of our stockholders, investors, and most importantly our consumers. My father, Simon, will be held responsible for the crimes he's accused of if he's guilty. But he is no longer a part of this company. We're going in a new direction with Jordan cosmetics and I'm pleased to announce that we're debuting a new and exciting line of makeup that will embrace the beauty of every woman in every hue."

Erik paused and smiled again. "Just keep in mind that Jordan Industries is more than one person. We're a family business that is starting over with an eye to the future and a nod to the past."

Ingrid started the video screen behind Erik. Red lips filled the screen, and now he wished that he'd looked at the video first. Not that it was in poor taste, it was just Sylvie. Whenever he saw red lipstick, he thought of her. His body remembered her and he wanted her all over again.

The presentation of the lipstick and the announcement of Logan's line went over well with the press. But when Ingrid ushered Erik away from the podium without allowing him to take any questions, an audible groan filled the room.

"What was that all about?" he asked when they'd entered his office.

"Leave them on a high note. You know every question was going to be about your father and not what we wanted the media to focus on." She pulled up a file on her phone. "I'm going to send every reporter who was here more information about the cosmetics line and a transcript of your statement."

"I don't like doing business this way." Erik shook his head as he paced. "I'd rather be transparent and take the tough questions than—"

"Questions about how you're a chemist and

not a businessman? Or questions about how you and your father's relationship will recover from this? Trust me, we'll be transparent when you sit down with a reporter we can trust. That would've been throwing you to the wolves."

Erik nodded. He paid this woman because she knew what she was doing, and now wasn't the time to question that. "Who are we going to do the interview with?"

She shrugged. "Not sure yet. Give me a couple of days and—"

A loud clang at the door caused them to pause their conversation. Erik focused his stare on Sylvie, who had dropped a bunch of charts and rulers on the floor. Crossing over to her, he assisted her in picking up her tools.

"Sorry, I thought you were still doing your press conference thing." She smiled as he kneeled in front of her.

"That's done for now," he said. "What is all of this?"

Ingrid rolled her eyes and cleared her throat. "Erik, do you want to go over the reporters who you want to do the interview with?"

"Let's meet for lunch. You can even pick the place. Sylvie and I need to figure out how long I need to be out of my office."

Ingrid released an exasperated sigh. "Fine, I'll go monitor the news reports and get with the staff about some press releases as well as uploading the video to social media." She turned on her heels and clicked out of the office.

"What's her deal?" Sylvie muttered.

"Huh?"

"Nothing. I thought you didn't want to be involved in picking out color swatches and what color the walls were going to be." She set the rest of her tools on his desk.

"Can't a brother change his mind?"

Sylvie shrugged. "I guess. But why did you really change your mind, Erik? From what I was told, this isn't your favorite project."

He was about to respond when his phone rang. "Hold that thought." Erik walked into the hallway before answering the phone. "This is Erik."

"You had to throw your father under the bus," his mother hissed.

"He threw the whole family under the bus with his stealing. Is he locked up in his hospital bed or in a jail cell?"

"Now you're concerned? Erik, why are you joining in this campaign against your father? After everything he's done for you? We're going to lose the house."

"Ma, you know I'll take care of you."

"In the same manner that you're taking care of your father? I don't think so."

"Are you involved in this?"

"What? How dare you?" Yvonne yelled. "Your father and I built this company and I'd rather see strangers run it than for you and your brother to destroy it!"

"Dad is the only one who's trying to destroy

anything. He stole from the company, he's behind the falling stock prices, and—"

"And you're responsible for destroying his good name when you could've looked the other way and voted for the sale!"

"Who are you and what have you done with my mother? The woman who raised me always taught me to do the right thing."

"Family comes first seems to be the lesson you forgot."

"I'm not the only one who doesn't know that lesson." Erik hung up the phone and shook his head. Now he was convinced that his mother was hiding something. How was he going to find out the truth, though?

Erik walked back into his office and watched Sylvie climb up on a step stool with a tape measure in her hand. As she inched forward to take window measurements, her foot slipped. He jetted over to her and caught her before she hit the floor.

"That was close," she said as she wrapped her arms around his neck.

"Why would you do something so reckless?" He brushed his lips across hers. Sylvie moaned as he captured her mouth in a smoldering kiss. She tightened her grip around his neck and reveled in the heat of his body against hers.

Erik fell into his desk chair, still holding on to Sylvie. Their bodies were a tangled mess of lust and he wanted every inch of her right then and there. But this wasn't the time or the place, especially when . . .

"Oh my God!"

The couple broke this kiss and looked into Olivia and Logan's shocked faces. Sylvia leapt out of Erik's lap.

"It isn't what you think. He just saved me from a fall. I, um, have to go get some . . . I'll be back." She dashed out of the office and Erik shook his head.

"Better learn to close that door," Logan quipped. Olivia punched her fiancé on the forearm.

"How about he learns that he and Sylvia are supposed to be acting like they're in a place of business."

Erik folded his arms across his chest. "What do y'all want?"

Olivia rolled her eyes. "Well, we wanted to come and congratulate you on your press conference, but it looks like—"

Erik held up his hand. "Liv, I know you and Sylvia are close, but trust me when I say that she isn't doing anything she doesn't want to do."

"Babe, you're going to have to let them do their thing without your interference." Logan stroked the back of Olivia's arm.

"I'm not trying to interfere. But since I've known this guy, he hasn't had a great track record with women." Olivia speared him with an icy look. "You treat them like interchangeable bed warmers, and I'm not going to sit here and watch you do that to my friend."

"Need I remind you that . . . Olivia, I'm not going to do anything to your friend that she doesn't want. I'm not sitting here promising to love and cherish anyone. Logan has that on lock."

She rolled her eyes, then turned to her fiancé. "I'm going to check on Sylvie."

Once the brothers were alone, Logan picked up a paperweight, which was shaped like a baseball, and threw it at Erik. "Whatever is going on with you and Sylvie, you have to stop it now. If I have to listen to another hour-long diatribe about you two being horrible for each other, I'm going to kill you in your sleep."

"What?" Erik caught the paperweight and set it on the edge of the small table in the corner.

"Olivia and Sylvia are more than just friends. So, she is super concerned about whatever this is between the two of you, which means I'm in the middle. Don't like being in the middle."

Erik glanced at the door to make sure they were still alone. "There's something about that woman that drives me crazy."

"Is it because she doesn't chase you like everyone else has? Or are you trying to get her back for that New Year's Eve tryst?"

Erik shrugged. "She's different. Sylvia isn't intimidated by shit. And she haunts me."

"Really?" Logan raised his right eyebrow. "This might be serious."

"Shut up, and if you tell Olivia anything I've said I'm going to kill you in your sleep."

Logan clasped his hand around Erik's shoulder. "But you know I never sleep. So, I win."

"Why are you really here, though?"

Logan perched on the edge of Erik's desk. "Came to jump-start this line and get the world talking about something other than Dad's arrest. You know, all that business shit we talked about last night."

Erik narrowed his eyes at his brother. "You know what, let's go to the lab and look at some color palettes. I swear you get on my last nerve."

"Sure I do. So, if Olivia and I had been about five minutes later, would you have ripped her clothes off and taken her on the desk or nah?"

Olivia cornered Sylvie in the coffee nook, where her friend was gulping down a bottle of cold water.

"I guess you do need to cool off. What's going on with you and Erik?"

"Nothing," Sylvie said after taking another gulp.

"Bullshit," Olivia said. "You two seem to keep having your lips touching all the time."

"That's not true. It's just he was there when I almost fell and . . . Didn't I tell you last night that I like kissing him?"

"Sylvie, I know that you're trying to act like

you're focusing on business and you don't want to fall in love with someone. But Erik is dangerous."

"You're being overly dramatic here," she said. Although, Sylvie was well aware of how dangerous that man could be. *A drug named Erik's dick.*

"I don't want to see you hurt, when I know you do want to give your heart to the right man."

"Says you. I'm good with this whole love thing. What's with you and my mama these days?"

Olivia folded her arms across her chest and shook her head. "Your mama wants a grand-baby. I want my friend to be happy. What's wrong with that?"

Sylvie shrugged. "I'm going to ask you the same question I asked my mother: Who says I'm not happy now?"

Olivia threw her hands up. "You're right. You're probably content as hell."

"The last time I put my happiness in the hands of someone else, we saw how that turned out." Sylvie raised her right eyebrow. "I don't need a man to make me happy. But a few orgasms isn't a bad thing."

"Stephen was an asshole, but you can't keep thinking that everyone is going to be like him."

"So, you're saying Erik shouldn't be judged?" Sylvie laughed. "Don't answer that. I don't want anything from Erik. And I certainly don't want a relationship with him. Besides, I think he has something brewing with the PR lady."

"What PR lady?"

"The one he's taking to lunch later today. She had him wear makeup during the press conference, can you believe that?"

Olivia laughed, then grabbed her own bottle of water. "You don't sound jealous at all."

Sylvie glared at her friend. "I'm not. It's just that I asked him to let me do a CEO portrait of him in makeup and he told me no."

"Umm-huh, not jealous at all."

"Again, I'm not. Listen, I don't care who he spends his time with, because according to office gossip, he's a man who wants the models. Ever heard of Madison Monroe?"

"Girl, that cokehead? If that's the kind of woman Erik wants, why are you spending time with him?"

"Eh, because I'm renovating this place."

"Whatever. Just be careful. I know you want this because of the national exposure for your company, but make sure you're not putting yourself at risk. Okay?"

"Don't worry about me. I have this under control." Sylvie almost believed what she said, until she saw Ingrid walk into the coffee nook.

"Hello, ladies," she said. Sylvie gave the woman a slow once-over and couldn't help but think that she and Logan looked alike. Maybe it was just her imagination. Olivia told the woman hello, then ushered Sylvie out of the room.

"Go to work, but stay out of Erik's arms."

She offered her friend a mock salute. "Will do, Captain."

When Sylvie returned to Erik's office, she found it empty. She was cool with it, because she could get her re-measurements without worrying about her lips being assaulted again. Well, *assault* wasn't the right word. Erik's lips were the magnets and she was the steel. Despite what she'd told Olivia, there was something about Erik that made her quiver. And she hadn't felt that since the beginning of her relationship with Stephen.

To think she almost married a man who wanted a Stepford wife. When she'd started talking about going into business for herself, he'd discouraged her at every turn.

"Sylvia, you don't need to work. I make enough money for us to live comfortably. Why do you want to turn a hobby into a business?" Stephen cut into his steak and she vowed that she'd never eat red meat again. Obviously the flesh of a cow made people stupid.

She closed her eyes and counted to ten before she responded to her soon-to-be ex. "My mother taught me that hard work is important, no matter how much you love your mate. Things happen and . . ."

Stephen dropped his knife and fork, then threw his hands up. "Oh my God, do I have to sit through this story again? Your father died after lifting y'all out of the slums of New Orleans and your mother worked hard to make sure you didn't suffer. I got it. Maybe if your father had planned better for your future, you wouldn't be sitting here feeling so insecure."

Without a second thought, Sylvie grabbed the steak knife from the table and pointed it at Stephen. His eyes stretched to the size of quarters, because neither one of them knew what was going to happen next. Part of her wanted to bury the knife in his shoulder. How dare he talk about her father? He never met her hero, and no matter what he thought, her dada did everything to take care of the family. But who can predict death? No one!

"Don't you ever mention my father ever again, you son of a bitch!" She dropped the knife and stalked away from the table. "How about you get out of my house?" Sylvie pulled her engagement ring off and tossed it across the room. "You will never be half the man my father was and you're not good enough to be my husband."

"And you're just a good piece of ass that I thought I could turn into a housewife. Clearly I was wrong." Stephen marched out the front door, leaving the engagement ring spinning on the floor.

The next morning, Sylvie took the ring to Magazine Pawn Shop on Magazine Street and got the seed money for her business. When she'd told her friend, Amanda Warren, that she wanted to start an interior design company, her friend had jumped in with a one-hundred-thousand-dollar investment. At the time, she and Amanda were determined to make it on HGTV with their *projects. The call never came, but the duo gained a reputation in New Orleans for creating magic.*

Behind the scenes, though, cracks were starting to form in the foundation of the company. Amanda thought her investment had exempted her from doing work. After Sylvie did a few high-profile projects, the spotlight shined on Sylvie exclusively.

But money was pouring into the new business, and Sylvie had no idea that Amanda was harboring resentment toward her.

Shaking her memories away, Sylvie decided that she had to renew her focus on work and forget about Erik's kisses.

"Sylvie."

His voice made her jump. Whirling around, she offered him a smile. "What's up?"

"I have a staff who can help you do those measurements. The last thing I need is you falling off that little stepladder when we have janitors who can help."

"I don't need . . . Thanks, Erik."

He crossed over to Sylvie and stroked her cheek. "You have to be the most stubborn woman I've ever met."

"Why would you say something like that?" She turned her head away from his hand and tried to ignore the tingles kissing her spine.

"Baby girl, you're short. But you thought you'd be able to use a three-foot ladder to measure those windows?" He nodded toward the floor-to-ceiling windows behind his desk. "Then I offer you a staff who will be at your beck and call, and you want to act as if you don't need the help? That is the definition of stubborn."

She rolled her eyes. "Don't you have a lunch to prepare for?"

"Maybe. But we still need to look over those color swatches, remember?"

Chapter 7

If he was honest, Erik didn't give a damn about wall coverings, or about colors and textures for the furniture that would decorate his office. All he wanted was to inhale her feminine scent and accidentally on purpose touch her arm or hand.

Damn, her skin felt like silk and he wanted to peel her clothes off and touch her all over. But he had to focus.

"Why would I want red walls in here?" Erik leaned forward and looked at the sketch Sylvie had designed.

"Hello, your logo. And red is a power color. You're a powerful man, embrace it."

Erik knew what he wanted to embrace and it wasn't power. "Maybe we can do a muted red. Add some gold trim and maybe put the company's logo on the wall."

She shook her head and eased a little closer to his chest. Erik inhaled deeply as her booty brushed against his crotch. Why did this woman have to smell like strawberries and sweet cream? He already knew how sweet she was, and his mouth was watering thinking about that yoni.

"Those walls are going to be super busy with trim and logos. Make a choice."

"I yield to your expertise."

"I knew you were a smart man." She turned around and faced him with a smile on her full lips. Erik noticed they were bare. No shade of red. Not even a nude gloss, but her lips were still tempting. He brushed his index finger across her cheek.

"Will you have dinner with me tonight?"

She expelled a sigh. "I'm not sure that's a good idea. I—"

"Why not? We've already gotten the sex out of the way and it's time what we get to know each other a little better."

"We work together, and that's probably not the best idea. We should just leave things on a professional level."

"I don't want to do that. There's something between us and I want to explore it. Tell me if I'm wrong about you feeling the same way and I'll back off."

She bit down on her bottom lip. "Erik, I . . ."

"Listen, I don't normally do this. But there's something about you that I can't get out of my head."

"This is going to be super complicated and we shouldn't even try it."

He stepped back and gave her a slow once-over. "What are you afraid of?"

"Nothing," she quipped.

Erik grinned. "Are you sure? Because a meal won't kill you and you know I don't bite."

"That's not true, because I'm sure I had a bite mark on my shoulder to ring in the New Year." She returned his grin. "Not that I was upset."

Erik folded his arms across his chest. "So, are we on for tonight?"

Before Sylvie could answer, Ingrid walked into the office. She gave Sylvie a cool glance, then plastered a smile on her face.

"Hope I'm not interrupting anything, but you owe me lunch." She crossed over to the front of his desk and looked down at the renderings Sylvie had been working on. "This will photograph beautifully. Good job."

"Thank you." Sylvie fought the urge to roll her eyes at Ingrid. It was official, she didn't like that uppity heffa.

"Damn, I know I promised you lunch, but I got so caught up here. Why don't we order in and meet in the conference room."

She shrugged. "Fine. Hope you're cool with sushi." Ingrid started toward the door and Erik followed her.

"Text me when everything is set up." Erik closed the door, then turned back to Sylvie. "Now, you have a question to answer."

"That was a little rude."

"Maybe, but I'm tired of being interrupted. Dinner or breakfast?"

She chuckled softly. "Why are you so relentless? Suppose I have plans?"

"Part of me wants to tell you to cancel them, but if you have something better to do, then by all means, let's have dinner tomorrow."

"We can do it tonight."

He raised his eyebrow and licked his lips.

"Dinner," she explained. "And nothing else."

Erik threw his hands up. "Didn't expect anything but a nice meal and some good conversation. But no talk of color swatches."

"So, unlike your lunch, this won't be a business dinner?"

He shook his head. "This is about me trying to have a funky good time with a sexy woman who haunts me." Erik crossed over to her and pulled Sylvie into his arms. "I can't promise you that I won't kiss you tonight."

She tilted her head to the side. "Why wait?"

Erik traced her lips with his index finger. "Because, I want to see these lips painted your favorite color."

"And what if I don't have a quality tube of red lipstick?"

He released her. "Hold that thought." Erik dashed out of his office and headed for the sample room down the hall.

* * *

Alone in his office, Sylvie wondered what she was getting herself into. Dinner with Erik had the potential to be dangerous. Clearly, she couldn't hide behind work. She had so many questions about him and where this thing was going. Where did she want things to go? Back to the bedroom? Sylvie couldn't allow herself to put her heart where it shouldn't be. And that was squarely in Erik's hands. What if there was more than business going on with him and Ingrid? Then again, she couldn't believe Erik would be that much of a dick to openly flirt with her in front a woman he was sleeping with.

At least she knew that he wasn't married. But he did have a reputation, and Sylvia didn't want to be another among the Jordanettes. She also wasn't trying to make Erik settle down with her—either.

Focus on your job! This is about building your brand and not falling in love with this man. Sylvie was ready to tell him that dinner was off and they needed to keep things strictly business.

Then the door to his office opened and Erik's smile made her want to melt. Then he crossed over to her and opened his hand. Now, she was going to melt.

"Is that *Yvonne Red*?"

"It is. And if you promise to meet me for dinner, these are yours."

She grabbed the lipsticks from his hand. "Does seven thirty work for you?"

Erik laughed. "Sounds great. Though, I feel really used right now. Oh, and these aren't for writing on mirrors."

"Are you ever going to let that go?"

He folded his arms across his chest and shook his head. "You're going to have to show me exactly what a *funky good time* is for me to let that go."

Sylvie shrugged. "I thought I'd taken care of that already." She looked down at her watch. "I have to go. My supplier and I have to meet about furniture for the waiting room."

Erik leaned in and kissed her on the cheek. "I'm looking forward to seeing you tonight."

She closed her eyes as his lips touched her skin. "So do I."

He walked her to the door and they shared a quiet moment. Erik opened the door and watched Sylvie walk away. "Damn," he muttered.

Sylvie felt as if she was floating when she left Jordan Industries. That had to stop. Just because the man gave her red lipstick, her favorite red lipstick, it didn't mean anything. They were sexually attracted to each other and that's where things ended. Olivia had warned her about Erik's player ways, and Sylvie wasn't going to get caught up in it.

But there was something so tender about that simple kiss on the cheek that made her feel all warm and cuddly inside. Shaking her head,

Sylvie put her focus on purchasing furniture for the project and not her attraction to Erik Jordan.

She wanted an art deco feel with a hint of elegance, something that would embody the Jordan brand. And she was focusing on color. Reds, orange, and blues. Part of her wondered what Erik's signature color was. She'd only seen him in formal wear or naked. He wore a lot of gray suits to the office. But a man who created the kind of makeup that Jordan Industries was known for had to have some kind of style that represented him. Sylvie wanted to incorporate that in the redesign because this place was his show to run now. She headed out of the office and to her favorite décor store.

As she drove to the store, which was less than three blocks from JI, Sylvie reminded herself to take a look at the stories about the shake-up at Jordan Industries and how Erik got the big job. She pulled into the lot across from the store and fumbled with her smartphone to pull up the internet browser.

When the app was about to open, she looked up and saw Amanda walking in her direction. The childish part of her wanted to trip her and watch everything in her hands roll into the middle of the street. But she was a mature woman who could ignore the bitch who had tried to destroy her company.

One thing was for certain, she wasn't going to

run. Standing inches from each other, Sylvie smiled. "Well, hello, Amanda."

She rolled her eyes at Sylvie and kept walking as if she didn't hear the greeting. As she took a step forward, Amanda dropped the cans of spray paint she'd been holding. Sylvie didn't even try to hide her laughter.

"I always told you not to use spray paint, but you never listened."

"Go to hell, Sylvia!"

"Oh, you can talk."

Amanda picked up her items and glared at her former partner. "What are you trying to do, gloat?"

"Why would I do that? Oh, because you left me in the lurch but I'm still here?"

"No one left you, because you don't know how to have a partnership. If you wanted it to be all about you then you can do it without my money."

"And I'm sure you're happy to know that I have done just that."

"What do you want, a cookie? You never meant for this to be a partnership, and you made it clear in that article."

Sylvie shook head. "Is that what this is all about? You didn't like the article I did about how I dealt with the death of my father? How this business helped me work through my grief?"

"There you go again, with the *my, my, my*! I mean, damn, Johnny Gill."

"I'm not doing this with you. If you were ever my friend, you would—"

Amanda rolled her eyes. "Yeah, let's not do this. Because you think you're the only person in the world who has ever had pain. Get over your selfish self."

"I'm selfish? Well, I guess you're the pot and I'm the kettle. You wanted credit for not doing any work. Your investment didn't mean you could just sit on the sidelines."

"My investment is why you made a name for yourself, and you tried to erase me from the company. So fuck you, Sylvie. And I'm not the only one who feels that way. Stephen and I were just talking about you."

If Amanda thought she was going to get a rise out of Sylvie with that little revelation, she was dead wrong. But inside, Sylvie was boiling.

"It's a shame that you two don't have anything else to talk about." She started to walk away.

"Oh, we do have other things to discuss, like our future son or daughter."

Sylvie stopped in mid stride. Spinning around on her heels, she saw that Amanda had a baby bump.

"Congratulations," she said, then quickly walked to her car. Sylvie climbed in the Jag and pounded her hand against the steering wheel. She tried not to allow her tears to run down her face. But of all the women in the world that Stephen could've knocked up, it had to be that tramp?

Stephen wanted kids when they were together, and Sylvie had wanted to give him a child. But the more they'd tried without success, the more her soul was shattered. Without telling him, she'd gone to her ob-gyn to find out if she had issues conceiving. It turned out that her infrequent periods were because she only had one functioning ovary. While her doctor told her that she could conceive, it would be difficult. The only person she'd ever shared the news of her doctor's appointment with had been Amanda.

Now, to see her standing there with a uterus full of Stephen's baby shook her core. Wiping a stray tear that slid down her cheek, Sylvie started the car and tried to pretend she didn't give a damn.

But it hurt, knowing that he had given Amanda the one thing she'd wanted when they had been together.

Chapter 8

Erik couldn't put his finger on it, but Ingrid had an attitude. Maybe it was the fact that she kept jabbing her sushi rolls with the chopsticks, as if they had stolen her money. They'd been sitting in the conference room for about twenty minutes and she hadn't said a word about what the company was going to do to make the launch of Logan's line the topic of conversation, rather than Simon's arrest.

"You all right?" Erik glanced at her over the rim of his cup of iced tea.

"Yes. I'm fine. Why do you ask?"

"Thought this was a business lunch, and you usually talk a mile a minute."

She rolled her eyes. "Excuse me for doing my job."

"Hold on. I know I've been leaning on you a lot lately, but if there's a problem, let me know."

"Sorry, Erik, I'm just a little tired. When do you think we can get Logan to come and talk about his line? Who's going to design it, by the way?"

Erik snorted. "Me, of course. Just because I'm CEO doesn't mean I'm going to give up my work in the lab."

"Isn't that what Simon did?"

"There are a lot of things my father did that I won't be doing."

"Has the board agreed to this?" Ingrid stabbed another California roll with her chopsticks. "You're going to have to dig the company out of this PR nightmare, reassure the stockholders that the company isn't going under and . . ."

"Keep someone from staging a hostile takeover. It's a good thing I'm able to multitask."

Ingrid snapped her fingers. "We have to show you doing the work. Maybe you and Logan should do a photo shoot in the lab. We can shoot a video and call it 'A Day in the Life of CEO Erik Jordan.'"

He popped a crunchy roll in his mouth and nodded. "I'll get Logan on the phone and make sure he doesn't plan to leave the country anytime soon, and get this going."

"Do we want to make this a scripted thing or just capture the real?" Ingrid took a sip of her tea and relaxed in her seat. "We can get together tonight and come up with a realistic script."

"Tonight isn't going to work. I have plans."

"With the interior decorator? Are you sure that's a good idea?"

Erik raised his right eyebrow as he dunked a California roll in eel sauce. "Yeah, I'm sure."

"What do you know about this woman? The last thing we need is to be opened up to another scandal. Suppose things go left with you two and you have to let her go or she decides that she wants to pile on to what we're currently dealing with? You're going to have to exercise more caution with your extracurricular activities now that you're sitting in the big chair."

Erik took a deep breath and thought about his response. While he could appreciate Ingrid's advice, he didn't need it.

Sylvie could've run to *TMZ* or any tabloid the day he walked into his office and found her measuring the floor. She didn't and probably wouldn't. "I got this."

"I hope you're right. Just keep in mind, she's not a disgruntled model making up stories because she didn't get her face on a new product. And in this climate, even the rumor of sexual harassment would be enough to bring you down."

"That's not going to happen, because I've never done anything with a woman that she didn't want."

She rolled her eyes. "Now might be the time for you to settle down and stop your serial dating."

"That's cute, you're worried about me."

"I'm worried about this company, and since you're now the face of it, I guess I do have to put you on my worry list." She licked her lips. "And I get that you're single, rich, and sexy. But you have more to think about now."

Erik grinned. "What are you suggesting? A fake marriage? A media-suitable girlfriend? I'm good with that because what I do outside of saving this company doesn't matter. Things are bad, so I don't plan to get serious about anything but work."

She smiled and nodded. "Then it seems as if we're on the same page." Ingrid grabbed the last California roll and handled it with less violence. Erik was sure that his PR maven was tired and made a mental note to try and make her job easier.

"Let's talk about this article that my father was so excited about doing. How are we going to frame this story and make it about the new direction of Jordan Industries and not the sins of the father?"

"Glad you asked. I have a few ideas, but I haven't written the report yet."

"Can you have it ready in the morning? I want to let the board know what we're doing to keep the company afloat."

She nodded. "Unlike you, I don't have a life, so I can work on this tonight."

"Ingrid, you've been working really hard. If you need to take the night off, you can get me the report by three tomorrow."

She rose to her feet and then bowed in his direction. "Such a benevolent taskmaster. I'll have it ready in the morning."

"Great." Erik glanced at his watch and realized that he needed to get down to the lab if he wanted to make any progress on Logan's line. "All right, I'm taking the CEO hat off and heading for the lab."

"Cool. I'm looking forward to this new line. If I can be candid, our cosmetics have been kind of stale and safe lately."

Erik sighed because this was the same conversation he'd been having with his father. "Well, things in the game have changed."

Sylvie snapped at the mover when a box toppled over. "If those chairs are damaged, you're paying for them!" She crossed over to the box and opened it. Her face flushed with embarrassment. The box didn't contain a chair at all. It was a few area rugs. She looked up at the young man and offered him an apologetic smile.

"I'm sorry," she said. "It's hot. Let's take a break and I'll spring for cool drinks for everybody."

The two movers shrugged and leaned against the truck. Sylvie had worked with this company her whole career and the last thing she wanted was to piss them off. But she'd been in a mood since her run-in with Amanda.

Sylvie pulled herself together and treated her moving crew to ice-cold drinks and protein bars. Her good-natured gesture calmed any bad feelings, leading Sylvie to believe that Kind bars and Smartwater were the key to world peace.

She even helped unload the chairs, especially the chairs she'd been coveting. While standing beside the truck, she peeled her wet T-shirt off and wiped the sweat from her face with it. She was glad that she'd opted to wear a sports bra underneath her shirt.

"Stripping in the parking lot is appreciated but not allowed," Erik said as he seemed to appear out of nowhere. Sylvie tossed her shirt at him.

"What are you doing, waiting around every corner when I take a piece of clothing off?"

"I prefer to see you when you take off everything. You're pretty hands-on with your job, huh?"

"When you're the boss, you have to do it all sometimes." She leaned in to him. "Especially when you piss your workers off because you're having a bad day."

"And why are you having a bad day?" Erik placed his hand on her bare shoulder. The heat that rippled through her body had nothing to do with the blazing sun overhead.

"Eh, it happens. Ran into someone who I could've gone the rest of my life without seeing. But the best thing that happened today was these chairs." She pointed to the red and black leather chairs lined up beside the truck.

"What's so special about these chairs?"

"You'll see when everything is in place."

"Have you thought about what you want for dinner? Because no matter how bad your day has been, I can make your night even better."

"I think I want a nice thick steak."

Erik took a step back. "And I thought you were a vegetarian or something."

"I am when I want to be. But again, I had a bad day and a good meal is going to make it better."

"All you need is a steak? Then your day couldn't have been that bad. We can trade war stories tonight. I have to get to the lab."

"Ooh, can I see it?"

"See what?"

Sylvie smiled. "Where all the magic happens."

"No. Sorry, but my lab has to be pristine and everything that goes on there is top secret."

She folded her arms across her chest. "Are you saying you don't trust me?"

"When it comes to my work, I don't trust anyone. Don't take it personal. Besides, you'd probably take off with samples of my red lipsticks."

"I do wear other colors, you know."

His gaze fell to her hot-pink sports bra. "I see that now. Pink looks good on you."

Before Sylvie could respond, one of the movers walked over to tell her that the floors in the lobby weren't dry enough to bring the new chairs in. Erik nodded at her. "Handle your business, Miss Lady." He blew her a kiss and Sylvie's knees went weak.

Pull it together, girl. Sylvie turned to her crew and directed them to get some of the industrial fans and set them up to blow on the lobby floor. She was grateful that Erik had given her carte blanche with everything. And it didn't go unnoticed that closing the lobby kept the media at bay.

Around four thirty, the floor was dry and the logo of Jordan Industries was shining in the center of the wooden floor. She loved the combination of the cherrywood and bamboo flooring. The red and black logo in the center of the room laid the foundation for the art deco look that she'd drawn up in her plans. Sylvie loved this part of the job, watching her ideas become real. Sometimes things didn't work out, but this project was turning out to be everything she wanted. She just hoped that Erik liked it as well.

It was after seven before Sylvie and her crew finished installing the chairs and clearing the walls.

"Good job, guys. Thanks for your hard work today."

"Miss Sylvie, you know we like working for you better than we did with Amanda. But you gave us a little flashback today," one of the men said.

Sylvie stroked her chin and muttered her apologies. "It won't happen again. This project is just so . . . It won't happen again."

"We all have bad days," the other man said as he nudged his partner. "See you tomorrow."

As the men left, Sylvie turned and looked at her handiwork. Then she remembered, she had to get home and get ready for dinner.

Dinner with Erik. She had to say a silent prayer that she could keep her hands to herself over the steak.

* * *

Erik glanced at his watch as his chef plated the medium-rare steaks and smashed potatoes. Sylvie was late, and now he was wondering if she'd stood him up. Leaving the kitchen, he laughed because he'd never had this kind of issue with a woman before. No one had ever captured him in this way, making him question if he was going to be stood up. And he couldn't remember the last time he'd actually wanted a woman in his house.

Granted, he knew going out anywhere would lead to flashing lights from the cameras of the paparazzi, especially after today's announcement. Maybe he and Sylvie needed to be out of the public eye. But she was the kind of woman he wanted to show off. Fine. Smart. Sexy. Something about her made him feel different. Made him think about things more than just sex and moving on to the next one. And for the life of him, he didn't understand why.

"Mr. Jordan," the chef said, breaking into Erik's thoughts. "I made two desserts, banana pudding and the chocolate cake you requested."

"Great. I think we're done here."

"You don't want me to serve the meal?" he asked.

Erik smiled. "I think I got this." He handed the man an envelope filled with cash. "Thank you for this."

"No problem, sir. I hope you all enjoy it."

"I'm sure we will." Erik walked the chef to the front door, then sent Sylvie another text with his address and the message that he was looking forward to seeing her.

Sylvie was late and lost. That's what she got for not charging her phone before turning her GPS app on. She couldn't even call Olivia and ask her how to get to Erik's place because she'd been in such a rush that she'd forgotten her car charger. Maybe that was a sign that she needed to leave Erik Jordan alone. She was about to turn around when she saw a sign for Jordan Way. Maybe hope wasn't lost after all.

When she turned down the private street and saw the house, Sylvie was taken by the beauty of his place—classic columns, wide porch. And some of the ugliest chairs. She couldn't help but think he had picked out those white wooden chairs himself. *Or an ex who only had taste in her mouth*, Sylvie thought as she pulled into the driveway.

She glanced at the clock on the dashboard. Super late. Somehow, she'd have to make it up to him, she thought as she walked to the front door. She was certain about one thing as she rang the doorbell. Whoever picked out this furniture could not be trusted.

A couple of beats passed and she realized there didn't seem to be any movement inside. She pressed the doorbell again. Nothing.

That man can't be this petty, she thought as she turned to leave. She'd walked down one step when the porch light flicked on and the door opened. Sylvie gasped when she saw him standing there, shirtless—his six-pack on display—wearing a pair of low-waist jeans and no shoes.

"I could've sworn I told you to come around the pool-side entrance."

Sylvie blinked and sucked her bottom lip in. Did he realize how breathtaking he was? "My phone died. It's amazing that I made it."

"And here I was thinking I'd been stood up." Erik ushered her inside. "Your food's cold."

"Sorry about that."

"You'll be happy to know the steak is seasoned to perfection."

"You ate without me?"

Erik nodded. "You do realize that you're two hours late? And you didn't call."

"Sorry to keep you waiting, Mr. Jordan. But it's actually your fault."

"My fault?"

"Yes, because I did such an amazing job with your lobby, I had to admire my work."

"You're serious?"

"Everything about my work is serious."

Erik placed his hand on her shoulder. "We're going to table this discussion because this isn't a business dinner."

She smiled. "You invite all of your dates to your house for dinner? Or is that why you keep a penthouse in Midtown?"

"Nope, just the special ones. They usually arrive on time," he quipped as he led her to the

French doors that opened out to the pool area. This felt like the real Erik. Sylvie drank in the deep earth tones on the padded furniture surrounding the Olympic-size pool. A wrought-iron table was set up near a fire pit with matching chairs surrounding it.

"You do a lot of swimming?"

"Every morning, unless it's snowing."

"It's Atlanta. There aren't many mornings when it snows."

He winked at her. "You're just as smart as you are beautiful."

"So, where is my perfectly seasoned steak?"

He pointed toward the sand-colored chaises near the edge of the pool. "Right over here."

Sylvie was impressed with the chairs. Clearly the person who purchased them was a smart person. "I'm really sorry that I was so late."

"All will be forgiven if you can swim."

"I don't have a suit."

He tilted his head to the side. "You don't need one. I've seen you naked twice."

She folded her arms across her chest. "That doesn't mean there's going to be a third time! And I'm not skinny-dipping with you."

"Okay, just keep your underwear on."

She raised her right eyebrow. "Who says I'm wearing any?"

Chapter 9

These days, not much shocked Erik. But Sylvie left him speechless as he looked at that pink-and-purple maxi dress she wore. Was she really naked underneath? Just the thought of it made his body hotter than July.

"The pool is heated, and global warming has made this a warm winter night." He closed the space between them and stroked her shoulders. "Your choice, though."

"I'm choosing to keep my clothes on. And eat my steak." She walked over to the chaise and sat down. Erik picked up the covered dish and set it on her lap.

"Would you like tea or wine?"

"Ooh," she said as she lifted the silver cover from the plate. "Wine for sure."

"Red or white? I'm just going to give you red, because that seems to be your thing." Erik's gaze fell to her lips, and for the first time, he noticed her lipstick. She had followed that request.

Those full lips were painted Jordan red. "That lipstick looks good on you."

She smiled. "Thank you. It feels good too. Did you add some kind of moisturizer to the formula?"

"Now you know I can't tell you that. But I'm glad your lips feel as good as they look. I might be inclined to name this color after you."

She cut into her steak and rolled her eyes. "Tell me, how many times have you used that line?"

"First time for everything. I'll be back with the wine." He headed over to one of the pool cabanas and grabbed a bottle of Ace of Spades rosé. Looking at the wine, he changed his mind and went for a bottle of 1992 merlot from the Jordan Winery. Tonight was special, and he wanted the drinks to be as well. Uncorking the bottle, he smiled as he thought about the imprint her lips would make on the rim of the glass. His body clenched as he remembered those lips sucking his dick on New Year's Eve. And then she had the nerve to tell him she wasn't wearing panties.

"It's just dinner. Just dinner," he muttered as he poured the wine, then headed for the door.

He was surprised to see Sylvie half done with her New York strip. "This is delicious," she said when they locked eyes. "If you tell me that you cooked this, I might just fall in love."

"Sorry to disappoint you. But I'd be happy to introduce you to my chef."

She took another bite of her steak and raised

her right eyebrow. "Is he cute? Anyone who can make a steak sing like this has to be my dream man."

Erik set her glass on the edge of her chaise. "You're telling me that all I have to do is learn how to cook and you're mine?"

"Cook like this and keep making me red lipstick, and maybe."

Erik sat down in the chair beside her. "You have a mouth on you."

She dropped her fork. "You say that as if it is a bad thing."

Leaning closer to her, he picked up her linen napkin and wiped a bit of sauce from her chin. "I like your mouth. A lot." Erik captured her lips in a hot and wanton kiss. Sylvie's moans urged him to kiss deeper, and his tongue danced with hers. Exploring her mouth as if he'd never been there before. She placed her hand on his chest, breaking the kiss and taking a deep breath.

"We need to make something clear. You can't keep kissing me like that if—"

"If I don't want to find out what's underneath that dress?"

Sylvie sighed. "Can we be serious for a minute?"

He nodded, though there was one thing he wanted to get serious about and it wasn't a conversation.

She relaxed her shoulders and Erik realized he was still holding her. And damn, it felt good.

"Working with your company is really important to my brand, and I don't want things to get confused. If we're going to give in to this heat between us, there need to be rules."

"I get it. But what kind of rules?"

She wiggled out of his embrace. "Nothing that happens after hours gets in the way of business. And maybe we shouldn't tell anyone about us."

"You got something to hide?" Erik folded his arms across his chest and leaned back in the chair. "I don't care who knows about us."

"But I do. I can hear the haters now: *She got that job because she's sleeping with him.* I've worked too damned hard to let that be a part of my narrative."

He nodded and reached for her hand. "All right. But you had your job before I had mine and long before I had you on New Year's Eve."

Sylvie inhaled sharply. "Is this just about sex? I mean, it's cool if it is. Because to be honest with you, I can't stop thinking about that night." She inched closer to the edge of her seat. But when her fork clanked to the ground, she eased back. Setting her plate aside, Sylvie joined Erik in his chair. He stroked her cheek, his mind still burning with her last statement. Sure, sex was on his mind. How could he forget the amazing night they shared a few weeks ago? But Sylvie made him want more. Her drive matched his. And that mouth. Her wit was amazing and kissing her was just as exciting.

"It's not just about sex for me, but if that's what you want . . ."

She didn't reply, she just ran her hand across

the fly of his jeans. "Remember I told you that I was having a bad day?"

"Yes. And I'd be happy to listen to what made you so upset." Erik stroked her cheek, genuine in his concern. But clearly, Sylvie didn't want to talk. She made that clear as she stroked his hardness through his jeans.

"I don't want to talk. I want you."

Erik moaned as she unzipped his jeans and eased down his body. But the moment she wrapped those red lips around him, he screamed. She took him deeper into her hot mouth and he buried his hands in her curly hair. Erik lost himself in ecstasy as she licked, sucked, and slurped him. He didn't mean to come, but that thing she did with her tongue across the head of his dick made him explode.

And Sylvie didn't stop. She lapped his seed and winked at him. Erik almost came again. "Damn, woman," he moaned. "That mouth. That mouth."

She wiped her bottom lip with her thumb and smiled. Rising to her feet, she straddled his body and brushed her nose against his. "So, you liked that?"

"Understatement of the year."

She ground against his hardness and wrapped her arms around his neck. "This is wild," she breathed against his ear. "You do something to me."

"That's my plan. That and finding out if you really aren't wearing panties." He slipped his hand underneath her dress and was excited to find that she wasn't just talking about skipping underwear. "Did you come here to seduce me?"

"No. I came to eat dinner. This is just a pleasant side effect."

"Hmm," he said as he slipped his finger inside her. Sylvie moaned as he brushed the pad of his finger against her throbbing clit. "Just a side effect, huh?"

"Ooh, you know what I meant."

He nodded as he stroked. She was wet. Soaking. And he was hungry. Needing to have her sweetness in his mouth. Removing his finger, he lifted her from his lap and rose to his feet. "Come with me."

"I thought I was on my way to doing just that."

Erik shook his head. "That mouth."

"Amazing, isn't it," she replied as she took his hand. Erik led her into the cabana and pressed her against the wall. He slipped the straps of her dress down, revealing her black lace demi bra. The dress fell to the floor in a flourish and he took a moment to admire her curves. Those thick thighs. He slipped his hand between them. Sylvie sucked her bottom lip as he stroked her.

"So soft," he whispered, then dropped to his knees to worship her yoni. She seemed sweeter than he remembered. She was definitely wetter. His tongue lashed her clit, making her call out his name. He sucked and licked until his face was wet with her need. Sylvie quivered as he locked eyes with her while his tongue danced inside her.

"Erik, Erik, Errr-ik!"

The look of pleasure on her face urged him to deepen his kiss, to suck, nibble and lick more. The more she screamed, the harder he got. The time for eating was over. He needed to be inside her wetness. He scooped her into his arms and crossed over to the futon in the middle of the room.

He laid her on the soft cushions, disrobed and then joined her. Wrapping her in his arms, he reveled in the feel of her skin against his. She was so smooth, obviously the inspiration for Carlos Santana. She snaked her legs around his waist.

"What are you waiting for?"

"Protection." He reached underneath the pillow and retrieved a condom. Sylvie took the package from his hand and opened it. Untwining her legs from around him, she reached for his thickness—rubbing her hand across the tip— then she slid the condom in place. He pulled her on top of him.

"Ride me." His voice was a deep growl and Sylvie followed his command. Mounting him, she expelled a satisfied sigh as he filled her and gripped her hips. They fell into a slow rhythm, grinding to a beat of their own. Fast. Then slow. Faster. Slower. And finally, explosion.

Sweat poured from their bodies as they fell

against each other. Erik traced a bead of sweat down the center of her chest and Sylvie shivered.

"Cold?"

"Aftershock." She kissed his chin. "I don't normally—"

He brought his finger to her lips. "You don't have to explain yourself to me, unless there's a husband waiting around the corner somewhere."

"That's the last thing you have to worry about." She snorted and shifted in his arms.

"Wait, there's a story behind all of this attitude."

She rolled her eyes. "No, there isn't."

Erik stroked her cheek. "Spill it, sista."

"Why don't we talk less?" She reached down and gripped his penis. "And play more?"

As much as he wanted to talk, her stroke brought his body back to life and stoked his desire to be inside her again.

When Sylvie woke in Erik's arms this time, she didn't feel the need to run out. But she was confused about what she was feeling. She liked him and she'd promised herself that she'd never risk her heart again.

After all, Sylvie wasn't supposed to see Erik again, but here she was in his bed. Well, his cabana. Glancing at his sleeping frame, she sighed and shifted her body. He tightened his arm around her waist.

"There are no mirrors in here, and if you use my lipstick to write on something, it's going to be on."

"Didn't plan on leaving a note this time," she quipped. "But it is late and . . ."

"We should go inside and relax on a real bed."

"Erik," she said with a sigh. "I have a big day tomorrow. And my client is going to be hounding me if I don't have his building photograph ready for a certain magazine."

"Your client will be fine. If I need to talk to this jerk, I will."

She stroked his cheek. "Well, since you say it like that. Maybe we can have a midnight snack. I never finished my dinner, and I think you mentioned dessert."

"Come on. I think there might be another steak in the kitchen. I'm sure the bugs are dining on your leftovers."

"Ugh. Why did I let you distract me?"

"Clearly, it was the other way around, doll face." Erik kissed her on the forehead and then rose to his feet. "Come on, I'll show you around."

Sylvie took his extended hand and stood up. "Don't you think we need to put some clothes on first?"

"Optional."

She laughed. "I do have a question."

"What's that?"

"Who gave you those god-awful chairs on your front porch?"

Chapter 10

As Erik showed Sylvie around his house, he felt judged by her silence. Also a first when it came to a woman who had the privilege of being inside his house. Of course, Sylvie was different.

"What's that look?" he asked as they walked into the living room.

"You said no business talk tonight, right?"

"Yes."

"But." She pointed to the pastel green walls in the living room. "This looks like a bad Throwback Thursday picture on Facebook."

"Well, glad my feelings aren't hurt."

She placed her hand on his chest. "Don't get me wrong. Your home is very neat."

"That is the most backhanded compliment I've heard in my life."

She shrugged and walked over to the white leather sofa near the bay window. "This sofa doesn't belong in this room—or this earth, to be honest with you. Who decorated this place? Your grandma?"

"That's cold. All I did was move in here and added the pool. The rest of the place was handled by my mother's old interior designer."

Sylvie brought her hand to her mouth. "I'm sorry."

"Don't be. I'm sure Clara Belle did the best she could at the time."

"When? The 1980s? You should think about redecorating this place. Because if you're going to have a huge profile done about you, people are going to want to see your home."

"Really? Know anyone up for the job?"

She rolled her eyes. "I can give you a list of recommendations."

"If you know Sylvia Gates, have her give me a call. In the morning."

"Why in the morning?"

"Didn't I tell you no business tonight? You keep breaking the rules."

"Isn't that what rules are for?"

"Not if you want this dessert." He winked at her, then turned toward the kitchen. As they walked through the formal dining room, Sylvie shook her head.

"Clearly she was influenced by Tim Burton."

"Stop being a hater," he said as they walked into the kitchen. This room was modern and she thought the first glimpse of the real Erik Jordan. Well, technically not her first glimpse, but more insight into the man.

The black and stainless steel appliances glistened in the soft lighting. Copper pots hung above the stove. If he hadn't told her about his chef, she'd think he was a cook.

"What now, Sylvie?" He watched her as she studied the kitchen.

"This is probably the only room in the house that looks like you. Even if you don't cook."

"Didn't say I didn't cook. I just didn't do it tonight."

She ran her hand across the marble countertop. "And what do you cook, Bobby Flay?"

A slow smile spread across his face. "My breakfast is legendary. Grits, eggs, French toast with almonds and hot maple syrup."

"That does sound good."

"Then it's settled, you're staying for breakfast."

She cocked her head to the side. "You're so presumptuous. And I can't be bought with food alone. What kind of coffee do you have?"

"Only the best beans from Hawaii. I love Kona coffee."

"You're tempting me to stay."

He closed the space between them. "I need to do more than tempt you. I need to convince you that walking out that door is going to be the biggest mistake you make tonight." Erik cupped her face in his hands. "Did I mention that smoked-applewood bacon?"

She shook her head. "You just lost me. I gave up pork the other day."

"What kind of monster are you?" he quipped.

Sylvie rolled her eyes. "Whatever. What happened to this magical dessert that you promised me? If I had to see all of that stuff around your house, I want my sweets."

He brushed his lips against hers. "So do I." He kissed her slow and deep, drawing her tongue into his mouth. Lost in the heat of the kiss, Erik pressed her against the counter, realizing that the only dessert he needed was another taste of Sylvie.

Greedy? Yes. But he couldn't get enough of this woman. Breaking the kiss, he lifted her onto the countertop, then spread her thighs.

"Is it all right if I get my sweets first?" He ran his finger across her inner thigh.

She nodded and took his hand in hers, then pressed his finger inside her. "Do your thing, Erik."

Slipping between her thighs, he kissed her wetness, lapping her sweet pearl until she threw her head back in ecstasy. Lick. Suck. Explosion.

Her body went limp and Erik lifted her into his arms. "Delicious as always."

"Umm. Your mouth should come with a warning label." She ran her index finger across his lips. Erik took her over to a bar stool and set her down.

"You good?"

"Will be as soon as my knees stop shivering."

He kissed her on the cheek and crossed over to the refrigerator, where he pulled out two huge slices of chocolate cake. Sylvie's eyes stretched to the size of quarters.

"How did you know I have a weakness for chocolate? Dark chocolate to be exact."

He held his arms out and smiled. "It wasn't hard to guess." Erik set a plate in front of her. "I'd like to think that you've enjoyed me more than you're going to enjoy that cake."

"Give me a fork and I'll be the judge of that."

He flashed her a cool glance before reaching into a drawer and handing her a fork. "Keep in mind that I have a male ego and even if the cake is better, it's okay to lie."

Sylvie laughed. "You're funny, and I'll happily protect your fragile ego." She dug into the cake and moaned as she took a bite.

Erik's ego was a little bruised because he'd heard those sounds of satisfaction coming from her earlier. He coughed. And she grinned at him with a bit of chocolate on her front tooth. He pushed his own cake aside and kissed the chocolate away.

"Finally found something that doesn't look good on you," he said when they broke the kiss.

"You know, you just could've told me that I had chocolate on me."

He shrugged. "I can't resist kissing you. You staying for breakfast?"

Sylvie licked her lips. "You're driving a hard bargain."

"Trust me, it's going to be well worth it. If for no other reason than I have the most comfortable bed in the city."

"Are you five-star-rated on Yelp?" she quipped.

"I'm not worried about your bed. All I know is, your breakfast better be as good as this cake or I'm leaving your walls pale green and adding white lace dollies to your tables."

"You wouldn't."

She nodded. "And I'll post the pictures to my Instagram with the caption that this was your idea."

"At least you're taking the job to make this place modern."

"I thought we couldn't talk business until tomorrow?" She raised her eyebrow.

Erik pointed to the clock on the stove. "Technically, it's tomorrow. But we can table this until the sun comes up."

"Or until I finish my cake?"

"Sun up, after you've fallen in love with my breakfast and coffee."

She polished off the last of the chocolate cake, replete with licking the frosting from the fork, and nodded toward Erik. "You better be right. It takes a lot for me to fall in love with anything."

"The way you destroyed that cake says otherwise." Erik took her plate and placed it in the deep sink. "Would you like milk, wine, or water to wash that down?"

"Since I have a business meeting in the morning, I'd better go with milk."

Erik grabbed two glasses and filled them with almond milk. When he dropped two ice cubes in his glass, Sylvie uttered, "Eww."

"What? I like my drinks ice-cold."

"That explains a lot."

"Meaning?"

She rubbed her forearms. "It's colder in here than it is outside."

"Don't worry, I'll keep you warm." He slid a glass of milk over to her and watched as she sipped it.

"Almond milk, huh?"

"You don't like it?"

She shook her head. "I do. It's just . . . Never mind."

"Tell me," he said with his brows furrowed.

"Why do you want me to spill my guts so bad? We're both adults and have had things that happened in our past."

Erik picked up his glass and downed his milk. "True. Sounds like you just dropped a hint. Guarded much?"

She raised her right eyebrow at him. "Don't get it twisted, I was talking about food only. Love is just another four-letter word."

"That's hardcore." He wrapped his arms around her shoulders and pointed her toward the spiral staircase. "Let's go to bed."

Sylvie thought Erik was going to probe further about her take on love, and when he didn't she was filled with relief. Tonight, she didn't want to think about heartache and pain. And that's what love was. Her heart had never recovered from losing her father, who, to this day, was the best man that she'd ever known. When he died and Sylvie's mother decided to leave their French Quarter home, she felt as if her mom didn't hurt as much as she did. Years later, when she was old enough to understand, her mother told her that the house held too many memories for her stay there without crying every day. She'd explained to Sylvie that her father would always have a place in her heart, no matter where they lived.

"Breathtaking, isn't it?" Erik said once they reached the top of the stairs. Sylvie had been so lost in her thoughts that she hadn't paid any attention to the Hogwarts-like portraits. It would've been different if the pictures were in nice frames instead of huge silver ones that clashed with the gold trim on the stairs and the crystal chandelier that flanked them.

"Who hurt you?" she quipped.

Erik laughed. "I don't think anyone has ever trash-talked my home the way you have."

"They just didn't do it to your face. It's all right, being rich allows you to have bad taste. That's why people like me exist."

Erik rolled his eyes as they headed for his dark bedroom. He wasn't surprised that she gave his bedroom a critical eye.

"This room isn't half bad," she said as she opened the blackout shades. "Earth tones and all of that. It's just a little dated. But it looks super comfortable." She crossed over to the bed and plopped down. "You might have been right about this bed. It is pretty amazing."

She stretched out and lifted her arms above her head. Erik inhaled as he gave her a slow gaze. Just having Sylvie in his bed made the room look a thousand times better. Like she belonged there.

What in the hell am I thinking? Erik joined her on the bed and drew her into his arms. "Are you done or are you finished?"

"Funny." She yawned and Erik fought the urge to kiss her again. How could a woman be that damn sexy doing something so simple?

"Are you going to be comfortable in that dress all night?"

She rolled over on her side and brought her face closer to his. "Normally, I sleep naked. So, I doubt I'll be comfortable at all."

"Sweet Jesus," he muttered as he stroked her cheek. "You're something else. Whatever you think, you say it, huh?"

Sylvie stroked his face. "Pretty much. I don't have time to care what other people think about me anymore."

Erik yawned, and though he wanted to ask her when and why she'd ever felt that way, he was too tired to deal with another deflection from her. "Well, if you need to feel comfortable and take that dress off, I don't mind." He kissed her shoulder.

"Whatever," she said as she inched closer to him. Erik wrapped his arms around her waist and realized this was the first woman he'd ever wanted to hold while she slept.

Sleep didn't come easy for Sylvie. Though she was comfortable in Erik's bed and his arms, her mind went back to the huge bomb dropped on her earlier that day. Amanda having *his* baby. How did those two even get together? Did they hate her that much that they decided to do this?

Sylvie almost laughed, but she hadn't wanted to wake Erik. She was the one with a grievance. Her so-called friend and the man she thought she'd spend the rest of her life with were having a baby. When she shivered, she did wake Erik.

"Are you all right?" His voice was thick with sleep.

"Umm, sorry. I didn't mean to wake you."

"I told you to get naked and be comfortable." Erik chuckled and closed his eyes. "Are you sure everything is all right? You've been tossing and turning all night."

She shrugged but didn't reply. A silent beat passed and she flipped over on her back. "Is it time for that breakfast you lured me into bed with?"

Looking down at his growing erection, Erik smiled. "You know French toast didn't get you here."

"You're right. It was the promise of Kona coffee." She rolled out of his embrace and chuckled. "Erik, thank you for last night. Dinner and . . . You're a great guy."

"This is starting to sound like a lipstick message."

Sylvie sat up and leaned against the headboard.

"No, it isn't. You're never going to forget that, are you?"

He shook his head as he propped up on a pillow. "When something like that happens to a man like me, one doesn't forget it. Especially when fate laughs and brings you back into my life."

"It's called a job, Erik. It's not fate. Though, if I ever tell my mother the whole story about this, she'd disagree."

"Why?"

"She's a stickler for the magic of midnight kisses on New Year's Eve. Guess that's the thing about being from New Orleans, you believe in magic."

"You're from New Orleans?"

She nodded. "Well, I lived there until I was fifteen. My father passed away and my mother moved us to Baton Rouge, then Charleston, South Carolina."

"I'm sorry to hear that." He stroked her arm as if she'd said her father died yesterday. There was something about the way her eyes dimmed that told him how deeply she was still affected by the loss of her father.

She shrugged his touch off and wiped away a stray tear. "It's fine. My dad and I were really close. Not to say that I'm not close to my mom. But I was a daddy's girl."

Erik nodded, remembering when he and his father were close. But those days were in the rearview mirror. Simon and Yvonne made it clear that they weren't in the mood to forgive Erik for trying to save the company.

He nearly snorted as he thought about the fact that Simon brought this shame on the family and somehow it was all Erik's fault that he'd been named CEO. It still baffled him as to why his father had been robbing the company for years.

"Hello." Sylvie snapped her fingers in front of his face. "My stomach is growling."

"Sorry. I'll start breakfast and you should take advantage of my shower. It's even more amazing than my bed." He winked at her and hopped out of bed. Sylvie stretched her arms above her head and yawned.

"Everything is amazing in here except the décor." She got out of bed and headed into the master bathroom.

"There you go with that mouth again," he called out as he headed out of the bedroom. Once he made it to the door, he turned around and watched Sylvie as she slipped her dress off. Again, he was taken by the fact that she had an amazing ass.

Chapter 11

Sylvia stood underneath the warm shower spray, and once again she found herself believing that Erik was right. His bed was amazing. His shower was magical, and if the coffee and breakfast were on point, she might be in trouble.

Turning the water off, she knew she needed to get her mind right. Just because he had a big dick and great sex didn't mean that she should offer him her heart on a silver platter.

What am I thinking about? This man is in the middle of a scandal and clearly just needs to release pressure and steam every now and then. There is no need to get the idea that this is anything more than two people having a good time.

She stepped out of the shower and realized that she'd failed to get a towel—again. Luckily, the linen closet was inside the bathroom and she didn't have to drip all over Erik's bedroom to get one. Sylvie had to admit it, the man believed in luxury. The plush towel she wrapped up in felt like a warm hug on a winter's morning. It didn't compare to waking up in Erik's arms, though. And she was afraid that feeling would become a habit.

She started to reach for her dress, then she saw it had been replaced with a white silk robe. Now, Sylvie liked to think of herself as observant, but she hadn't seen anyone come into the bathroom. She put the robe on and walked into the bedroom. She found a note on the bed telling her that her dress was being laundered and Mr. Jordan was waiting downstairs for her.

"Guess this is how Julia Roberts felt in *Pretty Woman*," she muttered as she headed for the kitchen. One thing she noticed as the sun filtered in through the huge windows was that the interior of Erik's house was even worse in the daytime.

"Ugh," she murmured as she walked into the kitchen. The scent of cinnamon and butter filled the air and made her forget that she'd spent the night in a place that needed a makeover more than a reality star trying to make people forget she'd gotten her fame from a sex tape.

"Good morning, again," Erik said. "I hope Betsy didn't scare you when she came upstairs."

"Is she a ghost? I didn't even hear her come into the bathroom." Sylvie hopped up on a bar stool as Erik flipped the toast in a copper pan. "Is that your cleaning lady?"

"She's more like an auntie to me. Miss Betsy has worked with the family for my entire life."

"Must be nice."

"I'm feeling judged right now," he said as took the toast from the pan and loaded the thick slices on a plate.

"No judgment from me at all. You were born into wealth, yet you're not an asshole. You and LJ are special men. Why hasn't he had a bigger role with the company before now?"

Erik shook his head. "We're not having that conversation until after breakfast. And your coffee is almost ready. I think Kona is best when French pressed."

"You're almost as fancy with your coffee as I am."

"Sounds like we're a match made in coffee heaven." Erik sprinkled powdered sugar and pecans over the toast. "Are you going to sit there and look pretty or do you want to help me?"

"I don't think that was part of the deal." Sylvie laughed. "Besides, my best work is done outside of the kitchen."

"Why am I not surprised?"

"Whatever." Sylvie walked over to the French press and pushed the plunger down. The aroma of the coffee nearly made her knees weak. "You're right. This is the best way to make coffee."

"I hope you're planning to share."

"After what you did for me this morning with my shower, of course I'll share." Sylvie filled the two white mugs beside the French press with the java and crossed over to the bar. She liked her coffee strong and black. Taking a sip, she realized that Erik had the magic beans. Before she could stop herself, she was reaching for his cup.

"Whoa!" he said as he set the platter of French toast, eggs, and bacon in front of her. "I thought you were sharing."

"This coffee is amazing."

"I know. That's why there's more in the French press." Erik took his cup and sipped it slowly. "I did a good job today."

"An amazing job. I'm sure if I had another cup, I could finish your building in the next fifteen minutes."

Erik shook his head. "Then you better sit down and get ready to eat. I can't have you walking around here on a caffeine high. Let me heat the syrup. And move the coffee out of your reach."

She rolled her eyes and grabbed the handle of his mug. "Don't think I won't drink your coffee."

"You're used to getting your way all the time, aren't you?" Erik grabbed his coffee mug and took a huge sip.

"I'm used to making my own way," she replied with a saucy smile.

"Somehow, I'm not surprised."

"People have a habit of underestimating me."

"Enough talking. It's time to make you fall in love."

Erik ushered her over to the breakfast nook and pulled out a chair at the table for her.

Sylvie shook her head and smiled. "You should add a new title to your résumé."

"What's that?" he asked when she sat down.

"Breakfast hype man. And it better live up to the hype, Flavor Flav."

Erik winked at her. "Get ready to eat your words, Sylvia Elaine Gates. Yeah, boyeee!" He crossed over to the bar and grabbed the platter of food. Then he reached for the nearly empty French press. Setting the food and coffee on the table, Erik nodded for her to take a bacon crisp first.

"This is turkey bacon, right?" She picked up a piece of the crispy meat.

He nodded, then took a slice of his own. He watched Sylvie bite into the bacon and reach for a slice of French toast. She slipped two slices of bacon between the sweet bread, then dipped it in the warm maple syrup. She moaned as she took a bite of the food. "Okay, you win. This took me back to my childhood." She wiped her mouth. "My grandmother's waffles used to taste like this."

"This is the first time I've been compared to someone's grandmother and been all right with it." He sat down beside her and poured the rest of the coffee into her mug. "You're welcome to the rest of the coffee."

"I could get used to this. Since I'm going to make this house look a lot better, you can make breakfast for me when I come in."

"I can do that. Especially on the mornings when you wake up here."

Sylvie sucked her teeth and hid her grin. "There

you go being presumptuous again. Who said that I'm going to ever spend the night here again?"

Erik nodded toward her empty plate. "I would say I found your weakness. Me and French toast."

"You're right about one part of that equation. I'm weak for the French toast. And don't forget the Kona coffee. You, on the other hand . . ."

He leaned into her and brushed his lips against hers. "Am the most irresistible man who's ever made you breakfast."

She stroked the back of his neck. "You're all right."

"Let me fix that." He kissed her slow and deep. Her lips parted and invited his tongue inside. Erik wanted nothing more than to slip that robe off her naked body and make love to her on the tabletop. But they both had work to do. However, the temptation of her kiss and the sliver of brown skin he saw through the robe made him reach for the sash. Then his phone rang.

"Damn it," he muttered as he broke the kiss. There was something about seeing Sylvie's lips swollen from passion that made him hard as his marble countertop. Running his thumb across her bottom lip, Erik was two seconds from kissing her again when he got an alert on his smart watch.

"I have to handle this," he said as he rose from the table. Erik headed to his home office and checked his missed calls and the text message. Both were from Ingrid.

The shit is hitting the fan. You need to get here immediately. Press is everywhere.

He punched in Ingrid's number and ran his hand across his face as it rang.

"Erik," she said when she answered. "Did you know your parents were going on *Good Morning Atlanta*? And of course, the national media has picked it up. CNN keeps calling. The board is asking me to get you in front of some cameras and—"

"Calm down. We will address this, but I need to see the interview first."

"What have you been doing all morning?"

"When I wake up in the morning, turning on a TV isn't the first thing I do." His mind floated back to being in bed with his arms wrapped around Sylvie's heavenly body. Yes, the last thing he'd wanted to do this morning involved reaching for a television remote.

"Maybe it should. I'm going to draft a statement. When you get here, I'll make sure to show you the interview and we can tweak the statement from there."

"Sounds good. I should be in in an hour or so."

After hanging up the phone, Erik wasn't surprised to hear Logan and Miss Betsy talking in the kitchen. His brother probably saw the interview, and knowing Olivia, she was probably telling Logan not to get involved with the company because it would be too toxic to his brand.

He couldn't blame her if she felt that way, but he hoped that Logan wouldn't allow her to pull the plug before things got started.

Olivia gave Sylvie a cool once-over as she sat down across from her friend and took the last piece of French toast from the platter in the middle of the table.

"Say whatever you're thinking because that look is annoying." Sylvie rolled her eyes because she'd really planned to eat that last piece of toast while Erik wasn't looking.

Olivia slowly chewed the bread, then shook her head. "I guess you ran out of red lipstick."

"What?"

"No notes on the mirror. You spent the night."

"Yes, I did, and got a wonderful breakfast and another assignment."

Olivia pointed to her friend's neck. "Also, a hickey."

Sylvie pulled the neck of the robe together and laughed. "That's a birthmark."

Olivia leaned back in her chair and crossed her legs. "I guess you were born last night, too."

"Whatever. What are doing here?"

"Have you had a chance to see *Good Morning Atlanta*?"

Sylvie shook her head and lifted her nearly empty coffee mug. "Nope. What did I miss?"

"Probably the reason why Logan doesn't have anything to do with his family. His parents did an interview basically calling Erik everything but a child of theirs and God. They explained away Simon's arrest as a plot by Erik to bring his father down."

"That is unbelievable." Her voice was a near whisper. What kind of parents went on TV to trash their child? Maybe the Jordans were the hot mess that Olivia warned her about.

"Tell me about it. Logan was so upset, because Erik loved working for the family company. Maybe he was too loyal, but what their parents did today shows that Logan has been right all along." Olivia shook her head. "You got some coffee to share? This is going to be a long day."

Sylvia stood up and started for the coffee-maker, but stopped when she heard raised voices coming from the area that led to Erik's home office. Olivia crossed over to Sylvie and shook her head. "And so it begins."

"What are you and Logan going to do?"

"I'm minding my business. Logan was so excited to work with Erik and the company. But he was hurt this morning. I'm thinking it's a good thing that you two were otherwise occupied and didn't see that interview. It hurt me and I'm not a relative, yet."

Sylvie reached up in the cabinet for a mug and fixed Olivia's coffee. She couldn't help but wonder how Erik was feeling. It's not as if she knew how close he was with his parents or if he even cared about what they said on that show. What was she supposed to do?

"Maybe I should leave," Sylvie said.

"Why? I know you and Erik are just casual or whatever, but he's going to need all of us supporting him right now."

She nodded and turned around to see Erik and Logan walk into the kitchen. It felt as if the air was sucked out of the room by the stern looks on their faces. Erik slammed his phone on the counter and walked over to the refrigerator and grabbed a beer. Before he could open it, Logan snatched it from his hand.

"We're not doing this. If you're going into the office to refute what Dad said, you need to be sharp and sober."

Erik shook his head. "It's not what Dad said. I can't believe Mom sat there and . . . Fuck it, I have a fire to put out and if he wants tell this story about me being power hungry, then I'm going to tell the truth about him being a thief."

Olivia crossed over to Erik and gave him a sisterly hug. "I know this is hard, but you have to go into this without emotion. Just stick to the facts."

Erik nodded and headed for the bedroom. Logan, Olivia, and Sylvie just stood in the middle of the kitchen looking at each other, trying to figure out what to do next. It took a few seconds for Sylvie to head up the winding staircase to get to Erik. When she walked into the room and saw him standing there without a stitch of clothes on, all of the supportive things she had thought to say on her way up the stairs floated out of her mind like butterflies in the rain.

"I-I, Erik, are you okay?"

He turned around and her knees went weak at the sight of his magnificent body. Even with the scowl on his face, that man was sexy beyond words.

"You need something?" he asked. "Your dress?" Erik pointed to the chair in the corner of the room.

"Yeah, I need something. Are you all right?" Sylvie walked over to him and forced herself to look into his eyes and not at his tantalizing body.

Erik reached for his boxers and slipped them on. "I'll be fine. The beauty business can be really ugly. Don't worry, though, you still get to—"

Sylvie threw her hand up. "Hold up. I came up here to check on you. Forget business. I'm sure hearing about what your parents said about you has you feeling something."

He nodded. "You're right, but I don't have time to cry about that now. I have to do what the board trusted me to do, and that's save this company."

Sylvia crossed the room and grabbed her dress. "Good luck." She dropped the robe and tugged the dress over her head. She didn't understand why she was upset. Erik owed her nothing. He didn't have to spill his feelings out to her. She sure hadn't opened up to him last night about her horrible day. How could she expect him to do what she wouldn't? Just as she was about to walk out of the room, she felt his hand on her shoulder.

"Sylvie, I'm sorry if I was terse, but this is new for me. Simon was the one who always taught us to keep family business out of the media. I'm feeling a little betrayed right now. And the fact that I have to go into the office and hear all the bullshit my father said about me to the world, in front of my employees, has me on edge."

Facing him, Sylvie wanted to pull him into her arms and tell him everything would be just fine. It wasn't as if she hadn't faced a similar betrayal. "I'm sorry. If . . . I don't want to be in your way or anything."

"You're not in my way at all. Thank you for being here this morning and I'm sure I owe you a bag of coffee."

She tilted her head to the side. "Well, if it's that Kona blend, then yes. Otherwise, I guess I'll wait and have another cup the next time you make me breakfast."

"Like in the morning. We're supposed to give this place a makeover too, remember."

"Then what time should I report for duty?"

"Around seven thirty tonight. I get the feeling that I'm going to need those arms and these lips to get me through the night." Erik leaned into her and brushed his lips across hers. "And you can't use the *I got lost* excuse for being late this time."

"Whatever." Sylvie cupped the back of his

neck and nibbled on his bottom lip. "I'd better let you get dressed."

"Yeah. Duty calls. I'll see you later, and if you wear those black jeans again, I might be tempted to have you for lunch."

She released him and smiled. "You're going to stop looking at my ass while I work."

"I'd tell you that I would, but I don't believe in lying." Erik gave her bottom a playful swat. "See you at the office."

Leaving the room, Sylvie felt as if she was floating. What was she really doing? This man was a client, about to face a shit storm of controversy, and she felt herself falling for him. Oh, this had to stop.

It's just sex, it's just sex. She walked down the stairs and kept telling herself that she wasn't going to get serious with this man. All being serious with Erik would do is open her heart up to pain again. After Stephen, she was done with all of that.

"Sylvie," Olivia called out. "Can I catch a ride with you? Logan is going to follow Erik to the headquarters, and I need to get to my computer in order to monitor the news coverage of this."

"Sure. We need to talk anyway."

"Yeah, we do." Olivia looked up at the top of the staircase, catching Erik gazing at Sylvie. "Somebody has a love jones going on."

Sylvie elbowed her friend in the side. "Let's go."

As they headed for her car, Sylvie turned to Olivia and sighed. "I ran into Amanda yesterday."

"Ugh, that bi—"

"She's pregnant." A lump started building in her throat. "And it's Stephen's child."

Olivia covered her mouth with her hand, holding back an angry howl. "That dirty tramp! Really? Of all the men in Atlanta and after what she tried to do to your business." Olivia reached out and hugged her friend tightly. "I'm so sorry."

"It's like the hits keep coming."

"And you keep coming out swinging. Forget her and sorry-ass Stephen. You're so far above them."

Olivia's pep talk would've worked if Sylvie didn't feel as if her life was about to spin out of control.

Chapter 12

Erik and Logan walked through the throng of reporters and cameras to get into the building. "Well, the lobby looks great," Logan said once they walked inside. "Sylvie's very creative. But I'm sure you know that already."

"Yeah, that's why she's going to redo the house."

Logan shook his head. "That's not why she's redoing the house, but if that's what you need to make it through the night, then cool."

"Come on, man, cut me some slack. I'm just having—"

"A woman stay over at your place. And then cooking her breakfast with your own hands is pretty much an announcement of love."

"You're going too far, little brother."

"I don't think so. Look at how she took off after you when you were sulking this morning. And you didn't toss her out like last night's garbage when I told you I was on my way. I'm used to seeing your women look like blurs of lace and weave."

Erik nudged his brother in the side with his elbow. "Don't be a dick."

"There are so many things I could say right now, but I'm going to let it go because we have business to attend to. But she's special, isn't she?"

Before Erik could reply, Ingrid dashed over to them. "Great, you're finally here. We need to draft a statement pretty quickly. This story is picking up all kinds of traction on social media. One of those gossip websites has reached out to a few of your exes or whatever you call them."

"Weave blurs," Logan quipped.

"Who was it and what did she say?" Erik sighed, ready for more drama to be piled on him.

"She kept saying that you're the real MVP. The video is quite comical. She seems high."

Erik hid his grin and made a mental note to send Chantelle a makeup gift basket with all the high-end moisturizers.

"Let's look at my parents' interview and then address those vultures outside." Erik and his crew walked into the conference room where Ingrid had a big screen attached to her laptop. She pressed her mouse and the screen filled with Yvonne and Simon Jordan.

"It's sad that a civil war has broken out in my family and my son is using these trumped-up charges against me to grab power. Let's be clear, I started this company and without me there is no Jordan Industries. My blood, sweat, and tears. Erik is a glorified chemist, what does he know about running a multinational company?"

The reporter was about ask a question when Simon interrupted her. "None. That's what he has, no experience to lead, and he's falling for the lies that a jealous board of directors is feeding him because they want to sell the company."

"Turn it off," Erik growled. "I can't believe he'd get on TV and lie like that!" He looked up at the screen and stared at his mother's blank face. Though she held her husband's hand, her eyes looked dead. Maybe Yvonne wasn't 100 percent behind his father like he thought. But she sure made it seem that way in the few conversations he'd had with her over the last few weeks.

Ingrid turned the feed off and chewed her bottom lip. "I watched the entire interview and drafted a release." She handed Erik her iPad. "Feel free to make any changes you feel necessary."

Erik gave the release a cursory glance, then shook his head. "Here's the deal. I'm not issuing a statement about Dad's lies. He wanted to sell the company and fighting back and forth in the media is going to drop the stock prices."

Logan held up his smartphone. "It's already happening."

Erik rolled his eyes. "That's why we're making the announcement about your line, today. I know that the press is going to ask questions about Dad, and I'll address them. But what we need to do is show that business is moving forward."

Ingrid and Logan exchanged shrugs. "You're the boss," she said.

"And it's time that everyone knows it." He

looked at Logan's jeans and T-shirt and shook his head. "You need to change your clothes."

Logan cocked his right eyebrow. "I'm an artist, I can wear whatever I want."

"But you have dried paint on your shirt," Ingrid pointed out.

"Shit. All right, what kind of monkey suit do I have to put on to stand in front of the cameras?"

Ingrid snapped her fingers. "Keep the jeans and maybe a sport coat and a tank top. I'll send one of the assistants to Macy's right now."

"T.J. Maxx," Erik called to her retreating figure.

"Or, I can just call Olivia and have her bring me another shirt. Y'all are super extra around here." Logan chuckled and sat down in one of the chairs around the table. "Did you see Mom's face?"

"Yeah. She doesn't seem to be on board with all of this."

"Then why won't she talk to us?"

Erik shook his head. "That's the million-dollar question. Have you tried calling her?"

"You know I had a hard time getting through to the parents before all of this started. I did an oil painting for their anniversary two years ago and sent it to the house. It was returned unopened."

"I believe that was all Simon. You know our father believes his way is the only way."

"So, why would he destroy the only thing in the world he ever seemed to care about? Because lord knows that selfish bastard didn't give a damn about us."

"Not that I'm defending our father, but you two don't get along because you're just alike."

Logan furrowed his brows and pursed his lips. "Are you on drugs or something?"

Erik held up his hand. "Headstrong. Only able to hear what they want to hear. My-way-or-the-highway, attitude-having motherf . . . Yeah, you are more like Dad than you want to admit. Think about it. He was ready to leave me in the lab because his plan was to mold you in his image. If you were taking over, he probably wouldn't be doing this press blitz."

"Shit, if I sat in the big chair, selling this company would be the least of our worries. One of the reasons why Olivia and I work so well together is because she has a brilliant business mind and I don't." Logan folded his arms across his chest.

"Bullshit. You were doing very well before you and Liv hooked up, and by the off chance that things don't work, LJ will be fine."

"I'd lose my mind if I lost my woman. Speaking of women, please tread lightly with Sylvie."

"First of all, Sylvie and I aren't some epic romance like you and Olivia. She made it pretty clear last night that she doesn't want titles and drama. Makes me think that we're on the same page."

"That's what they all say in the beginning. But I saw something today that proves both of y'all wrong."

"Oh, so you're a psychic now?" Erik sat across from his brother. "Enlighten me, oh wise one."

"You were smiling, despite what I told you. When you walked in the kitchen and saw that woman, you actually smiled."

Erik rolled his eyes. "No I didn't."

"Deny all you want. But Sylvie is different and you're intrigued. That's why you're trying to make her remodel everything, so you can spend time with her in close spaces. Give you a reason to look over her shoulder and possibly kiss it."

"You sound like a horrible Hallmark Christmas movie."

Logan rose to his feet and walked over to the window overlooking the city of Atlanta. "I sound like I'm telling the truth, and you don't want to accept it. But let me be clear: Don't fuck around with her and have that shit spilling into my relationship. She is Olivia's best friend."

Erik laughed. "So this is about you and not some cosmic love story. See, just like your pops."

Logan lost his smile as he glared at Erik. "Don't do that."

"Calm down, junior. I'm going to my office to listen to all the messages I'm sure the board has left, and get ready for this press conference."

"Think about what I said about Sylvie. Be open to letting her inside that icebox you call a heart."

"Yeah, yeah." Erik wasn't going to admit it to his brother, but she'd already opened the door to his heart. He just wasn't sure if she could really walk in, or if she wanted to.

Sylvie shook her head as she and her crew pulled up to the Jordan Industries building. At least she had finished the lobby, and if the cameras caught the beauty of what she and her crew created, that would be another feather in her design cap.

But she was really concerned about how this all was affecting Erik. Was he okay? Though she wanted to rush up the stairs and give him a hug, she had to focus on work and not his lips, hands, and tongue.

Get a grip, girl. She directed her driver to the loading dock on the right side of the building. Today she was going to tackle the executive suites. That meant she was going to have to deal with Ingrid the Annoying. Something about that woman just rubbed her the wrong way. Maybe it was the way she looked at Erik with stars in her eyes like a lovesick puppy. Sylvie knew she didn't have a right to be jealous. Yes, the man gave her orgasms, but he wasn't hers. She couldn't control what he did when he wasn't in her arms. And if Ingrid had the hots for him, she was probably just one of many.

Still, she didn't like her. "Stop being petty," she muttered as she hopped out of the truck.

"Boss, you over there talking to yourself, everything all right?" her driver quipped.

"We're good as long as I don't answer myself back."

The man laughed as he pressed the button to raise the door on the back of the box truck. "Damned shame that this family is at war like a soap opera. I thought I was watching *The Black and the Beautiful* this morning when I saw that interview. I know my grandma is probably mad as hell right now."

"Why?" Sylvie asked as she took inventory of the cargo.

"She loves Jordan cosmetics and she hates to see black people on TV fighting, unless she's watching one of those housewives shows."

"Your grandmother sounds like a hoot."

"She is. Wish I could get you to redo her place. But you're big-time now and I probably can't afford you."

"Please! You tell me when your grandma is ready, and if we can watch one of those hip-hop love shows together, and I'm there."

"Oh no! She watches enough of those shows and you can't be adding more to her schedule. You're a bad influence."

Sylvie checked off the last item on her clipboard and nodded for the two men on the back of the truck to start unloading. "I'm a bad influence? I think my feelings are hurt."

"Umm, it should be. Stop watching trash TV."

"I'll think about it," she replied as she tapped him on the shoulder. "Tell your grandma to call me, I got questions about last week's episode."

He shook his head and pointed his finger at Sylvie. "You're too much. I don't know why Amanda wanted us to believe you were stuck-up."

Sylvie fought the urge to roll her eyes. The things she could say about her former partner. But she was going to focus on the future and forget that lying, scandalous tramp. "That's why you should always judge for yourself." She smiled broadly at him and headed for the entrance.

As Sylvie and her crew got to work, she kept looking over her shoulder, hoping to catch a glance of Erik. The whispers in the hallway told her that she'd walked into a shit storm. Was it possible that the interview had been even worse than what Olivia had described earlier?

"That was really cold what Mr. Jordan did this morning," a woman said as she passed by the open door where Sylvie was standing.

"Yeah, he didn't just throw Erik under the bus, he drove it right over him."

"I'd be happy to help Erik lick his wounds. That man is too fine to frown."

"Kill that noise, he's your boss and he only goes for the model types anyway."

The other woman shrugged. "I just want to know if he lives up to that MVP status."

Sylvie furrowed her eyebrows. *MVP? What*

does that even mean? Shaking her head, she headed for the break room for a cup of coffee.

She wasn't surprised to hear more gossip when she walked in. "I know Ingrid is loving this," Sylvie heard a woman say in a loud whisper. "Now she gets to be up under Erik without having to come up with more public relations bullshit for us to do."

"Please, you're just mad because it isn't you. I wouldn't want to be in either of their shoes right now, and then this annoying remodel is going on. You know we have to get out of our office for the next three days."

Sylvie cleared her throat as she walked over to the coffee machine. The women looked at each other, sucked their teeth, and then left. It would've been comical if she weren't pissed about the *annoying remodel* comment. They should be happy that when they returned from three days of paid leave there would be a new and pretty thing waiting for them. She tried not to think about how jealousy flowed through her soul when she heard them talk about Ingrid's efforts to spend more time with Erik. Though she couldn't blame her, she needed Miss PR to back off. As Sylvie poured sugar into her coffee cup, she heard the click of high heels. Turning around, she locked eyes with Ingrid—who looked less than perfectly put together for once.

"Good morning," Sylvie said.

"Clearly, you haven't been watching the news. There is nothing good about this morning." She sighed. "I'm sorry. Good morning. How's the decorating coming along?"

"Great. If you're doing a press conference, you should use the lobby. It's done and beautiful, if I do say so myself." Sylvie gripped her coffee cup and headed back to the executive suites.

Erik sat at his desk reading the statement that Ingrid insisted he should have for backup. He knew exactly what he wanted to say and he didn't care if he went off script. His father was a thief. He didn't care if this back-and-forth in the media put a stain on the Jordan family. Simon was being strategic in his plan. But didn't he know that selling the company would do nothing but highlight his malfeasance? Did he even care? Rising to his feet, Erik started pacing. What made Simon think that he could get away with stealing? And what was behind it? Was it simply greed?

One thing Erik knew for sure was that he needed to get to the bottom of it. That meant he needed to have a one-on-one conversation with his mother. Before he could have another thought, the door opened and Logan walked in. Erik hid his grin as his brother tugged at his tie.

"This is ridiculous," Logan complained. "I hate wearing ties, but your PR chick has some horrible taste in clothes."

"She was probably trying to capture your personality or whatnot."

"Do I look like a man who wears floral shirts?" Logan cocked his right eyebrow. "I'm not Eric Benet."

"So where did this shirt come from?" Erik eyed his brother's plain white oxford shirt and blood-red tie.

"Olivia. She saved me, as usual."

"Think she can use some of that magic to save this family?"

Logan scoffed. "That ship sailed and sank a long time ago. I don't know what all of this means for the family. And to be quite honest, I don't care. Dad wanted us to be his clones. Then when you step up and do what's best for the company, you become his verbal punching bag. I don't know when Mom became his damned puppet. She won't even take my calls and she's always done that."

"We do need to talk to Mom, and the only thing I can think of doing is going to the house and making them face us."

Logan nodded. "I think you're right."

Erik sighed and stood up. "Let's get this press conference over with."

"Where are we hosting this dog and pony show?"

"In the lobby. That way we can go on and on about our new direction with our new look taking center attention."

"Damn, I hope you're paying Ingrid what she's worth."

"Actually, Sylvie gave me this idea."

Logan chuckled. "Of course she did. You better watch out. Next thing you know she's going to be giving you the idea to settle down and become a one-woman man."

"You're going to be that annoying-ass dude now? Because you're locked down in love, the rest of the world has to follow your lead?"

Logan shrugged. "If we can find some happiness in all of the madness around us right now, then you're damned right I'm going to push it."

Erik was about to deny that Sylvie was the answer to his happiness, but what if Logan was right? Sylvie had already gotten under his skin. She made him think about things that no other woman had ever placed on his brain.

He wouldn't say that he was in love with her, or even falling in love with her. It just made him want to peel back every layer of her until he got to the real core. He couldn't remember the last time he wanted to know a woman beyond the bedroom. Yeah, Sylvia Elaine Gates was different and he was beyond intrigued.

Logan's hand on his shoulder broke into his thoughts. "You all right?"

Erik nodded. "Yeah, let's do this." He stalked to the door, ready to tell his side of the story to the world.

Chapter 13

Yvonne Jordan felt tortured every time she saw a replay of the interview she and Simon did that morning. The last thing she wanted was for her sons to be humiliated by their father. She'd tried to shelter them for years. But seeing Simon carted off in handcuffs forced her to choose between her husband and her kids.

Yvonne thought she'd made the right decision. Simon told her that Erik was being influenced by his enemies on the board and couldn't see past his own ambitions. She didn't totally buy that, because her oldest son loved playing with chemicals. Yvonne smiled. Erik didn't want to hurt Simon, but Simon was making it his business to hurt their son. He'd already cut Logan out of their lives because he didn't live and bleed Jordan Industries. She rose from the empty dining room table and walked over to the painting LJ had sent her years ago. Over Simon's objections, she'd hung the painting her son made of her from her modeling days. He'd made her look like ebony Mona Lisa, dressed in Egyptian royal garb. She loved that portrait so much and was extremely proud of her son's success in the art world. It puzzled her why Simon was so against Logan chasing his dreams.

Yvonne snorted as she crossed the room. It was simple: Dreams that didn't match his were deemed wasteful and stupid. He'd even put an end to Yvonne's dreams when they'd started to outgrow his. Her modeling career had been about to take off after Logan was born, but Simon refused to allow another company to hire his wife for ad campaigns—whether it was for clothes or items unrelated to makeup.

When she'd relented and decided that she'd be the face of Jordan cosmetics, Simon dropped her lipstick line and claimed the company was moving in a different direction. Then he told his wife her only job would be focusing on the family.

And, feeling trapped, she followed Simon's plan for her. Family and the house became her main focus. She pretended that she didn't know about her husband's other women. She thought everything would be fine as long as no one knew what a lying dog Simon was.

Yvonne couldn't play the victim, though. Because she'd had a lover of her own. Well, two. But she did a much better job of hiding them than Simon did with his.

Things were different now and Yvonne needed to put her family together before it was too late.

"Mrs. Jordan," Tabitha, the family house-keeper, said.

Yvonne turned around and smiled at the comely woman. "I'm sorry, Tabitha, what did you say?"

"Mr. Jordan said that he won't be home for dinner and that you can send the staff home if you'd like."

"That's fine. Maybe I should have my sons over for dinner."

"It's been a while since they've been here. What do you want Chef to prepare?"

"Turkey meatloaf, macaroni and cheese, and cabbage. The boys have always loved that. I just hope they will accept my invitation."

Tabitha placed her hand on Yvonne's shoulder. "I'm sure they will. Families have their squabbles, but you guys will work it out."

"I hope so. I'm going to go into the garden and cut some flowers."

"You don't have to . . ."

"I just need some air," Yvonne said. "And I love to cut my own roses."

Tabitha nodded and headed for the kitchen. Yvonne grabbed her gardening shears and her cell phone. When she got outside, Yvonne dialed Erik's number. When the phone went to voice-mail, she was upset.

Had she ignored her sons so much that she was now getting the same treatment? It would be fitting, because she had taken Simon's side without question. She cut a few roses and slipped them in her woven basket. When she walked into the house, Yvonne set the basket of roses on the end table and touched her breast.

It wasn't as if she could feel the cancer there, but she felt regret. She'd hurt her sons and been a fool for her husband. But no more.

She crossed over to the portrait Logan had painted of her. Smiling, she looked at the image. Logan had turned her into an Egyptian goddess with a big smile. In the red background, there were images of her sons. It had been one of the first LJ originals that put him on the map. She'd asked Simon to use Logan's art on the new line of makeup. He'd refused, and when she'd suggested that Logan meet with his father, her husband told her he wanted nothing to do with it.

She pulled her phone out of her apron pocket and called Erik again. Still no answer. Yvonne closed her eyes and a few tears fell from underneath her lids. Had she alienated her kids and now they weren't going to be there when she needed them most?

Logan smiled as a reporter asked him about his latest collection that was going to be displayed at the Victoria and Albert Museum in England.

"I have a whole new collection that I created exclusively for the museum. It's my most personal collection and I'm excited to share it with the world."

Erik tried not to yawn, but he was over this

press conference. But he was happy that the questions had been directed to Logan. It was amazing to him that so many people didn't know that LJ the artist was related to the Jordan family. Olivia and LJ had done a great job keeping those family ties secret. Erik couldn't be mad that they didn't want to be associated with a family who didn't celebrate the fact that he was a damned genius.

"Erik," a reporter called out. "Does this new direction with your brother mean that you're moving the company closer to being all about family?"

"It means that it is a new day at Jordan Industries. We're going to be more transparent with our investors and stockholders. We're going to continue to celebrate black women and their beauty with new lines of makeup and skin care products. Not only that, but we're providing places in our company for qualified women to become leaders. So, let me be clear: Jordan Industries is stepping into the twenty-first century with a new direction."

"Does your father have a role in this new direction?" a reporter called out.

"He does not." Erik waved his hand. "And we're done because we have work to do. Thank you for your time today."

Erik and Logan turned to leave the podium and Ingrid began telling the media that she had kits available for them about the new line, and a copy of Erik's initial remarks.

"Mom called a couple of times," Erik said, once they were out of earshot of the media.

"Think she was watching the press conference and wanted to tell us what a good job we did?" Logan laughed. "Are you going to call her back?"

"Seems like the right thing to do, right?"

He shrugged. "She might be rethinking what she did with Dad this morning."

Erik reached into his pocket and pulled out his smartphone and dialed his mother.

"Erik, I'm so glad you called me back," Yvonne said, forgoing a hello.

"What's going on, Ma?"

"Are you and Logan together? I want you two to come over for dinner tonight."

Erik snorted. "Seriously? You and Dad went on television to tell the world that I'm not shit, and you think I want to break bread with you?"

"Erik, I need to see my sons and I didn't know your father was going to use the interview to . . . I'm sorry, Erik. But I really need to see you and Logan. I want my family to come together sooner rather than later. Chef is making your favorites."

Logan took the phone from Erik's hand as he noticed the scowl on his brother's face. "Ma, is everything all right? Really? And Simon isn't going to be there? We'll be there. What time?"

Erik waved his hands as if he was landing a plane. "No."

"All right, seven. We'll be there." Logan ended the call and handed it back to Erik. "We're having dinner with Ma and you're going to like it."

"Is our father going to be there?"

"Nope, and we do need to hear why Ma is on his side so hard."

Erik folded his arms across his chest. "It's been that way our whole life. Why do you think something is going to change now?"

Logan shrugged. "Because. Look, man, she's our mother and we need to have at least one parent we talk to. When's the last time that Ma asked us over for dinner?"

Erik rolled his eyes. "Fine." He was about to say something else when Sylvie walked toward him. She was working those black jeans as if they were a second skin. And speaking of work, she looked as if she'd been doing a lot of it. Her hair was a bit out of place and there were sweat stains across her chest. Still, she looked delicious.

"Hey, guys." She stopped in front of Erik. Her smile nearly blew him away.

"How's it going?" Erik asked as he stroked her cheek.

"Very well. Do you want to see what we've gotten done in the executive suite?"

"I'd love to, but I have some things to take care of right now. What do you say to a cup of Kona later?"

"Totally say yes. And just FYI, that coffee you have in the break room is pure trash." Sylvie thrust her hip into his then took off down the hall.

Logan didn't hide his amusement as he watched

the banter between Sylvie and his brother. "There's something happening here," he sang off key.

"Shut up."

"I'm surprised you didn't invite her for dinner. Ma would've been shock to see you with a woman who isn't a model."

"You know I never take girlfriends home."

Logan raised his right eyebrow. "Did you say the G-word? Are you calling her your girlfriend? Damn, she is magical."

"I didn't say she was my girlfriend and I'm not doing this with you."

Logan doubled over in laughter. "The last time I saw you act like this about a woman was . . . never."

"Get out of here and go make some art or something." Much to Erik's dismay, Logan followed him into his office. "I got work to do and I don't have time to go back and forth with you."

"Here's the deal. I know if I walk out that door, you're going to come up with every excuse in the world as to why you aren't going to dinner."

Erik tilted his head to the side. "Didn't I say I was going to be there?"

"You have a lot of your father in you. You say things that you don't mean."

"That was low." Erik took a seat at his desk and noticed that the chair was different. "What the hell? This is not my chair." He leapt up as if he'd sat on a pillow of thorns.

"You're really tripping over a chair? You know you have issues, right?"

"This is Dad's old chair. I thought I threw this shit away." Erik pressed the intercom button on his phone and called out to his assistant.

"Yes, sir?"

"Who brought this damned chair into my office?"

"I think Sylvia did, but it was . . . Hey, Sylvia, I think you need to talk to Mr. Jordan."

"I thought he was busy," he heard her say.

"Please send her in," Erik bellowed.

A few moments later, Sylvie walked into the office with her hand on her hip. "Is there a problem?"

"Why is this chair here?" he asked coldly.

She furrowed her eyebrows. "So you can sit down. I'm having your other chair refitted to match the color scheme that we're going to do in here. What's the problem?"

"On that note, I'm going to the snack machine," Logan said as he rose to his feet. Sylvie shrugged as she and Erik watched Logan walk out the door.

"Again," she began. "Is there a problem?"

Erik dropped his head, realizing how ridiculous he would sound if her told her why he hated that chair. "I'm sorry. This is an old chair that I thought I'd gotten rid of and . . . Forget about it."

Sylvie walked over to the chair and ran her

hand across the back. "This is a piece of classic furniture. I thought I was doing you a favor when I saved it from the garbage pile." She smiled wistfully. "My dad had a chair like this. Always made me think he was the boss of everything."

Erik rolled his eyes. The chair did belong to his father, and he didn't have fond memories of him like Sylvie had of her father. "It was going to be trashed for a reason."

"You want to talk about it?"

"This was my father's chair and I want it gone. End of story."

Sylvie threw her hands up. "Say no more, I'll have it removed. But I do need access to your office tomorrow."

"And I'm going to need access to your lips tonight." Erik crossed over to her and wrapped his arms around her waist. He didn't care about the sweat, the mussed hair or bare lips. He needed to kiss this woman more than he needed to breathe.

"I guess I can make that happen. Tonight." Sylvie wiggled out of his embrace. "But right now, I have to get to work."

"One more thing," he said as she started for the door. "I guess I need to give you a key to my place so you can get in and out when I'm not there."

"Umm, yeah, I guess."

"And if you ever get tired and need a place to sleep, you know the direction to my bedroom."

Before Sylvie could reply, Ingrid appeared in the doorway. "Am I interrupting something here?" She shot a cold look in Sylvie's direction.

"No, come in," Erik said. "Sylvie, make sure you get that key from me before you leave."

She smiled, then nodded. "Will do."

As Sylvie sauntered out of the office, Ingrid turned to Erik. "What's that all about?"

He shrugged. "My business."

"With all the eyes on this company right now, the last thing we need is another scandal."

"I don't need you to police what I do."

Ingrid raised her eyebrow. "So, there is something going on with you and Sylvia Gates?"

"Ingrid, I know you didn't come in here to question me about our interior designer."

She folded her arms and shook her head. "Actually, I came with good news. The announcement about LJ's line is trending on all the social media sites, and the beauty bloggers are losing their minds about this." She turned her smartphone around to him. Erik grinned as he looked at the picture of him and Logan, which had been shared nearly a million times.

"Maybe we ought to look into doing a men's line," Erik mused.

"These comments are hilarious."

"I'm sure Olivia is going to have something to say about this one," Erik said as he pointed to one talking about what the commenter would do to a naked Logan.

"Well, look at what they think about you," Ingrid quipped as she pointed to another comment a woman made about letting him lie on her chest to get over his daddy issue.

"Social media makes everyone so bold and over-the-top."

"And buyers." Ingrid pulled up another file on her phone. "The preorders are through the roof."

"This is a good thing. Maybe this line is what we need to get back in the black."

"Hopefully. We should plan a launch party."

"Yes. And make it exclusive. But let's capitalize on this social media interest and run some sort of contest."

"I was thinking the same thing. I'll get my social media crew on it right now. Do you want to meet this evening and see what we came up with?"

Erik shook his head. "I have plans, but first thing in the morning, we can have a breakfast meeting."

"Plans with Sylvia?"

"Though it's not your business, I'm having dinner with my mother. Ingrid, why are you so invested in my personal life?"

She laughed nervously. "I'm not. Like I said, I'm trying to make sure that we don't get hit with another controversy. What do you really know about Miss Gates?"

Erik placed his finger to his lips. He knew a lot about Sylvie. She tasted like honey. Her smile made his dick throb. She had the most amazing lips he'd ever tasted.

"What do you know about her that you think I should know?" he finally said.

"Would you be offended if I did some research? I mean, Simon hired her, and who knows why she took the job?"

Erik silently counted to ten before responding. Of course Ingrid didn't know that he and Sylvie had a connection before he found out that she'd be working on the remodel of the Jordan Industries headquarters. Erik was 100 percent sure that Sylvie wasn't going to be a problem.

"If that will make you feel better. Go for it."

"All right. And I want you to know that this is for the company and nothing else."

"I trust you're doing it for the good of Jordan Industries and nothing else. Now, I'm going to the lab to make the palettes happen." Erik left the office and went where he was most comfortable.

Granted, he took the CEO mantle because the board thought a Jordan still needed to run the company. But he wasn't going to give up working in the lab. Especially when he had a new inspiration. Sylvie. She made him see colors and want to make every woman feel as soft as Sylvie did. If he could bottle everything about her, he would, and probably keep it for himself. Smiling, he walked into the lab and looked at the people who were his coworkers a few weeks ago.

"Aww, look, the boss man decided to visit us today," Derrick Coleman said. He was one of the head chemists.

"Keep it up," Erik said as he reached for a lab coat and protective eyewear. "You know I can fire you now."

"Then who's going to help you make this new line that everyone is talking about?"

The two men shook gloved hands and Erik prepared his workspace. "We got this, and we have to make it the most successful thing that we've ever done."

"How did you get Logan to actually cop to being a Jordan and working on this line?"

"All it took was a change at the top. I always thought my father and Logan could've made magic together. For whatever reason, Simon didn't agree."

"The way that guy has blown up, Simon has to be kicking himself for rejecting that idea."

"Let's not talk about that. We have work to do."

For the next four hours, Erik and his crew created new foundation and lipstick mixes. When one of the newer chemists showed him a bright red lipstick color formula, he had an amazing idea.

"Guys, we're going to introduce a new line of red lipstick and we're bringing the Yvonne red back." He pointed to the formula that the new chemist had showed him. "And I know just what we're going to call this color."

* * *

Sylvie stood at the entrance to the executive suites and smiled. The work she and her crew had done was pretty amazing. The deep purples and reds that lined the walls gave the area a royal feel. It made sense to her that it should feel like a kingdom because she noticed that these folks spent a lot of time at work. She could understand putting in long hours, Lord knows she'd done it a lot herself in the last few months. Her mind went where she wished it wouldn't. Amanda. Her pregnancy. Sylvie inhaled deeply as she placed her hand on her midsection. Knowing that it was unlikely she'd ever have a baby filling her womb, she felt a wave of sadness wash over her. She didn't equate womanhood with becoming a mother, but she wanted a family and had thought that Stephen was going to be the man who gave her that. Now, he was going to have that with another woman. Not just anyone, but the woman who tried to bring down everything that Sylvie worked for.

"Hey, boss," one of her workers asked as he touched her shoulder. "You all right?"

She turned around and smiled at her. "I'm good and I'm loving this look. Thank you for suggesting the purple."

She nodded. "Well, I know you like bold colors. It turned out really well."

"Better than well. It's exquisite. I think we're done for the day."

"Sylvie, I have to say, working with you has been a lot better than working with Amanda ever was. It was always her way or the highway."

Sylvie threw up her hand. "We don't have to cross that road ever again. And if all of your ideas are this brilliant, we're going to be doing a lot more collaborations. I hope Erik likes it as much as I do."

A few moments later, Sylvie was packing up her tools and ready to leave for the evening. She couldn't help but think about going to Erik's place again. She made herself think it was simply a business thing. But this man had gotten under her skin and she knew if he asked, she'd stay the night. And she'd get naked again.

What in the hell am I doing? she thought as she rubbed her hand across her face. Heading to her car, Sylvie pulled her cell phone from her pocket and called Olivia.

"Hello?" her friend said when she answered the phone.

"You sound stressed, is everything all right?"

Olivia sighed. "No. I really want to punch Logan in the face right now. I'm fielding so many questions about his ties to the Jordan family. Ugh. I know this is my job, but who knew people would be so interested in this?"

"I've been working, so I haven't seen any of

the news. I know they had a press conference here at the headquarters."

"And it looked amazing. You did the shiggidy on that lobby. Sylvie, you do realize this is going to launch you into the atmosphere with the elite designers."

"From your mouth to God's ears. You want to meet for coffee? I really need to talk to you about something."

"Is it Erik?" Olivia laughed.

"No," Sylvie said. Her voice took a serious tone. "I just need to talk, if you aren't too busy."

"Is your mom okay?"

"She's fine. I just really need to talk, but I'm not trying to interrupt whatever you have going on right now."

"This sounds serious. Like, Dancing Goats serious."

"Then let's meet at the Ponce de Leon location in twenty minutes."

"See you there."

Sylvie ended the call and headed for her car. Then she realized that she'd ridden to the office in the truck, and her car was at her house. Just as she was about to pull out her phone and order an Uber, she noticed Erik walking in the hallway. There was something sexy about him in that white lab coat. And that walk. The grace of a jungle cat and the swagger of a man who knows how to make a woman scream.

"Hey, Sylvie," he said when he noticed her watching him.

"Oh, hi."

"You're done for the day?"

"Yeah. Clearly I didn't plan this well. I rode on the truck with the furniture and now I'm stuck here. Thank goodness for ride sharing."

"You headed home?"

She shook her head as she gave him a sly once-over. "Olivia and I are meeting for coffee."

"I'm about to head out, you want a ride?"

She inhaled sharply because the kind of ride she wanted had nothing to do with his car. Then again, the last time she'd been in his car she'd gotten one hell of a trip. "You don't have to. I'm sure you have other things to do."

"Yeah, and what's your point? Besides, I can't have you missing when you have me excited about what you're going to do to my house." He leaned into her. "And my body." Erik took her hand in his and placed it on his chest.

"How presumptuous you are." Her voice was nearly a moan because he had already done something to her body. She was soaking wet and glad she was wearing jeans.

"But am I wrong?"

She licked her bottom lip. "Maybe."

"So, do you need a ride?"

"I do. I'm supposed to meet her at the coffee shop on Ponce de Leon."

"Dancing Goats, huh?"

Sylvie nodded. "Almost as good as that magical Kona that you have at your place."

"And you're welcome to another cup in the morning." Erik winked at her as he took his lab coat off. "I need to grab something out of my office and then I'll be ready."

"Mind if I come in with you? I want to look at the layout again. I think I want to do something different than what I'd originally planned."

He held his hand out to her. "Let's go, beautiful."

She took his hand and smiled. "So, what's up with the lab coat? Don't tell me the CEO is still mixing chemicals."

"Yes, I am. I love that part of the job. This CEO shit isn't my true wheelhouse. Besides, I came up with something today that is going to be next level."

"Ooh, you're willing to share?"

Erik opened the door to his office and shook his head. "Nope."

"I sure hope y'all didn't come in here to do something strange," Logan said.

"Why are you still in here?" Erik snapped as Sylvie crossed over to his desk.

Logan rose from the chaise in the corner and smiled. "Good to see you, Sylvie. Make sure my brother doesn't stand me up for dinner."

She glanced from Erik to Logan. "What am I missing here?"

"My brother is being annoying. I said I'd be

there and I will be. But Sylvie and I have some work to do right now."

Logan sat back down, picked up his sketch-book and held it up. "I'm working too. But if y'all need some privacy . . ."

"Get out of my office," Erik barked.

Logan chuckled under his breath as he packed up his charcoal pencil set. "If you're late, I'll give Mom my story as to why."

"I can still kick your ass!"

"That's what you think, but we all know better. Sylvie, see you later. And please tell Liv that I want whole beans. I know she's going to buy some coffee."

"You mean to tell me that Erik doesn't share his—"

Erik brought his finger to Sylvie's lips. "If you ever want another cup, you're going to have to keep that information to yourself."

She kissed the pad of his finger. "Will do."

Logan shook his head and left the office. Once they were alone, Erik pulled Sylvie into his arms. "Now that we're alone, let me do what I wanted to do when you walked in here." He captured her lips in a gentle kiss. But when his tongue brushed across her bottom lip, Sylvie's knees went weak.

His kisses were lethal, and the look on his face when he broke their embrace told her that he knew it as well.

"So, umm, did you get what you needed?" Sylvie asked.

"Sure did. I'm ready if you are."

She nodded. "Ready to go."

"I can't believe you didn't drive your Jag today. That car looks like it was specially made for you."

Sylvie smiled wistfully. "I need to put the old girl in the shop. People keep telling me I should get rid of my Jag, but I'm not going to."

"It's a beautiful car. You shouldn't."

"And it was my dad's, so I'm going to ride her until the wheels fall off. And then I'll put new wheels on her."

Erik took her hand in his as they walked out of the office. "A true daddy's girl, huh?"

She raised her right eyebrow. "Is that a problem?"

"Not at all. If anything, I'm a little envious. You see what my relationship with my parents is like." He ran his thumb across the back of her hand. "I have a friend who specializes in classic cars. Maybe he can help you with the upkeep of your Jag."

Sylvie stopped in her tracks and looked up at him. "Are you really this nice?"

"Come on, what kind of question is that?"

Sylvie's mind filled with the image of Stephen and the argument they had every time she took her car in to get a part replaced or when she'd drive hours away from her home to find a part for her car from some junkyard.

"You're spending more money on that hunk of junk. Why don't you get a new car? That Jaguar belongs in a scrap yard," Stephen said as they walked down the overcrowded aisle of Pull-Your-Part.

"I didn't ask you to come."

"I was hoping you'd head to a dealership and get a real car. Why are you holding on to it? You're not going to bring your dad back."

Sylvie stopped in her tracks. "Stephen, I swear to God . . . Why does it matter to you if I want to drive my father's car? I've always loved this car and if I have—"

"I worry about you, Sylvie. You do a lot of traveling and I don't want that hunk—car to leave you stranded and I can't get to you."

Her anger melted away for a moment. "That's sweet. But I'm still not getting rid of my car."

"Fine. But I'm not traveling all over the Southeast looking for parts with you anymore."

Erik's hand on her shoulder brought her back to the present. Why was Sylvie feeling some kind of way about Stephen having a baby when he hadn't given a damn about her feelings when they were supposed to be in love? He never cared about her and it was clear as day right now.

But she was not falling in love with Erik. No. Way.

"To answer your question, I'm nicer than you think. But when I'm pushed, I will push back."

"Gangster CEO. Duly noted," she quipped.

"And I'm fiercely protective of what I love."

Sylvie raised her right eyebrow, but didn't say a word. This whole love thing was just a fantasy she was building up in her head. And that was dangerous. Besides, he loved his company and his family. She wasn't dumb enough to believe that some hot sex had made this man fall in love with her.

Chapter 14

Clearly Sylvie was some kind of magical being. What in the hell did he just say? He wasn't a guy to throw the L-word around and he wasn't trying to lock Sylvie down like Olivia had done with Logan. That's it! He'd been spending too much time with his brother and these stupid ideas of falling in love with the most intriguing woman he'd ever met. Without even thinking, he took her hand in his as they headed out the door.

"So, how did you and Olivia meet?" Erik asked as they made it to his car. He couldn't help but remember the last time they'd gotten into his car. Stealing a look at her thighs when she slid into passenger seat, Erik remembered those fishnets.

"What's that look?"

Erik raised his head and smiled. "Admiring some very nice thighs."

"If anyone else said that, I'd probably punch them. Consider yourself lucky." She reached for his hand as he sat down and placed it on the center of her thigh.

"I'm a very lucky man." Erik leaned over and kissed her slow and deep. Her mouth was sweeter than honey and he was unapologetically addicted. Sylvie's moan made his body tingle. Made his dick hard and his need for her grow like a wildfire.

She pulled back from him and stroked his cheek. "We'd better get out of here before I allow you take these pants off and cause a scandal in your parking lot."

"And I'm not going to say no." Turning back to the steering wheel, Erik started the car and headed for the coffee shop. As he drove, Sylvie played with the radio until she stopped on a '90s station that was playing a sexy Jodeci song.

"Oh my goodness. This used to be my jam!" She started dancing in her seat and it was all Erik could do to keep his eyes on the road.

"Bet you had a crush on DeVante Swing, like every other sister did back in the day."

Sylvie shook her head. "I was a Mr. Dalvin girl, to be honest. But secretly, I would've gone out with JoJo."

"That's kind of gross. Glad your taste has evolved."

"Excuse me?" She gave him a slow glance. "If I squint, you remind me of JoJo."

"If I were less of a gentleman, I'd stop this car and let you walk."

She shrugged. "That's fine, I mean, the coffee shop is right there."

Erik pulled into the parking lot and shut the car off. "You know I'm the sexiest man you've ever seen."

Sylvie leaned into him. "You're right. JoJo has nothing on you."

"But if you promise to do those moves tonight, I'll play Jodeci's greatest hits until the battery in my phone dies."

"Don't you have to go eat with your mama?"

"I'll get there, but first . . ." He captured her lips again, hot and wet. Erik wanted to devour every inch of her lips. Wanted to feast on her until he'd gotten over his Sylvie addiction. But he was convinced that wasn't going to happen.

She placed her hand on his chest and broke the kiss. "We'd better stop."

"For now. I'll call you after dinner and we can go over your design ideas, then get naked."

"You don't care about my ideas, you just want me in your bed."

"That's only half true. I really do care about your ideas." Erik winked at her as she opened the door.

"And I'm going to go over my plans in extreme detail. See you later." She climbed out of the car and he watched her hips sway as she walked into the coffee shop. Pure magic.

It wasn't until a horn blew that he realized he'd been blocking the driveway. Moving out of the impatient driver's way, Erik knew if he didn't start for his parents' house, he wouldn't go.

What did his mother want, after going silent for so long? She'd been on Simon's side and turned her back on him, and now she wanted to have dinner with him and Logan.

"She wasn't thinking about us when she went on that damned talk show," he muttered as he merged onto Interstate 285.

When Erik pulled up to the Jordan estate, he looked up at the colonial house and smiled. At least he had happy childhood memories that were full of light, and he could always recall them instead of the bullshit that was going on now. He pulled into the seven-car garage and thought about how he and his father would sit out there tinkering with cars. Simon used to offer him manly advice, told him to follow his dreams. It helped a lot that Erik's dreams had a lot to do with being a part of Jordan Industries, unlike Logan.

It seemed as if the moment Logan picked up a crayon and started drawing, Simon lost interest in his younger son. But Yvonne had been Logan's rock for a long time. At least until he'd gained fame, and then she'd started acting like her husband. Aloof and distant.

Erik tried to pretend that he wasn't bothered by the way his parents had treated Logan. But he knew it hurt his little brother. That's why he made every effort to keep their relationship as close as possible.

As he exited the car, his cell phone rang. "Yeah?"

"You better be on your way to Mom's," Logan said.

"I'm in the garage."

"With or without Sylvie? I was just about to tell Ma all about her, but since you're here I'll let you do it."

Erik ended the call and shook his head. He wasn't telling anyone a word about Sylvie. How could he explain something he didn't even understand?

When he walked inside the house, Erik started for the dining room, but he heard his mother call his name.

"We're eating in the kitchen. Like the old days."

He turned around and gave his mom a long look. At least her smile was real, unlike when she was on TV that morning. She looked relaxed in her capris and tunic. "Been in the garden?"

She nodded. "My roses are looking amazing. And from the hints Logan kept dropping, I might need to cut you a few for your new lady."

"Don't start that."

"Well, I'm not going to be upset if both of my sons want to settle down. That just gets me closer to grandma status."

Erik sighed, unable to allow the elephant in the room to keep wandering around. "And when would you see these grandchildren, since Dad wants nothing to do with us and you seem to be falling right in line with his nonsense?"

Yvonne dropped her head. "I guess I deserved that. But I was hoping we could get through dinner before you called me on the carpet."

"How can I, *Mother*? You sat there this morning looking as if you were agreeing with your husband's lies about your son. How am I supposed to feel about any of this? We got through the holidays without a word from you and tonight you want to have a family dinner?"

"Erik, can we please just eat?" Logan said as he walked into the hallway where Yvonne and Erik were standing.

"No, we can't just eat," he snapped, then focused an angry stare on his mother. "Why are we here, when you made it clear that we weren't welcome?"

"I was wrong." Yvonne's eyes filled with water. "I-I . . . For so many years, I went along with everything your father wanted, and I'm trying not to . . . I don't want to make things worse between us. I love you boys and I'm sorry that I listened to your father when he was the one who brought this on himself. Erik, you didn't do anything wrong when you turned him in."

"Why did it take you so long to figure that out?"

Logan placed his hand on his brother's shoulder. "Chill out. This is our mother and you're on the line of disrespect."

Yvonne shook her head. "No, Logan. I'm the

one who has been disrespectful, to both of you. I can't change the past and I can't undo the hurt that I see in my son." She reached up and stroked Erik's cheek. "But I have to make things right. And since I sent the staff home, we better eat before the food gets cold."

Erik chuckled. "Still afraid to use a microwave, Mom?"

"They cause wrinkles!"

Logan and Erik doubled over in laughter and then Erik wrapped his arm around Yvonne's shoulder. "You're lucky that you have a son who can crack the anti-aging code. As a matter of fact, I did that today."

Yvonne smiled proudly. "Then I'm sure a lot of women are going to be praising your name."

"Pretty sure he just wants one to do that," Logan said, then scooted away from his brother's glare.

Yvonne tilted her head to the side. "Are you going to tell me about this special lady he keeps mentioning?"

"Where's that food?" Erik diverted. "I'm hungry."

"Her name is Sylvie!" Logan called from the kitchen.

"Nobody asked you!"

Yvonne linked arms with her son and patted his hand. "She must be special if Logan met her."

Erik nodded. "She's definitely one of a kind."

"Maybe I'll get to meet her one day."

He glanced at his mother and offered her a

fake smile, but didn't respond. It wasn't that he
didn't want to rave about Sylvie and how special
she was becoming to him, but he wasn't sure if
he wanted to bring her into the shit show that
was his family.

"Oh," Yvonne said quietly.

"We'll have to see what happens." He was sure
that his mother didn't miss the double meaning
of his words. When they got into the kitchen,
they laughed at Logan's plate, which was over-
flowing with macaroni and cheese and cabbage.
Just like when he was a kid, he'd poured ketchup
on everything.

"The more things change, the more they stay
the same," Yvonne said. "I hope you left enough
for the rest of us."

"Just a little bit." He nodded toward the pan
with the meatloaf in it.

Erik grabbed a plate and filled it with the
savory meatloaf and veggies. He wasn't a huge
fan of mac and cheese, but cabbage was his favorite. He glanced at his mother, who hadn't
placed anything on her plate. "You're not eating?"

Yvonne shook her head and walked over to
the refrigerator. "I'm doing a smoothie cleanse
right now."

"Why?" Logan asked with his mouth half stuffed
with food.

She pulled out a tumbler filled with a green
liquid that reminded Erik of vomit and took a
huge sip. He and Logan shuddered.

"Ma, that looks disgusting," Erik said as he took a seat beside Logan. "Probably tastes worse than those SlimFast shakes we used to steal at night."

Logan nodded as he swallowed his food. "Which is why I have to double check everything chocolate to this day."

Yvonne placed her tumbler on the counter. "It's healthy and I . . ."

"Is something wrong?" Erik asked as he set his plate down.

She looked out the window and took a deep breath. When Erik saw the tears in his mother's eyes, he crossed over to her. Drawing her into his arms, Erik hugged his mother. "What's going on?"

Logan dropped his fork and crossed over to them. "Ma, why are you crying? What's the matter?" He glanced at his brother and shrugged.

"I wanted y'all here tonight because . . . I got some bad news last week and . . ." Yvonne started sobbing. Erik held her tighter, thinking that this had everything to do with his father. He'd been tamping down his anger at Simon, but if he'd hurt his mother, all bets were off.

"What did he do?" Erik demanded.

"What?"

He rubbed her shoulder. "What did Dad do to make you this upset?"

"Your father has nothing to do with this." She

wiped her eyes with the back of her hand. "I have breast cancer."

Erik felt his lungs constrict. Logan held on to his mother's elbow and led her to a chair at the bar.

"Why are you just now telling us this?" Logan asked.

"It wasn't as if we were on the best of terms when I found out. But I just can't keep this bottled up when I know that . . ."

"We can get you the best specialists and you can beat this," Erik said. "What did Dad say?"

"I haven't told him yet." Yvonne's voice was barely audible.

"You haven't told Dad? Why?" Logan questioned. "He needs to be there for you. All of us do." He shot Erik a cold look.

"We do have to have your back on this, Ma. All of us need to be here for you and help you beat this."

Yvonne rubbed her face and shook her head. "There's not much we can do. The cancer has metastasized to my brain and my liver."

"What does that mean?" Logan asked.

"The doctor said that I may have eighteen months to a year, tops."

Erik wiped his face and shook his head. "I'm not going to lose you, Ma. First thing in the morning, I'm calling my boy at Emory and we're going to get some answers."

"The only answer is that I'm going to die and

I want my family to be whole before I'm gone." She broke down again and Erik felt as if he was going to die right then. He couldn't remember seeing his mother cry. Couldn't remember his heart breaking like glass, ever.

"You can't give up, Ma. We're going to help you fight." Erik turned away as his eyes filled with tears. He knew he needed to be strong for his mother. And this fight was going to mean that he'd have to forgive his father.

"We can't fix this," she said, then rose to her feet. Yvonne paced the length of the bar. "And your father can't know about this. The last thing Simon is capable of is dealing with hardship right now."

"This isn't a hardship, Ma." Logan slapped his hand down on the countertop. "This is your life and—"

The sound of the alarm alerting them that the front door had been opened stopped all of the conversation. Moments later, Simon walked into the kitchen.

"What in the hell are they doing here?" he boomed as he looked at his sons.

"They are our children," Yvonne said. "I thought you weren't coming home tonight."

"My house, I can come and go as I please, but these Judas-ass bastards aren't welcome here. We've talked about this, Yvonne, and I want them out."

Erik glared at his father. "You son of a bitch.

I'm here to see my mother and I'm not going anywhere."

Simon stalked over to his son and stood nose to nose with him. "What did I say? Get out of my house!"

"Dad," Logan called out. "Do you even care why Ma invited us to have dinner with her tonight?"

Simon gazed at Logan and snorted. "Why are you even here? You don't give a damn about this family, yet—"

"Shut up! All of you shut up! I wanted to have dinner with my children and I did. Simon, just leave us alone."

Simon turned to his wife and pursed his lips. "We'll talk about this later." He started for the back door and Erik punched his father in the face.

Yvonne gasped and Logan rushed over to his brother, grabbing his shoulder. "This isn't the time," Logan said.

Simon attempted to punch Erik, but he ducked out of the way of his father's fist. Shaking Logan's hand off him, Erik charged at his father and knocked him to the floor. "You don't want this fight, *Simon*."

"You think you're a big man? Think you're doing something by running my company. Boy, you ain't shit."

"Then I'm just like you! You don't even know what's going on in your own house and you want to come in here and act like a caveman?"

"Don't be here when I get back." Simon slowly rose to his feet and then left the house.

Yvonne shivered and cried. "This isn't what I wanted this night to be. I hate seeing this. You two have to stop being angry at your father."

Erik sucked his teeth. "After all of this, you're still taking his side?" Shaking his head, Erik stalked out the door.

Chapter 15

Olivia drained her coffee cup, then burst out laughing. Sylvie was not amused.

"You're falling for Erik Jordan and you don't want to admit it."

Sylvie rolled her eyes and drummed her fingers against the coffee cup. "That's a lie. I said I like him and I enjoy having sex with him. Where in that do you get that I'm falling for him?"

Olivia rolled her eyes. "Sylvie, I know you. This role that you're trying to play right now is a farce. You're not a casual-sex girl. Had that been the case, you would've dropped Stephen years before you did. And if a son of a bitch deserved to be dropped, it was that bastard."

Sylvie cast her eyes downward as she felt a few tears threatening to spring forward. "I'm not falling for Erik. But he is a really nice guy. Besides, we have business between us and this could get really complicated."

"You should've thought about that before you

slept with him again. Obviously, there's a spark between the two of you that goes beyond sex."

"What if it isn't?" Sylvie shrugged. But she knew it was deeper than that. After all, the man wanted to help her fix her car. A car that meant more to her than getting from point A to point B. That was big, wasn't it?

"I'm happy for you. Because after Stephen, I thought you were going to bury yourself in work and pretend that you didn't want a happily-ever-after. You know you deserve one, right?"

"Sorry, everyone can't be like you and LJ. I'm still blown that he's a Jordan and hid it from the public all of these years."

"Clearly you haven't watched his father's interview today. Logan dodged a bullet that Erik took head-on."

Sylvie shook her head. "I haven't watched it because this is so sad. Erik clearly wants to be close to his family, and for them to come against him like this—it's not a good look."

Olivia picked up her empty cup. "But you're not falling for him, yet you're feeling some kind of way about how his family is treating him. But it's just casual?"

Sylvie narrowed her eyes at her friend. "Can I be honest for a second?"

Olivia nodded.

Sylvie took a deep breath and closed her eyes. "I'm pretty sure my relationships are going to have to be casual for the rest of my life. I found out a few years ago that I'm not going to be able to have children."

"Sylvie," Olivia said, then brought her hand to her mouth.

"Stephen and I wanted a child and we tried for about a year. After I found out that I only have one functioning ovary, that's when our relationship went from bad to worse."

"What do you mean?"

Sylvie closed her eyes to hold back her tears. "Stephen wasn't supportive at all. You get the worst news you could ever hear and the minute you have a disagreement he brings it up."

Olivia rolled her eyes. "I swear, if I see that fucker on the street I'm going to run him over."

Tears welled up in Sylvie's eyes. "You don't want to do that. His child is going to need a father."

"His child?"

"With Amanda."

Olivia's mouth dropped open. "Sylvie, are you all right?"

She wiped her eyes. "I'm fine. Okay, that's a lie. It's not that I'm holding on to some feelings for him, but knowing that those two are about to have the one thing I know I can't have makes me feel some kind of way, and I don't want to set myself up to be hurt by any man who wants the one thing I can't give him."

"Which is? You have a big heart, you love with your whole soul, and there are more ways to have kids. And guess what, there are men in this world who don't want kids."

"But what if I do? What if I want to give my mama that grandchild she keeps hinting about?"

"Then your rich future husband will have all kinds of specialists come in and get you tested."

"My what?"

"If you and Erik want to have a baby, he will make that happen. Calm down."

"Who said I wanted to . . . You know what, I'm not doing this with you."

"Doing what?" Olivia shrugged.

"Building a fantasy life with a man who has more drama going on than *The Young and the Restless*. And it's not that serious between us. We're just . . ."

"Falling in love. Now, you know I'm not one to gossip, but in the three years that LJ and I have been together, I've never seen Erik with the same woman twice. I mean, he's a love-them-and-leave-them type of guy. But you have the keys to the castle. Don't miss out on something special because you're trying to be hardheaded."

"Really? You're that girl now?"

"The girl who wants her friend to finally be happy in every aspect of her life? Yes, yes, I am. I will say this—you've been smiling a whole lot more these days."

"That's because my business is booming. Things are finally looking up for me, despite what Amanda tried to do. I'm a survivor out here."

"Start singing and I'm going to walk out that door as if I don't know you."

"That's fine. It's not like I can't take an Uber or call Erik, since we're meeting at his house tonight."

"That's what we're calling it now?" Olivia raised her right eyebrow. "You're going to spend the night with him and show him paint swatches while y'all are naked in bed. I get it. It's a working affair."

"You make me sick." Sylvie didn't hide her grin. "But that is a good way to make him go along with all of my plans."

"Eww, you're really going to use your body to renovate that man's house?" Olivia laughed. "Get him, girl!"

"I'm not getting him. We're just . . ."

"Falling for each other like a ton of bricks. It's okay. Act like it's something casual and meaningless. That way I can always rub this in your face."

Sylvie rolled her eyes and sighed. "I need to go home and change." She glanced at her watch. "Hopefully dinner with his mother didn't end up in a hot mess."

"Knowing those people, I wouldn't be surprised if they didn't get in a fight. But I hope LJ and his mother can find their way back to each other. He misses being close to her."

"I couldn't imagine not being close to my mama."

Olivia nodded. "So, what's wrong with your car now?"

"I need some specialty part that's available at a parts store about four hours away from here."

Olivia sighed. "Have you ever thought about just making the Jag a weekend car?"

"No. You know I love that car. I feel really close to my father when I drive it. Sometimes it's like we're riding together and I hear him speaking to me. Or I'll hear a song that he and Mom used to dance to, and I know it's going to be a good day. Sounds crazy, doesn't it?"

"No. But I still think you need a vehicle that's a little more reliable. I'm still blown away that you drove all around the Southeast finishing those jobs without that car breaking down on you."

"I guess Daddy was looking out for me." Sylvie smiled. It wasn't that she couldn't afford another car, or hadn't thought about it. But she didn't want to get rid of her father's car.

"You can keep that car and get a new one. It doesn't mean any less to you if you do that."

Sylvie nodded. "I know. I'll think about it. But for now, I'm leaning on my friends and using this Uber app."

"As long as you don't drive that big truck around town, I'm happy. Oh, wait. I have to get those beans for Logan."

While Sylvie waited for Olivia to make her purchase, she pulled out her cell phone and sent a text to Erik.

Hope you have some dessert at your house for
our meeting.

She and Olivia headed for the exit.

When she arrived at home, Sylvie realized
that Erik hadn't replied. She couldn't help but
hope he and his family had made peace. Heading for the garage, Sylvie stood in front of the
Jag and rubbed her hand across the bumper.

"All right, Dad. Tell me that this guy isn't
going to break my heart." She laughed. "I guess
you and Mom wrote the book on being able to
find the love of your life, huh? Things are different these days. It's hard to know who to trust.
But Erik seems different. Or maybe I'm just
fooling myself."

She reached into her pocket and pulled out
her cell phone. No response from him at all.
That was strange, or maybe it was the sign she'd
been looking for. Or she was doing it again,
trying to keep herself from falling in love with a
man who would certainly break her heart.

Sylvie hadn't told Olivia, but she did google
Erik, and saw what a serial dater he was. Models,
movie stars, social media mavens. Everything
that Sylvie wasn't. Mind you, it wasn't as if she
didn't think she couldn't compete with anyone,
but she didn't want to wake up and see that she
lost herself to love again.

Nope. She wasn't going to risk that again.
What did she have to show for the last time

she fell in love? A broken heart and wavering self-confidence. That's why she had poured herself into her work and swore that she was going live her life with very little drama and extreme success. To her, love brought drama. What she felt right now, glancing at her phone every five seconds because she was waiting on a text, she was living through drama.

Why hasn't he responded to me yet? Sylvie stomped inside and kicked her shoes and jeans off. This was about to relax in a bubble bath and get ready for tomorrow. Where she would run right into Erik.

I knew this was a bad idea. Now I'm going to have to act professional and pretend that I don't care that he didn't text me back.

Normally when she decided to take a long bath she would take her phone into the bathroom with her. But tonight she was going to leave it all behind.

Erik paced back and forth on his mother's front porch, trying to wrap his mind around everything that had happened over the last few hours. He really threw a punch at his father. His mother had cancer, and he didn't know how to deal with all of this.

Logan walked over to Erik and placed a hand on his shoulder. "You need to calm down."

He glanced over at his brother. "How can you be so calm?"

Logan shrugged. "Because seeing you punch Dad made my day."

Scowling at him, Erik continued pacing. "We have to get Ma to take her health care seriously. I don't like the fact that she's basically given up."

"I don't like that either. But what can we do? Dad's probably in her ear with some bullshit about us right now. Going through this alone probably feels like the best choice."

"Why do we find keeping secrets a viable option in this family?"

"You're really asking me?" Logan grunted. "My existence as an artist has been an entire fabrication." He ran his hand across his smooth face. "We have to do something to help Ma. Even if that means forcing her out of the house and checking her into a treatment center against her will."

"Don't think it works like that, but you're right. We have to do something."

Logan glanced down at his watch. "Shit, I was supposed to meet Olivia an hour ago."

Erik squeezed the bridge of his nose. "Sylvie was supposed to come over tonight. Damn it, where is my phone?"

"Haven't seen it," Logan said with a shrug.

Erik patted his pockets and his phone wasn't there. "Hand me your phone." He held his hand out for Logan's phone.

"Now, wait a minute, how are you demanding my phone to call a woman you're just kicking it with? You're not acting like a dude who's not falling head over heels for a woman."

"Stop being a dick and hand me the phone."

Logan laughed and handed Erik his smartphone. "Make it quick, because I need to call my fiancée."

Erik was surprised that he had memorized Sylvie's phone number, and when he saw the number was already stored in Logan's phone, he almost said something rude. But Logan was about to marry her best friend.

And why was he acting as if he had a right to be angry about another man calling his woman? Well, technically, she wasn't his. *What am I thinking?* he thought as the phone rang in his ear.

Sylvie sank into a tub of jasmine bubbles and lavender oil. Just as she was about to dip her head under water, she heard the ringtone she'd set for Olivia vibrate through the silence.

"Ugh! She would call now." Pulling herself out of the tub, she drip-dropped down the hall to grab the phone. Seeing that it was LJ's number, she got nervous. Had something happened to Olivia? Why was he calling?

"Hello? LJ? What's going on?"

"It's not Logan, this is Erik."

Sylvie reminded herself to breathe. Then she thought that something even worse probably happened. "Why are you calling me from your brother's phone?"

"Because I can't find mine. I know I should've reached out to you sooner, but dinner with my mother took a turn for the worse."

"So, that's why you chose to . . . Wait, is everything all right?"

"Where are you right now?"

"I'm at home." She looked down at the water on her floor. "And I . . ."

"Sylvie, I need to see you. Not to talk about colors or patterns or chairs. I just need to see you."

All of the random evil thoughts she'd had about him ignoring her floated away as she gave him her address. "Just give me a few minutes to put on some clothes. I'll text you my address."

"Sure, and thanks."

After ending the call, she rushed upstairs, let the water out of the tub, then dried the floor. Next, she dried off and pulled on a cotton dress. She tried to calm her heartbeat as she waited for him to arrive. Here she was acting all mad and the man had a family emergency. *That's what I get for jumping to conclusions.* Sylvie headed for the kitchen and started a pot of coffee. She didn't know what she was supposed to do in this situation. It wasn't as if she knew his family situation—well, only what she'd seen on TV. But there had to be more to why a man would turn his back on his sons for no reason like that. And then the situation with Logan not even claiming the Jordan name. But there was no way she could ask him these questions, it wouldn't be polite. She was just going to lend him a shoulder and an ear. And a damned good cup of coffee.

By the time the doorbell rang, Sylvie had two mugs of coffee and a plate of cookies sitting on the round coffee table in the den, John Coltrane's *A Love Supreme* playing on low, and a cinnamon candle burning in the corner of the room. She started to blow the candle out because it felt as if she was setting the wrong kind of scene. But she simply wanted to make him feel comfortable. That meant her questions didn't matter. She walked to the front door and opened it.

"Hi," she said.

Erik pulled Sylvie into his arms and hugged her tightly. She stroked the back of his neck as she inhaled his masculine scent. "Are you okay?" Her lips brushed against his ear.

"I've been better." He broke their embrace and stroked her cheek.

"Well, I have coffee and cookies."

"Did you bake them? It smells amazing in here." He glanced at her and smiled. "Unless that's just you."

Sylvie took his hand and led him to the den. "You smell my favorite candle." She nodded toward the corner. "Cinnamon relaxes me and . . ."

Erik brushed his finger across her lips. "You're a special lady, Sylvie Gates. And the Coltrane?"

"Who doesn't like Coltrane? If you say you don't, I'm going really question this thing we have going here and believe that you picked all of that stuff that you have in your house."

He took a seat on her soft sectional sofa, then reached out and stroked her bare leg. "Never said I didn't like Coltrane. But I've always been more of a Miles Davis man myself."

"Why? 'Cause you think you're cool?"

"And slick. For about ten minutes in high school, I tried to play the trumpet." His hand slowly inched up her thigh. "But there were other things I wanted to do with my lips and fingers."

Sylvie inhaled as his hand reached the top of her thigh. "That's why," he continued, "I think Miles is the man."

"May-maybe I should play some of *Birth of the Cool*." She took a step back from his touch because he was making her weak.

He patted the cushion beside him. "This is fine. More than fine."

Sylvie sat down and reached for the platter of cookies. "You want to talk about what happened tonight?"

He took one of the chocolate chip cookies and broke it in half. "Well. My mother has cancer. She acts like she plans to give up and not fight. She hasn't even told her husband."

Sylvie furrowed her brows at the way Erik said *her husband*. That was his dad, right? She set the cookies on the table and stroked the back of his hand. "What are you going to do?"

"What can I do? Logan said we should kidnap her and force her to get treatment. And all of the stress of this bullshit with the company can't be good for her."

"Then you should make peace with your father so your whole family can rally around your mother."

Erik snorted, then bit into the cookie. "Doubt that will happen since I punched my father in the face today."

Sylvie's mouth dropped open. She wanted to say something, but how do you respond to that? He polished off his cookie then reached for one of the coffee mugs. "We are not a Norman Rockwell–painting family."

"Maybe it's time for you guys to give it a try. Erik, I don't know what your relationship is like with your mother, but I couldn't imagine my life without mine."

Erik sighed. "There was a time when I felt the same way about my mom, maybe I still do. I'm just confused about the woman she's become."

Sylvie tucked her legs underneath her and faced him. "What do you mean?"

"How she went along with my father when she spent her life protecting us—especially Logan—from his bullshit. It's as if he turned into Jim Jones or some shit. But maybe she was trying to keep sanity in the house because she's sick."

Sylvie nodded. *At least he has time*, she thought. When her father died, it was without warning. No time to prepare for a life without him.

"Hey, hey," Erik said, then wiped a tear from her cheek. "What are those tears all about?"

She hadn't realized that she'd been crying until he touched her.

"I didn't want to unload on you and make you cry."

She shook her head, then dabbed at her eyes with her fingers. "I was just thinking about my dad. When he passed away, there was no time to prepare. It just happened. One day he was bigger than life and the next day he was gone."

"And here I come with—"

She brought her finger to his lips. "We deal with things differently." Sylvie shrugged her shoulders. "Clearly, I'm a crier."

"But a beautiful one." He leaned in and kissed her damp cheek.

"You need to work things out with your mom, while you still have time. I get sad when I think about losing my father. But I don't regret anything. The last thing I said to him was *I love you*."

"You're right, I don't want to have any regrets if something were to happen."

"And you got to make her fight."

Erik smiled. Something about the way Sylvie poured her emotions into life made him understand a lot more about her. And damn it, it made her sexy as hell. "You know what, I don't want to talk about that anymore." He took a sip of the lukewarm coffee.

"I can reheat that if you'd like."

"Nope, this is fine. As a matter of fact, this

might be added to my coffee collection. What is this again, reindeer dance?"

"Funny. It's Dancing Goats. I can't believe you've been in Atlanta all your life and aren't hip to these delicious beans here."

"Haven't been in Atlanta all of my life. I spent part of my childhood in Chicago." Erik's voice rose an octave.

"Guess you had some good times in the Chi?"

"Heck yeah, the block parties, the food, and when we'd put on the makeup shows, my dad's take on the Ebony Fashion Fair shows, it was amazing. And Mom would come out as the show-stopper. She'd have on the new Yvonne color and people would go wild.

"I remember my mama talking about those shows. She's still pissed about the Yvonne lipstick."

"Tell your mom I have something coming that is going to blow her mind."

Sylvie raised her eyebrows. "Tell me."

"Nope."

She folded her arms across her chest and poked her lips out. "You're so wrong."

"You think so?" He inched closer to her and pressed his lips to hers. He nibbled on her bottom lip, then their tongues touched and she moaned as he pulled her closer to his hard body. She ran her hand across his chest and wrapped her leg around his waist. Pulling back from him, Sylvie stroked the side of his face. "There you go with those dangerous lips again."

"Like you're not over there with two soft lethal weapons of your own. Never had a woman kiss me until I was weak before. So, checkmate."

"Whatever. The coffee is cold now."

"I don't want any more, anyway. I need you." He ran his finger down her cheek. "When I wake up in the morning, I need you in my arms."

She nodded. "Okay." Sylvie attempted to move, but Erik shook his head.

"Let's just be here right now. Listen to that sax."

Chapter 16

Hours passed and Erik still had Sylvie in his arms with the music still playing. They'd moved from Coltrane to Miles and now Charles Mingus.

"You have a great collection of music." They swayed back and forth on the sofa. They'd switched their position and she was leaning back on his chest. Erik's arms rested around her waist.

"Something else I learned from my dad."

"He sounds like a good man." Erik kissed her on the cheek.

Sylvie nodded. "Want a drink?"

"Sure. But no more coffee."

"What are you thinking? Wine, whiskey or . . ."

"Surprise me."

As Sylvie rose to her feet, he watched her walk into the kitchen. He watched her hips sway as she walked. It seemed redundant to keep thinking how sexy she was, but how could he not?

"Damn. I got to make sure that I don't mess this thing up." He shook his head, surprised by his thought. What thing? Was he really falling for this woman like Logan kept saying? *Nah, this is me thinking too hard about this thing. Sylvie doesn't want to be mixed up in this mess and I'm not trying to bring her into this.*

Moments later, Sylvie returned to the den with two glasses of merlot. "Is this okay?" She set the glasses in front of him.

"Perfect."

"Great. So, are you feeling all right?"

Erik nodded. "Thank you for letting me talk your ear off tonight."

"One day I'm going to need you to return the favor."

"Anytime you need me, I'm right here for you."

She patted his thigh and his dick sprang to life.

Erik shifted in his seat and expelled a sigh. Damn, he wanted this woman, but he couldn't have sex with her every time they were together. He brushed his finger across her bottom lip. "I plan to hold you to this. And you know what, I don't mind being held at all."

"Is that so?" She gazed at him over the rim of her wineglass.

Erik took the glass from her hand, then smiled. "Yes, so why don't you wrap those arms around me."

Sylvie followed his directive and snuggled against him, wrapping her arms around his waist. They sipped the wine and talked about everything but his family and color palettes. He kissed her forehead and felt her shiver against him. This woman made him think about long walks in the park, overnight beach trips, and roses. He'd never sent a woman roses. But he wanted to send Sylvie dozens of roses, plant the flowers in her yard so that every time she went outside she'd think of him.

"More wine?" she asked, breaking into his thoughts.

"No, I think I've had enough. It was very good."

"My collection doesn't compare to yours, but I like a nice bottle of something vintage around the house every now and then. Tonight seemed like a good time to share."

"My wine cellar is always open to you."

"Don't say it if you don't mean it," she quipped.

"I never say things to you that I don't mean." Erik stroked her cheek.

"Are you tired?" she asked. "Seems like this has been a really long day for you."

"It has. Think it might be time for me to go."

"You don't have to, unless you just want to sleep in your bed."

"That I do want. But I don't plan to sleep alone. Why don't you pack a bag and come with me? After all, we do still have a meeting."

"I think you're holding this meeting over my head so that you can keep me coming back for more."

"More what?"

She ran her finger across his bottom lip. "Those, for starters. Then that Kona coffee."

"I feel like the coffee is the main reason you

came over. But it's fine, I like to see you coming."
Sylvie raised her right eyebrow. Erik was certain
she'd picked up on the double meaning behind
his words. "If you're just as tired as I am, we can
just sleep. But I do want to wake up with you in
my arms."

"Then you're going to have to stay right here,
because I've already gotten my lavender-scented
candles burning upstairs."

Erik furrowed his brows.

Sylvie dropped her head, hiding a smile. "So,
before you explained what happened after dinner
with your mom, I was kind of pissed with you. I
thought I'd been stood up."

"And you burn candles when you're angry?"

"It's for the oil, and don't you think that's
better than burning down someone's poorly decorated house?"

"You don't have that in you, do you?" he
quipped.

"Act right and you will never have to find out."

Erik rose to his feet and downed the rest of
his wine. "I knew there was something scary
about you."

"Trust me, on that tip, I'm all talk and no
action." She stood on her tiptoes and kissed him
on the cheek. "Besides, if you stay here, you get
to see what an adult's bedroom is supposed to
look like."

"That was harsh. You know what, let me get
the full tour."

She picked up their empty wineglasses. "We'll

start with the kitchen." They walked into her ultramodern kitchen with stainless steel appliances, a smart refrigerator, and a marble island. The vaulted ceiling made the room seem larger than it was. Erik was impressed with the space in the kitchen and her industrial-looking coffeemaker.

"More Dancing Goat over there?"

"A few surprises. This is probably the least used spot in my house. I'm not a big cook."

Erik nodded. "I can see that."

She nudged him in the side as she placed the glasses in the sink. "And what's that supposed to mean?"

"That you're always busy, running around doing work and building that brand of yours."

She smiled. "So, you googled me, huh?"

"Not yet. I just recognize your drive. And it's pretty impressive."

"Wow, that's the first time someone has actually said that to me. I'm usually told that I'm doing too much."

"Whoever said that was an idiot. And in my humble opinion, you're better off without him."

"What makes you think some guy told me that?" she asked as she shut the lights off and led him to her sitting room.

"Because that's some dumb shit a man with no vision would say. People like to pretend that a woman is supposed to dim her light to allow others to shine. Life doesn't work that way." Erik sighed as he thought about his mother and how she'd done just that for Simon. What had it gotten her in return?

Nothing.

There was no way he'd ever ask the woman he loved to give up on her dreams and what she wanted just so he could feel like a big man. Watching his baby soar would give him just as much satisfaction as anything else.

"Erik?" Sylvie said, breaking into his thoughts. "Are you all right?"

"What?"

"I clearly asked you a question and you just stood there."

"Sorry, darling. What did I miss?"

"You need to go to sleep. We can finish the tour in the morning." She stood on her tiptoes and kissed his cheek.

"I can't go to sleep without a true good-night kiss," he said as he pulled her against his body. Erik brushed his lips against her soft ones. He felt her shiver in his arms, then captured her mouth in a hot, soul-searing kiss. Her moans made every nerve in his body stand on end. But he needed to prove to himself, and in a sense, to her, that tonight wasn't about sex.

But damn it if he didn't want her—especially when her tongue tasted like manna from heaven. He pulled back and stared into her sparkling eyes. Maybe Logan was right. It was quite possible that he was falling in love with Sylvia Elaine Gates.

Something electric happened and Sylvie wasn't

sure if she even understood what was going on. Just the way Erik looked at her, the way he seemed to pierce her soul and make her shiver with want. But as much as she didn't want to admit it, what they had was more than physical. She tried to pretend that she didn't have deeper feelings for this man, that she was protecting herself from being hurt, but in this moment, she had to admit that it was all a lie.

"If you want to take a shower, I have a towel warmer in the hall."

"You're fancy, huh?" He stroked her cheek and Sylvie wanted to melt in his arms. "Point me to the bathroom and I promise not to make a mess."

"Yeah, I'm not like you. I have to clean up after myself." She'd hoped that her teasing would ease the crackling sexual tension in the air. But when he sucked his bottom lip, all she could think about was when he'd buried himself between her thighs.

"Keep in mind, I did offer to whisk you away to a place where someone else picked up the towels." He winked at her as they headed for the staircase.

"Welcome to the real world, Mr. Jordan."

Once they made it to the top of the stairs, Sylvie turned on her disco-ball hallway light. Erik burst into laughter. "What's the story behind this light?"

She shrugged. "I had a club in Charlotte that I redesigned for Christmas. I ordered a bunch of

lights and fixtures and the company sent this."
Sylvie pointed up to ceiling. "I didn't want this
for the club. Didn't even order it. Called the
company, because they are one of my favorite
vendors, and told them about the mistake. They
said keep it."

"And you installed it here?"

Nodding, she hit another button and caused
the ball to spin. "Now, only special people know
that it does this. After I've finished a good project
or had a good day, sometimes I put on some old-
school disco and have a party in the hallway."

Erik turned to her and drew her into his arms.
"So, you're going to show me some moves or
nah?" He thrust his hips forward and swayed
side to side.

"And I thought you were sleepy." She placed
her hands on his shoulders and did a sexy two-
step. "You sure you can handle this?" Sylvie
dipped herself, turned around and pressed her
backside against him.

When she dropped down and slowly rose up
against his crotch, Erik nearly lost his mind. He
bounced back as if he'd been scalded. Didn't he
tell himself that he wasn't here to have sex with
this woman?

"You might be right, I can't handle those
moves." He winked at her. "Tonight, anyway."

"When you're ready, it's on."

"I feel like I was just challenged to a dance-off."

She sucked her teeth. "Like you could even

see me on the dance floor." She did a super sexy snake, then transitioned into the hustle.

"This sounds like a battle that needs to happen outside of your hallway."

"Whenever you're ready." Sylvie smiled, then pointed down the hall. "The bathroom is right there. Make sure you use the massage setting on the shower head, because when we do this dance battle, I don't want any excuses about why you lost."

"Oh, my beautiful hostess, I won't lose." Erik turned toward the closet and grabbed a warm towel. No matter how warm the towel was, he knew he needed a cold shower before he could climb into bed with Sylvie. Though he did wonder if she slept in something silky or lacy and transparent. What he really needed was for her to sleep in flannel. That way he'd be able to just wrap his arms around her soft curves and go straight to sleep.

He ducked into the bathroom and glanced around at the forest-green room. It was an interesting color choice, because he'd expected yellow or pink. But the dark green added depth to the room. It seemed as if every room in her townhouse showcased her skill as a designer.

Maybe her redesign of Jordan Industries would blow the media's mind and they'd ignore the brewing storm around the family and the company. Before misplacing his phone, Erik had been getting alerts about the SEC's investigation into Simon. Maybe that had fueled his rage at his father and that had been why he punched him.

Erik still couldn't understand why his father had single-handedly destroyed something he'd spent his life building. There had to be an explanation. But he was sure that he'd never get one. Not one that made sense anyway. Erik stripped out of his clothes and turned the shower on. He couldn't understand Simon and why he thought he could rob his stockholders and put such a spotlight on the business in a negative way.

Stepping underneath the lukewarm water, Erik exhaled and allowed it to beat down on him. He wished that he could spend the rest of his life without his phone, but he knew that he had to get back to work—tomorrow. Tonight he was going to wrap his arms around Sylvie and pretend that he was living a normal life with his woman.

Chapter 17

Sylvie couldn't understand why she was nervous about Erik sleeping in her bed tonight. Things felt different, more intimate. She wasn't sure that she was ready to be emotional with this man. Look what happened the last time she'd given her all to a man in the name of love. She'd ended up heartbroken and betrayed. Sylvie stroked her belly and thought about the baby Amanda was about to have.

How could she think about getting serious with a man when . . . Not having a child didn't make her less of a woman, but Erik seemed like the type who wanted a family. He seemed close to his mom, and he was definitely close to his brother. Would he waste his time with a woman who couldn't give him a legacy of his own? Would anyone?

Stop feeling sorry for yourself. You're a grown woman who won't be judged by the fact that you have kids or not.

She turned down the rose-colored comforter, then fluffed the goose-down pillows while she waited for Erik to leave the bathroom. Sylvie told herself that she was putting the cart before the horse and she needed to take things one day at a time.

"Hey, Sylvie." Erik's voice from the doorway made her nearly stumble. But when she looked up and saw his damp chest and the towel wrapped around his waist, her knees did buckle.

"Yes?" she found the voice to say.

"Where's your laundry room? I'd hate to waste this clean body smell by putting on dirty clothes in the morning."

"I'll put your clothes in the wash, if you want me to."

"Nah, my hands aren't broken. I can actually wash clothes." He winked at her. "My grandmother wasn't rich and didn't plan on having lazy grandsons."

"Your grandmother sounds like a winner."

Erik nodded. "She was. That's why I don't understand why my father has done . . . Not going to go there."

"The washroom is in the basement. But you don't have to do laundry tonight. We can have breakfast and get your clothes clean."

Erik crossed over to Sylvie and took her hands in his. "Now, if a brother has to sleep naked, you're going to have to keep your hands to yourself."

"Then a brother should be thankful that I have a pair of sweatpants he can slip on."

Erik tilted his head to the side. "Do you really think I want to put on another man's pants?"

She shrugged as she released his hands and walked over to the closet. "They're actually my pants." Sylvie pulled out an extra-large pair of Clark Atlanta University sweatpants. "Remember when everybody was on the TLC tip and wore pants that were way too big?"

"Don't tell me you walked around with condoms pinned on your clothes too," he quipped.

Sylvie sucked her teeth. "I didn't. But I did rock that T-Boz haircut for far too long in undergrad."

"Please tell me there are pictures."

"None that you'll ever see." She tossed the pants to him. Erik dropped his towel and Sylvie drank in his masculinity. Ripped abs, thick dick, muscular thighs, and that chocolate skin. Her mouth watered thinking about all of the places that she'd kissed and licked on that man. Noticing her stare, Erik did a 360 spin.

"Make sure you get a really good look before I put all of this away."

"Oh, whatever." She turned away as heat rushed to her cheeks. "Let's go to bed."

Erik slipped into the well-worn sweatpants and walked over to the bed. "Sounds like a plan to me. Which side to you like?"

"The middle."

He grinned, then plopped down on the bed and opened his arms to her. "Rest your weary head on my chest, darling."

Sylvie eased onto the bed beside him and snuggled against his chest. Erik ran his fingers through her curly hair and started massaging her scalp. "Ooh, that feels good," she moaned. "You know if you ever need a second career, you should consider massage therapy."

"Nah. These hands are reserved for special people. Not for everybody."

"So, you think I'm special?"

"Oh, I know you're special. You have a glow about you and you seem pretty unstoppable. Some dude is out there right now wondering how he let you get away."

Sylvie snorted. "I seriously doubt that. Most men think I'm too much, and that's their problem."

"Good thing I don't have that affliction. You're more than enough and—"

"Erik, don't fill my head with sweet nothings that are going to . . ."

He stopped massaging her scalp and brought his finger to her lips. "True confessions time. Sylvie, I feel something for you that I've never felt before. And I never expected this."

"Erik."

"We owe it to ourselves to see where this goes."

She propped up on her elbow and stared at him. "Are you sure? You have a lot going on and I don't want to be another issue."

"How could you be an issue? Do you realize what you did for me tonight?"

She shrugged. "Fed you cookies and gave you wine."

He tweaked the end of her nose. "You turned a shit day into a good night. Let's be real, fate keeps pushing us together. Did you think we'd see each other after you left that note on the mirror?"

Sylvie laughed and shook her head. "You're right. But I thought we weren't going to talk about that note ever again."

Erik stroked her back. "Never said that. It's going to be my go-to argument killer."

"I don't argue. Fighting isn't my thing. I'm more about the prevention of arguments."

He stroked her back. "Tell me something about you that I don't know."

"What do you mean?"

"When did you know you wanted to be a designer?"

Her heart swelled as he held her. Other than her friends and family, no one ever took an interest in her career choice. "I think I knew it was what I wanted to do when I got my first dollhouse."

"Really?"

"Yep. My dad didn't put the roof on it, so I could look in the house from the top, and seeing all of the empty rooms just gave me so many ideas. Of course, it was hard to put all of my vision in there. Then I asked my parents if I could redo my room. My mama was against it at first—I was ten years old. But my pops promised to help and the idea stuck."

"Wow. So, all your life you knew what you wanted to do. Wish I could say the same was true for me."

"You didn't want to work in the family business?"

"It wasn't as if we believed there was a choice. You were either going to work for Jordan Industries or work for Jordan Industries. And if you did something else, it was as if you sent a slap in the face to what was supposed to be our family legacy."

She rubbed her hand against his chest. "Did you have another dream?"

"Until I became CEO, I was living my dream. I got to make women beautiful and I did it all behind the scenes."

"You don't like the spotlight? Even when you were dating the models?"

Erik chuckled. "I see I wasn't the only one who went on Google."

Sylvie shrugged. "It's the way of the world these days. We're all just a few clicks on the Internet."

"Let me guess. You're one of those people who checks in everywhere on Facebook?"

Sylvie laughed. "Only when I want people to know where I am. Mostly when I'm doing a project or finding a new restaurant with really good food and coffee."

"Then no more Kona for you. Can't have you giving my address to your thousands of followers."

She pinched his nipple. "Like I'd want to let the world know your address. I'm special, remember."

"Of course you are. So, since you're going to redesign my place, don't you think it would be a good idea for you to move in?"

She raised her right eyebrow. "You know that's not how I normally do things, right?"

"I'm not a normal client either. Being that I'm

giving you carte blanche to my house, don't you think you should spend more time there to get a great feel for what I need?"

It was Sylvie's time to laugh now. "You just want nights like this on a regular basis, huh? Or are you trying to pay me in coffee beans?"

"If it makes you more comfortable, I won't give you any coffee that doesn't come from a can."

"Hush your mouth, man! That's offensive." She laid her head on his chest. "I'll think about it. We're almost done with the headquarters, so I'll have a little more time to devote to your ugly house."

"I don't know how many more of those ugly-house comments I'm going to take."

"Luckily for you, I only have a few more."

He kissed her on the top of her head. "Thank you for your mercy."

Sylvie closed her eyes and tried to tell herself that she wasn't going to fall in love with this man. But she already knew she was on her way to being wrapped up in Erik Jordan's world.

Sylvie drifted off to sleep and Erik couldn't do anything but watch her. This was new for him. It excited him to want a woman this much. When she shifted in his arms, Erik made sure she was comfortable instead of letting her go. This wasn't his standard MO! When he looked down at her sleeping figure, Erik decided that he was going to stop pretending that he didn't want to fall in love with this woman. She was everything that he didn't know he wanted. Everything that he didn't know he needed. He held her a little closer before he closed his eyes and drifted off to sleep.

When morning arrived, Erik almost thought he was dreaming. Sylvie's body was wrapped around his and their lips were pressed together in a near kiss. He cupped her chin and brushed his lips against hers.

Sylvie's eyes fluttered open and a smile spread across her face. "Good morning."

Erik nodded. "Yes it is."

"What do you want for breakfast?"

He eased his hand down her hip. "That's a loaded question. But I'll have whatever you normally have for breakfast."

"Coffee and cornflakes it is."

Erik shook his head. "That's terrible. Guess I'm going to have to cook for you again."

Sylvie stretched her arms above her head. "You must be a magician. Haven't been to the market in a week."

"We can figure something out."

"Then we're going to have to get out of bed."

Neither of them moved an inch.

Ingrid was worried and livid. She'd been calling Erik all night and it was unlike him to ignore her calls, especially with everything that was going on. It had to be because of that woman.

She didn't want to be jealous, because she had no right. Her crush on Erik was so unrequited that it didn't make sense to cause a scene about him being with a common chick like Sylvie Gates. So, when she typed Sylvie's name in the search bar of the Google homepage it was for research and to make sure this woman didn't have an ulterior motive when it came to Erik. It wasn't about jealousy. It was about business. Jordan Industries didn't need another scandal—especially since the story about Simon's stealing and the family drama was gaining steam.

"Ingrid?"

She turned around and smiled at her mother, Violet Graham. Violet had come to Atlanta two days ago from Los Angeles. Ingrid loved her mother's free spirit and the fact that after all of these years, she was still trying to break into the entertainment industry. While Violet would get a bit part here and there or a role in community theater, she wasn't a starving artist. Ingrid never understood the source of her income and she didn't ask. She also didn't press her mother about why they had different last names. After all, her mother's excuse had been that she didn't want Hollywood producers to know how old she really was. So, she'd given Ingrid her grandfather's surname, at least that was the story.

"Hey, Mom. I hope I didn't wake you."

"No. I'm finally on East Coast time now. I was going to take a run. What are you doing?"

"Checking out this woman who's digging her claws into Erik. Just trying to make sure she doesn't have any skeletons that're going to come back to bite us with everything that's going on."

"Are you sure that's the only reason? You do know that it is a bad idea to mix business with pleasure and—"

"This is strictly business, Mom."

"Be sure that it is. You can do a hell of a lot better than Erik Jordan."

Ingrid closed the lid on her laptop. "Why do you think I like him?"

Violet crossed over to her daughter and placed her hand on Ingrid's shoulder. "Please tell me that you don't. Ingrid, I have to tell you something, something I should've told you years ago."

Before Violet could say anything else, Ingrid's phone rang. "Mom, I have to take this. It's CNN." Picking up her smartphone, she walked out of the room. "This is Ingrid."

"Hi, Ingrid. This is Bradley Simmons, I'm a producer for *CNN Money*. We're doing a story about the indictment of Simon Jordan for stealing from the company and his feud with Erik. Can you make Mr. Jordan available for an interview, or do you-all plan to release a statement?"

"When is this story going to air?"

"We plan to run it on today's show and we'd love to do a live interview with Erik."

"I'll talk to him, but this better not be some ambush. If Simon Jordan is going to be on the set, we're not doing it."

"I guess you haven't heard. Simon was arrested again today. This morning around four, they found him at the airport attempting to board a flight to Angola."

Ingrid's mouth dropped open, but no sound came out.

"Hello?" Bradley said. "Are you still there?"

"Yes, I'm here. I'll get with Erik and see if we can make the interview. What time do we need to be there?"

"It's a little short notice, but if you-all can be here by one this afternoon, we can go live."

"All right." She looked up at the clock on the wall. She had five hours to find her boss, write a press release about Simon, and prep Erik for whatever was going to happen next. Her mother was going to have to talk to her later. Maybe she could set up a nice dinner for them to talk once this day ended.

She dialed Erik's number and it went straight to voicemail. "Where is he?" she groaned as she hung up the phone. Ingrid dashed into her bedroom and dressed. She needed to get to the office and find Erik. She also needed to gather all of the information she could about Simon's arrest.

Chapter 18

To say Sylvie's cupboards were bare was the understatement of the decade. She didn't even have the cornflakes she'd jokingly promised Erik.

"You just eat out all the time, huh?" he asked as the dryer beeped.

"Most of the time, or I go home with Olivia when her mom cooks. Mama B packs up enough food to last me at least two weeks."

"She's an awesome woman. I'm surprised we never ran into each other over one of her meals at Modele's."

"How often do you eat there?"

"Not as often as I'd like to. I try not to take advantage of my brother's future in-laws. But after that New Year's dinner, I think I'm going to make more of an effort to visit with Mama B."

Sylvie broke out laughing. "Olivia invited me to dinner on New Year's Day. That would've been awkward as hell."

"I don't think it would've been any more

awkward than me finding you in my office with your booty in the air."

She pinched his arm. "Why don't we go get breakfast from Modele's, since your clothes are dry now."

"Good idea. And maybe I'll find my phone after I eat." Erik headed for the laundry room and Sylvie walked into the den to get her dose of morning news.

As Erik slipped into his pants, he heard Sylvie call his name. Dashing into the den, he looked up at the TV and saw his father's face on the screen.

"Former Jordan Industries CEO, Simon Jordan, is behind bars again after FBI agents found him at Hartsfield-Jackson International Airport attempting to board a flight to Angola, a country that does not have an extradition agreement with the US.

"Jordan was on bail after being arrested for stealing from the company that he started and defrauding stockholders. Jordan Industries is currently being run by Simon Jordan's oldest son, Erik. Good Morning America *attempted to reach Jordan Industries for a comment, but we haven't heard back from the company."*

Erik shook his head. "Damn it. I have to get to the office. Rain check on breakfast?"

"Yes. I know you're going to be busy for the rest of the day, but I'll drop some food off at your office." Sylvie gave Erik a tight hug. "I'm sorry you have to deal with all of this."

He held her out a few inches. "Guess this is what it means when they say you have to pay the cost to be the boss. I can't believe he's this fucking selfish. My mother needs him and he's trying to flee the country." Erik brought Sylvie's hand to his lips. "I'll see you soon, all right."

She nodded and watched him gather his keys and head out the door.

Erik hopped into his car and headed straight for the office, not caring that he was wearing wrinkled clothes. He imagined that he'd been getting calls from the board, Ingrid, and everybody else that knew about Simon's headlines. Any regrets he had about punching his father had been replaced with the need to do it again.

Even if Yvonne hadn't told that son of a bitch about her cancer, Simon needed to be the man he'd always told his sons they should be, and face his wrongs. He created this mess, and it wasn't Erik's job to fix it.

He arrived at the office in record time and darted inside. He didn't acknowledge the strange looks he got from his employees as he headed for the elevator. When he entered his office, he wasn't surprised to see Ingrid pacing back and forth in front of his desk.

"Where the hell have you been?" she demanded.

"I've been calling you all morning. This is a crisis and—"

Erik held up his hand. "Take a breath. I lost my phone and I just saw the news about Simon's arrest."

"We have to get out in front of this. CNN wants to do a live interview with you, and I think you should do it."

Erik nodded. "That's fine."

"We also need to get something out to the stockholders and calm them down." Ingrid picked up her iPad from the edge of Erik's desk. "Our stock is falling like a lead balloon."

Erik groaned. "We can turn this around, I hope." The office phone rang, and as much as he wanted to ignore it, he answered. "Erik Jordan."

"Monsieur Jordan, this is De'Leon Bisset."

Erik gritted his teeth and clutched the phone harder. The last thing he wanted was to talk to the CEO of De'Leon Cosmetics, the French company that had been trying to buy Jordan Industries. "I don't have time to talk to you today."

"I'm sure. I've seen the American news today, and your father is making headlines that aren't good for business."

"What do you want?"

"Jordan Industries. Here is your way out of this mess."

"Go to hell." Erik slammed the phone down.

Ingrid sighed. "Should've warned you, the vultures are circling."

"The last thing that I'm going to do is sell this

company. Not now." Erik rose to his feet and crossed over to the window and looked out over the city. "All my life, I was told this was my legacy. This was supposed to be everything. He spent so much time here that I barely saw my father. I wanted to be close to him. That's why I took the job here." He banged his hand against the window. "Why in hell did he destroy it all?"

"We're going to save this company." Ingrid walked up behind him and placed her hand on his shoulder. He turned around and faced her.

"Thank you for all of your hard work and believing in what we have here."

Ingrid leaned forward as if she was about to kiss him.

"Knock, knock," a voice from the door said. Erik sidestepped Ingrid and saw his mother standing in the doorway. "Am I interrupting anything?"

"Ma, what are you doing here?" He crossed over to her and enveloped her in a tight hug. Ingrid cleared her throat and headed for the door. "I'm going to get things together for the interview. I'll see you later."

Yvonne watched Ingrid walk out the door. "I thought your special lady was an interior designer."

"She is."

"Then what did I just walk in on?"

"Nothing. Ma, why are you here?"

Yvonne sighed. "I wanted to tell you to your

face that I didn't know what your father was planning. I hate him so much right now."

Erik led his mother to his desk and nodded for her to sit in his chair. "I need you to focus on your health and not him. This is business. Whatever happens, we can come back from it, but if you don't get treatment . . ."

"Erik." Yvonne closed her eyes as tears rolled down her cheeks. "With our assets frozen and your father's bail being revoked, I can't afford to go to the doctor."

"And you think I'm not going to help you? That Logan won't help you pay for your treatment?" He kneeled in front of his mother. "Mom, don't give up."

"I don't want to be a burden to you boys. I can't do that to my sons after I've failed you both so many times already."

"You've never failed us." He placed his hand on her knee. "But I do have to ask you a hard question."

Yvonne nodded. "Go ahead."

"Did you know what he was doing with the company?"

She laughed. "No. God, no. After your father decided that my lipstick line and my face no longer belonged here, I stopped paying attention to the business. Had I been a smarter woman, I would've walked away from him too. But I stayed for you and your brother."

"We would've gone with you."

"I'm not trying to make you feel guilty, because what happened between me and your father wasn't for you and Logan to worry about. You two were children and I wasn't going to put my adult problems on your shoulders."

"But we grew up and . . ."

She stroked his forehead. "You're always going to be my baby. And you were so close to your father. I didn't want to come in between that relationship."

"And now?"

"You see who that man really is and you can make your own decisions about how to deal with him, going forward."

Erik stood up and smiled. "You need to make an appointment with your doctor and let me or Logan know when we need to get you there."

"Yes, son," she said as she stood up. "If you're going on TV, I hope you plan on changing your clothes." Yvonne reached into her purse. "After you punched your father, you dropped your phone. Tabitha found it this morning."

Erik leaned in to his mother and kissed her. "Thanks. Got a feeling I'm going to need this."

"I'm going to roam around a little bit. I like what you've done with the place."

Erik smiled again. "That's all Sylvie's work. I just let her work."

"Do I get to meet her?"

"Ma."

Yvonne held up her hands. "All right, I'll wait. See you later."

* * *

Sylvie wasn't surprised to find Logan and Olivia in Modele's. They probably met there every day for some of Mama B's amazing dishes. Sylvie had offered to redesign the restaurant for free, but Mama B was a creature of habit and she didn't want to change anything in her space. Sylvie could respect that, because there was something comforting about the old-school wooden tables and plaid tablecloths.

"Good morning," she announced as she crossed over to the couple.

Logan grunted and Olivia shrugged. "Good is relative," Olivia said.

Sylvie pulled up a chair and sat down. "I saw the news."

"Once again my dad shows what a selfish bastard he is." Logan brought his coffee mug to his lips. Olivia placed her hand on top of his.

"It's going to be all right. And we're going to figure out how to keep your brand from being damaged by all of this."

He slammed his cup on the table. "Liv, I don't give a damn about a brand, right now. My mother has cancer, my father was trying to leave the country, and you think I give a damn about my *brand*?"

She snatched her hand away. "I know you're upset, so I'm going to let this slide."

"Babe, I'm sorry. Sorry."

Sylvie looked from Logan to Olivia. This was serious because she'd never seen these two fight at all. Olivia rose from her chair and headed to the counter. Logan closed his eyes and squeezed the bridge of his nose.

"And this is why I stayed away from them for so long," he mumbled. "Did Erik see this bullshit?"

Sylvie nodded. "He's at the office right now. I came here to get him some breakfast. Are you and Olivia all right?"

"Yeah, yeah. We'll be fine. I'm just charged up right now and I need to apologize to her. Excuse me." Logan stood up and walked over to his fiancée. When Sylvie saw them hug and share a kiss, she released a sigh of relief. They needed to stick together, because if Logan and Olivia couldn't make it, there was no hope for anyone else.

"Sylvia!" Mama B called out. "Girl, if you don't come over here and give me a hug!"

She sprinted over to her friend's mother and hugged her. "How are you?"

"God woke me up in my right mind, so I'm great. It's good to see you. How are things going?"

"Great. I promised my client one of your breakfast platters today."

Olivia cleared her throat. "That's what we're calling him now? A client?" Logan laughed, then turned away from Mama B's stare.

"So, you have a boyfriend now?" Mama B asked.

"I-I . . ."

Olivia nudged her mother. "It's Erik."

"Erik Jordan? I can see that." Mama B wagged her finger at Sylvie. "He's a good guy and almost as intense as you are. Olivia, you should've hooked them up years ago. But why are you calling him a client?"

"Because I'm remodeling Jordan Industries." Sylvie smiled proudly. "And my offer still stands for you."

"No, baby. Sometimes you just have to leave a classic, a classic." She waved her meaty arm. "Everybody knows this place this way, and loves it. One day, my lovely daughter will come back and take over. Then I'm sure you two will change everything in here."

"Never," Olivia said.

"Never what? You coming back or you remodeling the place?"

"I wouldn't change this place or run it," Olivia quipped. Mama B playfully swatted her daughter's shoulder.

"Let me go get these platters together." Mama B disappeared into the kitchen and Sylvie shot her friend a cold stare.

"Can I go on record and say—to both of y'all—that Erik is not my boyfriend."

Logan laughed and Olivia rolled her eyes. "You and my brother have inspired an idea for a painting. Living in denial."

"I know, right," Olivia chimed in.

"I don't have to take this from y'all. I have to go to Asheville in a few days, but I don't know if . . . Has Erik found his phone yet?"

Olivia and Logan exchanged a knowing look.

"You can call your client at his office, right?" Olivia quipped.

Sylvie rolled her eyes. "Y'all make me sick."

A few moments later, Mama B returned to the dining room with two of her famous breakfast platters—grits, cheesy eggs, sausage, and pancakes.

"I put blueberry preserves in there instead of syrup because Erik loves my preserves. Y'all need to come by for dinner one day soon, okay?"

"Yes, ma'am," Sylvie said as she paid for the food.

"Give Erik my love," Mama B said as Sylvie headed out the door. The smile that lit Sylvie's face didn't go unnoticed by anyone in the café.

Once again, Sylvie was driving her work truck because she hadn't had a chance to get the part she needed to fix the Jag, but she would get it soon because this truck drank gas like a hungry kitten lapped milk. Setting the food on the passenger seat, she pulled out her phone and called her mother.

It was time for her to accept that she'd met someone who she could possibly see a future with. Sylvie hadn't had these feelings in years, and this time it felt as if she'd be giving her heart to the right man.

The connection she and Erik had was simple, sweet, and sexy. If anyone had a right to be arrogant, or at least be an arrogant jackass, it was Erik Jordan. But he was down-to-earth and loyal. She could tell that he was torn up by his family drama, especially his mother's illness. There was something about a man who was loyal to his mother. Even if Erik had been a serial dater, he didn't seem disrespectful to those women. And the way the blogs loved a Jordan scandal, someone would've spilled the tea.

She had to admit that she was looking forward to seeing where this thing with Erik went. Sylvie could finally let go of the past.

Erik was her future. Or maybe she was moving too fast in her mind when she should just go with the flow. *Take it one day at a time*, she thought as she turned onto the freeway interchange known as Spaghetti Junction.

When she arrived at Jordan Industries, Sylvie was happy to see that her crew had made it on time to get started on the executive suites. She'd have a little time to eat breakfast with Erik if he wasn't too busy putting out the fire that had exploded around the company. Her heart broke for him and his relationship with his father. She couldn't imagine not having the relationship she'd had with her dad. Or worrying if her mother had been keeping secrets from her about things her father had done. She parked the truck and hopped out with the food. Heading for the elevator, she heard someone call her name. Turning around, she offered Ingrid a plastic smile while she wondered what this woman wanted.

"Can we talk?"

Sylvie nodded. "I'm just heading up to Erik's office to drop off breakfast. I can meet you afterward in the break room. What are we talking about?"

Ingrid smiled. "We'll go over that once you drop off that meal. And Mrs. Jordan was in the office with her son when I left. Not sure if she's still there or not."

"Duly noted," she replied as she pressed the up button on the elevator. Now, Ingrid needing to have this little talk was giving her pause. So many things ran through her mind. Was she going to tell her that she and Erik were a couple and he'd been using her to make Ingrid jealous? Was she going to throw down the gauntlet and tell Sylvie that she wasn't qualified to be with Erik? Why did she have to throw it in her face that his mother had been in his office? Did that mean Ingrid and his mom were cool, and she'd immediately hate Sylvie or view her as the help?

By the time the door opened to the executive suite, Sylvie had worked herself into a frenzy. But the moment she walked into Erik's office— without knocking—and saw him standing there naked, she saw red.

"Erik, what in the hell is going on?" She gave him a slow once-over and gritted her teeth.

"Changing for my CNN interview. You could've knocked if you didn't want to see me naked."

"What's the deal with you and Ingrid?"

He raised his right eyebrow as he grabbed

his boxers from his desk. "She's my PR guru. There is nothing going on with us that isn't business. Why?"

Sylvie shrugged and set the bags of food on the desk. "This is me overreacting. I'm sorry."

"Did she say something to make you think . . . No, here's the better question. Have I done anything to make you think that there is another woman in my life not named Yvonne Jordan or Sylvie Gates?"

She stroked the back of her neck. "You know how you go on a job interview and they ask you what your biggest weakness is? These days, mine seems to be jumping to the wrong conclusions."

Erik slipped into his perfectly pressed gray slacks, then crossed over to her. "Sylvie, with me what you see is what you get. I'm not about playing with you, and I hope I can get the same thing from you." He cupped her cheek. "Don't break my heart."

"Only if you promise the same."

He brushed his lips against hers. "That's one promise I can definitely keep. And for the record, I don't mix business with pleasure unless I'm doing it with Sylvie Gates."

"Well, if you're still hungry, I brought you Mama B's breakfast platter with blueberry preserves for your pancakes."

"You're a saint and Mama B is a queen for sending the preserves." He reached back for the bag. "And I smell sausage."

"She said we should come by for dinner one

night, since Olivia and Logan made . . . She knows we're seeing each other."

Erik nodded as he opened the container and stuck his finger in the small container of preserves. "Come here."

Sylvie shot him a questioning look. "What are you up to?"

Erik took two steps closer to her. "I love Mama B's pancakes, but I think there is something else these preserves will taste better on." He smoothed the sticky jelly across her lips then licked her bottom lip. "Yep."

Before she could reply, Erik had captured her lips in a hot kiss that made her swoon. Breaking the kiss, he smiled at her. "I'm thinking that those preserves will taste better in so many other places."

"You're too much. And I have to get to work."

"Who's going to check you?"

She ran her hand down his bare chest. "My crew. We can pick this up later." Sylvie winked at him and sauntered out the door. She'd almost forgotten about the talk she and Ingrid were supposed to have until she passed the break room and saw her.

"Sylvia, did you forget about our meeting? I even made you a cup of coffee."

"Can we just get to the point? I have work to do." Sylvie folded her arms across her chest and tilted her head to the side.

"Fine. And please don't take this the wrong way, because I'm just asking these questions from a PR perspective. What's your end game here with Erik?"

"How is that a public relations question?"

"Sylvia, you're a businesswoman and I know you're aware of what's going on here. I'm just making sure we're not going to have another storm brewing if you and Erik get in a fight. Just thinking about the good of the company."

"Sure you are. Ingrid, if you think I'm here to cause trouble for this company or for Erik, knowing what he's facing right now, then you should do a deeper Google search. And I don't share my personal business with the world."

"And you've never dated anyone like Erik before, so . . ."

Sylvie shook her head. "Thank you for your concern, Ingrid. But you don't have to worry about me." Rolling her eyes, Sylvie walked away from Ingrid and she couldn't help but wonder what she was going to tell Erik about their encounter. Did it even matter? Erik said she was just an employee, and maybe she was simply doing her job. Sylvie pushed it out of her mind and headed to the site where her crew was working.

Chapter 19

Yvonne sat at the bar of The Lawrence in Midtown and nursed a peach martini. Looking around the restaurant, she watched couples having lunch, girlfriends laughing over drinks, and hipsters drinking craft beer.

"Are you sure you don't want to see a menu?" the bartender asked her.

"No thank you. I'm just going to enjoy my drink."

"All right. But if you change your mind, let me know."

Yvonne nodded and brought her glass to her lips and took a sip of the sweet drink. She was about to ask the bartender for a menu when *she* walked over to the bar and stood beside her.

"Yvonne, I'm surprised to see you looking so slim. When Simon removed you from the cosmetics campaign, I thought it was because you'd gotten fat."

Yvonne gripped her glass as if she was contemplating tossing the contents in this woman's face. It wasn't often that Yvonne could say that she hated someone. But when it came to Helen Graham, she wished nothing but ill will for this woman. When she'd left Atlanta twenty years ago, Yvonne had hoped she would've fallen off the face of the earth. But here she was, alive and standing in her personal space.

"Why are you here, Helen?"

"Wanted a front-row seat to see what was going on with Jordan Industries. I can't believe you and Simon are throwing everything away."

"Get away from me." Yvonne took a small sip of her drink, and to her dismay Helen sat on the empty stool beside her.

Helen waved for the bartender. "I'll have what she's having."

Yvonne scoffed at her. "I see nothing has changed at all—you always want what I have." She set her glass down and gave Helen a slow once-over. Obviously, the woman had been under the knife a time or two. Helen never had natural curves, now she did? Whatever. Her full lips looked plastic and her face looked as if she'd had one shot of Botox too many. "My job, my husband, and now my drink. One day you'll be able to find your own identity."

Helen rolled her eyes. "I had all of those things. Why not try the drink as well?"

That did it. To hell with decorum or not making a scene. "Have the drink, please." Yvonne tossed the remainder of her cocktail in Helen's face, then pushed her off the stool. "You arrogant bitch!

Don't you dare come at me telling me that you're celebrating my family's issues. I turned a blind eye to your bullshit years ago, but not this time. You need to crawl back under the rock where you came from."

The bartender rushed over to the women. "Ladies, is there a problem?" He reached down to help Helen to her feet.

"You really should watch the trash you allow in here," Yvonne said. "And the drinks are on that tramp." Rising to her feet, Yvonne slowly walked toward the exit.

"When Simon gets out of jail, why don't you ask him about our daughter!"

Yvonne stopped in her tracks and whirled around. "Your what?"

Wiping her face, Helen smirked at her nemesis. "Maybe you met her. She works for the company, because my child was going to have a part of her father's legacy just like your sons."

"You are such a liar."

"Don't believe me? Then ask your husband. So, yes, Yvonne. I've had everything that you thought was yours. The money, the family, and the man."

Yvonne tore out of the restaurant. She had expected that she'd cry, but if she was honest with herself, she'd known for years that Helen and Simon had been carrying on an affair, but a child? He had a child with this bitch. She needed answers, even if that meant she had to go to the jail and confront her husband.

* * *

Erik sat in the CNN studio being fitted with a microphone and listening to Ingrid telling him to relax. "Just answer all of the questions honestly and—"

"Ingrid, I got this. Do me a favor, check the stock prices, and do another release on the new line with Logan so that we can get some positive press today."

She nodded and pulled out her cell phone to call the office. Erik touched her hand after he'd been mic'd up. "Thank you for everything, Ingrid."

"No problem. I'm just doing my job. If I can't be great in a crisis, then I'm in the wrong business."

Moments later, the CNN Money host walked into the studio and shook hands with Erik. "Thanks for being here."

"Thank you for allowing us to tell the whole story," Erik replied.

"We're going live in ten seconds."

Erik listened to the producer's countdown in his ear. Then the interview began.

"Good afternoon, and welcome to *CNN Moneywise*. I'm Leo Carpenter, and today we're in the studio with Jordan Industries CEO Erik Jordan."

"Good afternoon," Erik said.

"Your company has been in the news for a number of reasons lately, and most of them not good. Your father, former CEO Simon Jordan, is facing charges of stealing from the company and defrauding stockholders. Two larger companies have expressed interest in buying Jordan Industries, but you're steadfast in not selling—despite a big drop in your stock prices. Why is that?"

Erik cleared his throat. "Our cosmetics mean a lot to a population of women who have been ignored and marginalized by society in general. Jordan Industries has celebrated women of color since our inception, and I don't want that legacy to be erased or diluted. We're going to rebound from the mess that has happened these past few months."

"And how do you plan this rebound, especially after today's news of Simon Jordan attempting to skip out on his bail?"

Erik could hear Ingrid telling him to smile, so he did. "We're taking the company in a new direction with some innovative skin-care products and a makeup line inspired by famed artist LJ."

"That's a good start, but how are you going to regain the confidence of your stockholders?"

"How do you make stockholders happy? You increase profits. I'm banking on this new line and the skin-care products to do just that. It is a new day at Jordan Industries, and I'm happy to lead this company. Our stockholders can also expect more transparency in our reports, and our board is behind the changes that we're making because we're no longer a company that one man runs like a dictatorship."

Leo nodded. "Is it hard to come in and take over for your father because of his wrongdoing and not because he retired?"

"It's not. Doing the right thing is never hard. It may not be what I want, but it had to be done."

"Mr. Jordan, thank you for being here today, and we look forward to seeing the rise of Jordan Industries."

Erik had never been happier to see a light go off. He pulled his mic off and shook hands with Leo. "That was a great interview," he said to the host.

"My mother, grandmother, and sister told me not to mess this one up. They love your makeup. There is one question I was told to get an answer for today, though."

"What's that?"

"What happened to the Yvonne lipstick?"

Erik laughed. "Tell them to stay tuned." Looking to his right, he saw Ingrid standing in the wings shooting him a thumbs-up signal. Crossing over to her, he gave her a slight hug.

"You did good, Mr. Jordan," she said with a smile. "We should celebrate with a nice lunch."

He looked at his watch. "I have a meeting in twenty minutes, but if you want to hit up your favorite sushi place on me, go ahead."

"That's all right. I probably should go check on my mother. She came for an unannounced visit and said we needed to talk about something."

"Why don't you take the rest of the day off and spend it with your mom?"

"Are you sure? Don't we have some other—"

"You've been working like a dog, and while this thing isn't over, you need some rest."

"I think you're getting this boss thing down. Thanks, Erik." She started to walk away, then she turned around and faced him. "Before I go, I want to tell you about a conversation I had with Sylvia."

He shook his head. "What happened?"

"I just wanted to make sure that she wouldn't be another attention-grabbing headline and I hope you don't think that I overstepped my boundaries."

Erik shook his head. "If this came from a place of business, then you didn't overstep. But in the future, my personal life is off limits."

"Got it. Well, I'm going to grab my mother and feed her sushi, on you—right?"

"You got it. See you tomorrow."

Sylvie snapped pictures of the progress that she and her crew had made in the executive suite. She loved the colors that they'd ended up going with: red, gold, and green. She decided to save the purple for Erik's office.

Erik's office. Naked Erik standing in the middle of the office and blueberry preserves. She hadn't realized how much she was smiling until one of her workers crossed over to her.

"We're doing that good of a job?" he joked.

"Ha! Actually, yes. And we're so ahead of schedule on this project."

"Easy to do work when the boss actually shows up with ideas and not attitude."

Sylvie turned away, knowing that he was talking about Amanda. She had no idea that her former partner had been that bad. But it didn't matter anymore. She was running her business her way, and things were going better than she'd ever imagined. Just as she was about take another picture, her phone rang.

"This is Sylvie," she said when she didn't recognize the number.

"Sylvie, it's Myra Jennings from the Sweet Spot."

"Hey, Myra! How are you?"

"Girlfriend, I'm amazing. We're expanding our business."

"Ooh, congratulations! Seems like there is a lot of that going on right now."

Myra laughed. "And I know you don't think so, but I do credit your redesign with a lot of my business turnaround."

"Come on, Myra, you have some of the best pastries on the East Coast. I have nothing to do with that."

"Well, I'm taking my treats across the pond."

"What! That's amazing."

"I need you to design my place. I'll pay for your trip to London and your housing while you're here."

"When are you opening the shop?"

"Next month. Please tell me you have space in your schedule for me. I really want to bring a piece of Brooklyn to London."

"When do I need to give you an answer? I have a project that I'm finishing up in Atlanta, then I should be free."

"If you can let me know by the end of the week, that would be great."

"Will do," she said. "And thank you for thinking of me for this job."

"Sylvie, there is no one else I'd want to create this space for me."

After hanging up the phone, Sylvie did her happy dance. London! She had a chance to be international! This would be another feather in her cap and she'd be on her way to the success she deserved.

What about Erik? The thought startled her. Granted, they had just started seeing each other, but would going to London change things? *He knows that I'm a businesswoman and he'll understand.*

But what if he doesn't want you to go? "Why does it even matter?" she muttered.

"You say something, boss?" one of the workers asked.

"No, no. You guys can go once this room is finished. I need to talk to Mr. Jordan about the photo shoot and everything."

"Cool."

Sylvie headed toward Erik's office. When she

heard raised voices coming from the other side of the door, she stopped short of going inside.

"Ma! What were you thinking? You know there are cameras everywhere these days."

"I've always hated that bitch, and for her to tell me that she and your father have a child together. I can't believe this."

"She probably said that just to get a reaction out of you."

"She said it after she'd hit the floor. Maybe she bumped her head and was just talking out of her ass."

"Ma, this is the last thing we need right now."

Sylvie felt like an interloper, so she knocked on the door instead of continuing to eavesdrop.

"Come in," Erik bellowed.

She walked in and smiled. "Hi, Erik."

"Sylvie, what's up?"

"It's not that important. Didn't mean to interrupt. We can talk later if you're busy."

His mother turned to face Sylvie. "I was just about to leave," Yvonne said as she rose to her feet. Sylvie couldn't help but notice her lipstick. And it wasn't red.

"Oh, no. Don't leave on my account."

Erik stood up and walked over to his mother. "I'm going to walk my mom outside and I'll be right back."

It didn't go unnoticed that he hadn't bothered to introduce Sylvie to his mother. So, what were all of those sweet words about earlier? Did he think that she wasn't good enough to meet his mother? She crossed over to the window and tried not to get lost in her thoughts. But her mind flashed back to Stephen.

"Listen, my mother is judgmental. You not meeting her is a good idea."

Sylvie folded her arms across her chest and pouted. "If we're building a future together, why wouldn't I meet your family, Stephen?"

He rolled over on his side. "Go to sleep, Sylvie. You're making a big deal about nothing at all."

She scoffed and climbed out of bed. "Why are we together? What are we doing here?"

"I'm going to sleep, so if you want to have this argument, do it alone. Downstairs."

Erik's hand on her shoulder brought her back to the present. "Hey, you all right?"

Sylvie whirled around and looked into his eyes. "Thanks for introducing me to your mother."

He sighed. "Today wasn't the day. My mother made it onto *TMZ* and Worldstar today because she got in a fight at a Midtown restaurant."

"What? Your mother was out there brawling?"

He stroked her shoulder. "Oh, it gets worse. She was fighting with the model who replaced her years ago. Just think about how this narrative is going to play out in the media. First my father tries to jump bail, sending the stock plummeting, and now my mama is out here acting as if she's auditioning for a Real Housewives show."

"Sorry."

"No, I'm sorry, I had the day from hell and I've been edgy."

Sylvie gave him a hug. "It's all right. Why don't we go have a drink when you're done with work and try to put this day behind us."

"You've had a bad day too?" He stroked her cheek. "Tell me about it."

"Actually, I've had a good day. One of my first clients called me and wants me to decorate her new shop."

"That's great, babe. Looking at what you've done here, I'm not surprised that people keep coming back."

"And you'll also be happy to know that we're almost done here and under budget. I just have one last office to tackle."

He tugged at the waistband of her jeans. "There was always one thing I wanted to do in this office, on that desk."

"You know that desk is the first thing that's going to go, right?"

"Then you should really help me live out my fantasy." He lifted Sylvie in his arms and carried her over to the wide oak desk. She tugged at the buttons on his shirt, then stopped.

"You should probably lock that door."

"Right." Erik dashed to the door and locked it. Then he crossed over to Sylvie and untied her work boots. After slipping them off her feet, he laughed when he saw her Mickey Mouse socks. "Now, you're the only woman I know who can make the mouse sexy."

"Stop it," she joked.

He spread her legs and stood between them. "Then again, you could make a brown paper sack look sexy."

"Is that so?" She reached for his shirt and pulled at the few buttons that she hadn't undone. "Then I guess that's something we have in common. The way you looked in my sweatpants this morning was beyond sexy."

She slipped the shirt down his shoulder, then leaned in and kissed his smooth skin.

Once his shirt hit the floor, Erik made quick work of removing her T-shirt and her bra. He ran his hand down the valley between her breasts and Sylvie sighed with delight.

"Can't wait to taste my yoni," he said as he unbuttoned her jeans. She placed her hand on top of his as he slipped his finger inside her. With her urging, Erik went deeper and deeper inside her wetness.

"Yes," she breathed as his finger brushed across her throbbing clitoris.

"Lift those hips for me so these pants can get out of my way."

She followed his instructions and Erik snatched her jeans and her panties off in one swift motion. He dropped to his knees, spread her thighs and buried his face in her sweet yoni. Sylvie tried to muffle her cries of passion, but when his tongue circled her throbbing bud, she screamed in delight.

"Erik, Erik, Erik," she repeated like a mantra

as she came. He looked up at her, his face shining with her essence.

"Delicious. Maybe I need to put you on my pancakes."

She licked her lips. "So, what else did you want to do on this desk?"

"I'm thinking that chair, which you cannot get rid of, might do better for the next part of this fantasy." Erik crossed over to the other side of his desk and rolled the chair out. "I want you to ride me."

A slow smile crept across her face. "Absolutely. Drop those pants, first."

"Yes, ma'am," he said with a mock salute. Erik quickly kicked out of his slacks and boxers, then sat down in his chair. Sylvie knelt in front of him. She stroked his erection until he threw his head back in delight. But when her mouth covered his hardness, it was Erik's turn to scream. Deeper. Wetter. Deeper. She stopped and locked eyes with him, then licked the head of his dick as if he were a chocolate ice cream cone on the verge of melting.

Sylvie took him all the way inside her mouth, never taking her eyes off him. When she felt him tense up, as if he were about to climax, she stopped and rose to her feet.

"Now, it's time for the ride of your life. And for the record, that chair is the first thing that's going to go."

"Umm, at this point, I'll go along with everything you say."

She mounted him, holding on to the leather headrest as she ground against him. Erik gripped her hips, hitting every spot that made her wetter and wetter. Sylvie bounced up and down as she came closer to another orgasm. Fast. Slow. Faster. Then they exploded together like firecrackers on the Fourth of July.

It wasn't until they caught their breath that they realized how reckless they'd just been. "We really should've used protection," Erik mumbled as he stroked her back.

"I know. Well, there are two things you don't have to worry about on my end. No STIs and not a chance that I'll get pregnant."

Erik furrowed his brows. "How do you know that?"

"Because I had my yearly physical last week and got a clean bill of health."

"That's not what I'm talking about."

Sylvie jerked out of his embrace, wishing that she hadn't said a word about a baby. One day she planned to tell him, but not today. And not while they were naked.

"It's not important."

"That's not something you drop on someone and then say it's not important."

She tilted her head to the side. "Was it your intention to get me pregnant today? Why does it matter?"

"You want me to say that it doesn't matter? If you have a health issue, maybe it's something I can help you with or . . ."

"Didn't ask for your help. I was just trying to ease your mind." She rubbed her hand across her face. "I'm sorry I said anything."

"I'm not. But let me be clear, nothing changed because of what you said."

Sylvie grabbed her clothes and dressed quickly. "I have to go." Her mind filled with rejection, or the day Erik came around with a baby he had with another woman. Right now things might be the same, but there was going to come a time when things changed. Isn't that how it always went?

Not even bothering to put his boxers on, Erik leapt up and blocked Sylvie's exit. "Stop. Don't leave like this."

"Like what? I have stuff to do."

"Don't leave thinking that what I feel for you has changed or I'm looking at you differently or that I'm going to do whatever he did to you."

She sucked in a deep breath and tried to fight back her tears. Erik cupped her chin and forced her to look into his eyes. "If we decide kids are in our future, we'll make it happen. Trust me on that."

Tears flowed freely down her cheeks as she nodded. "I'm sure this wasn't a part of the fantasy."

Erik kissed her on the forehead. "Reality is fine. Even better than the fantasy. Dinner at your place tonight?"

"If you mean takeout from Modele's, then yes."

"And I'll bring ingredients for breakfast. Because you still owe me a tour."

"All right." She wiped her eyes and stood on her tiptoes to give him a peck on the lips. "You'd better get dressed before I open that door."

"Good idea, because I'm sure Ingrid is going to be in here sooner or later." Erik crossed over to his chair and grabbed his slacks. After he was dressed, Sylvie unlocked the door and waved to him as she headed out.

"See you for dinner."

"And I look forward to having you for dessert," he said with a randy wink.

Chapter 20

Erik was about to pack it in for the day when Ingrid walked into his office. "Why did your mother attack my mom?"

Erik furrowed his brows. "Your mother?"

"Yes, I saw the video after taking all of those calls about two former models from Jordan Industries fighting at a restaurant. I just want to know why your mother attacked mine."

Erik rubbed his forehead. "I don't know. I didn't even know that was your mom. I thought you said your mom's name was Violet?"

"Yes, it is. She uses Violet professionally now, has since I was a little girl. Do you think it's true what people heard them say?"

"About my dad having an affair with your mother?"

Ingrid wrapped her arms around her midsection and hugged herself. "I don't even want to go home and talk to her about this."

"Maybe this will all blow over in the media

pretty quickly and we can focus on what's important."

"Erik, my mother is important and I want answers as to what's going on. This is bigger than Jordan Industries!"

Erik stood up and pointed his finger at Ingrid. "Stay away from my mother. She's going through enough and she doesn't need you harassing her about some age-old bullshit. Talk to your mother and leave it at that."

Ingrid turned on her heels and stormed out of the room. Erik felt bad for talking to her so forcefully after everything she'd done for him and the company over the past few weeks, but he wasn't going to allow anyone to go after his mother while she was battling cancer. He wished Yvonne hadn't fought with Helen, but he had questions of his own now. The only person who could answer them would be his father. But did he want to know the truth? One thing he'd always believed was that Simon loved Yvonne.

The way she stood by him over the years, Erik couldn't believe that she'd been rewarded like this. If this woman had a child with Simon . . . The thought popped in his head like a gunshot.

Was Ingrid his sister? Erik picked up the phone and called the federal prosecutor on the case.

"Ronald Taylor."

"Mr. Taylor, this is Erik Jordan."

"Mr. Jordan, it's a little late. What's going on?"

Erik sighed into the phone. "I need to know where my father's being held."

"You don't watch the news much these days, huh? Despite my objections, the judge decided to release your father on bail this afternoon."

"What? Isn't he a flight risk?"

"I did get his passport confiscated and he is confined to his home. One violation of that and he's going to be in jail until the trial begins."

"Thanks," Erik said. "I have to go." Hanging up the phone, Erik wondered if it was a good idea for Simon to be in the house with Yvonne. He grabbed his cell phone and called Logan as he rushed downstairs to his car.

"What's up, E?" Logan said when he answered the phone.

"We need to get to the parents' house now."

"Man, I'm not in the mood for Jordan drama today. Olivia and I have resorted to watching old-school cartoons on Netflix to avoid all of the news about the family today. But we did enjoy your interview."

"Then I guess you aren't aware that Dad's under house arrest and Mom is probably still pissed about her fight with Helen."

"Wait. What?"

"Turn the cartoons off and meet me over there. Please."

Logan started speaking under his breath in French and Erik rolled his eyes. "I'll be there," Logan relented.

Erik hopped in the car and started the engine.

Before he drove off, he texted Sylvie, telling her that he might be late for dinner. Speeding out of the parking lot, Erik hoped that he would get the truth out of his father for a change.

Sylvie walked into her house and tried to pretend that Erik's text didn't take her back to that dark place where she was when Stephen ended their relationship because she couldn't have a child. What if Erik was trying to distance himself from her—slowly and deliberately.

"The man said he's going to be late for dinner. Calm down," she muttered as she went upstairs to take a shower.

Before she started the water, her phone rang—Olivia's ringtone. "What's up, Liv?"

"Where are you?" her friend asked.

"At home about to take a shower. What's going on?"

Olivia sighed. "Have you seen the latest Jordan news?"

"You mean Yvonne Jordan's fight at The Lawrence?"

"Since you're at home, why don't I come over so we can talk?"

"Okay. But where's Logan?"

"He and Erik went over to their parents' house. Wine or ice cream?"

"Is it that bad?"

Olivia's sigh filled Sylvie's ear. "I'll bring both."

After hanging up with her friend, Sylvie took

a quick shower and changed into a pair of cotton leggings and a tank top. She was on edge as she waited for Olivia. What if something had happened to Erik's mom? Had their father done something else that was going to make headlines?

She said a silent prayer for the Jordans, especially Erik. Part of her wondered how much more he could take. He'd been thrown into a job he hadn't wanted, and every day there seemed to be some kind of firestorm surrounding his family.

And you want to add yourself to the equation? Even if Erik wanted to have a future with you, it's going to be hard to move forward. And then there's this job in London. Who knows what's going to happen while I'm there?

When she heard the doorbell, Sylvie assumed it was Olivia. Although she wondered how she'd made it to her place so quickly. Opening the door, she was shocked to see Stephen standing on her doorstep.

Had he not seen her, she would've left him standing or maybe even called the police because he was trespassing. But she wasn't going to be petty right now. Sylvie cracked the door open and glared at her ex.

"Why are you here?"

He folded his arms across his chest. "Are we at a point where you can't even invite me inside your home?"

"You're lucky that I'm allowing you to stand on my front steps. What do you want?"

He sighed. "I know that Amanda told you about the baby. I didn't want you to find out that way, and I certainly don't want you to think that something was going on between the two of us when you and I were together."

"I really don't give a damn about what you're doing or who you do it with."

Stephen rocked back on his heels. "Then why are you harassing Amanda? She's in a tough situation and having a high-risk pregnancy. The last thing she needs is to be confronted on the street by you because you're jealous."

Sylvie scoffed. "Jealous? Seriously? You weren't the man for me and I've dealt with my mistake. I'm not carrying some torch for you, nor am I following Amanda around *harassing* her. I have a business to run."

"Aww, yes, your business. Nothing has changed, huh?"

"Get off my steps and don't ever darken my doorway again."

He shook his head. "We'd still be together right now if you knew what was important. You're never going to be happy or satisfied with that business alone. Anyone can move furniture and slap paint on a wall. There's nothing special about you or what you do."

Sylvie closed her eyes and took a deep breath. "Thank you for your irrelevant opinion about my life. If there was a time when I gave a damn about what you thought about my life, trust me, those days are gone. I wish you and Amanda the best and I want her to have a healthy baby. But you'd better forget that you know me, know my address, my phone number, or anything about me at all."

"So, you're a tough girl now? You can't even let go of an old car because your father drove it. I know you're wishing that you were the one having my child, but it just isn't that way."

Sylvie laughed. "If I'm the one who can't let go, why are you here? I saw Amanda in passing. She announced that she was pregnant and guess what, the sun came up the next day and life moved on. For the last time, leave." She slammed the door in his face and released a triumphant sigh.

A few months ago, seeing Stephen and hearing him say those things about her might have devastated Sylvie. But tonight, she was going to do her happy dance. And pop a bottle of champagne.

The next time the doorbell rang, it was Olivia. "Okay, what's with the bubbly?"

Sylvie held out a glass to her friend. "Stephen came by."

Olivia grabbed the glass and gave Sylvie a questioning look. "And that caused you to break out the champagne? What the hell is going on and why is that loser coming to your house? If you tell me that you two are getting back together, I'm going to make you wear this."

"Take a sip and chill out. I am not getting

back with Stephen. Hell would have to freeze over and Satan himself would need to hit me in the face with a snowball. But seeing him on my doorstep did nothing to me. Hell, I didn't even let him in."

Olivia took a sip of the champagne. "Oh, this is good. Keep telling the story."

"He had the nerve to tell me not to harass Amanda."

Olivia lowered her glass. "And you didn't slap the hell out of him? Okay, that's some growth right there."

"I saw that cow once, and she was the one trying to make me feel some kind of way. He then went on to tell me that I'm going to be alone forever because I don't know what's important. You know, a few months ago, I'd be crying or breaking glasses on my patio."

Olivia nodded. "I know. And I would've been in Europe, so no one would've been here to reel you in. Now, this newfound devil-may-care attitude—does it have anything to do with a certain man named Erik?"

"I'll give him ten percent of the credit for this. But at the end of the day, I have to accept that I've moved on from disappointment. There's no need for me to think of what could've been with a man who went out of his way to hurt me time and time again. When I needed him most, he didn't even stand by my side." Sylvie walked over to the sofa and set the bottle of champagne on the table. "I almost let him kill the romantic in me."

"Thank goodness you didn't. And I love you, but we are not having some corny double wedding because we fell in love with brothers."

Sylvie held her hand up. "Pause. Who said I was in love?"

Olivia drained her glass, then grabbed the bottle for a refill. "Girl, we are not in Egypt and stop living in denial."

"Do I like him a lot? Yes. But I'm not ready to use the other L word. Thank you."

"Hmm," Olivia said before taking another sip of her champagne. "What brand of bubbly is this? Because clearly it is magical."

"Can you stop being overly dramatic?"

"As soon as you stop acting like you don't love Erik Jordan. It's time to woman up even more, and let that man know how you feel."

"Well, I do have another reason to celebrate."

Olivia raised her eyebrow, then took a seat on the sofa. "Spill it, sister."

"Remember the Sweet Spot in Brooklyn?"

"Yes. What about them?"

"They are expanding into London, and guess who she wants to decorate the place?"

Olivia screamed, leapt to her feet, and danced around the table as if she'd been the one who'd gotten the job. "This is so awesome! Please tell me her shop is going to be near our favorite princess."

"Clearly, she's a duchess, and I don't know where it's going to be, but she said she's going to pay for travel and housing while I'm there."

"What does Erik think?"

Sylvie poured herself a glass of champagne and took a big sip. "I haven't told him yet."

"Oh."

"What's that supposed to mean?"

"Nothing, but things are so new with you two, I'm just wondering if—"

"Hold up. You know I'm not putting my career on hold for any man. No matter how much . . . He'll understand. Unlike someone else I know, he admires my drive."

"As he should. Every man should admire women who make their own way without begging for a handout." She snapped her fingers. "And if I can be honest, you gave Stephen way too much of your time when he wanted to control everything about you."

"My bad. We all make mistakes. Need I remind you of Damien Crosland? Look how long you allowed him to talk you out of starting your own business."

"Ugh. Don't remind me of all the frogs I had to kiss before I found my prince."

Sylvie tipped her glass to Olivia. "On to bigger and better things."

"Thank God for the Jordan brothers. But I would've never thought that you and Erik would fit so well."

"I'm glad you had the good sense not to play matchmaker."

Olivia waved her hand. "To be honest with you, I hadn't spent a lot of time with Erik because LJ was so estranged from his parents. He and Erik would talk on the phone when we traveled, but it wasn't until we came to Atlanta this time that I got a chance to see another side of him. But if he hurts you, brother-in-law or not, I'm going to kick his ass."

Sylvie leaned in and kissed Olivia on the cheek. "That's why I love you."

Chapter 21

Erik heard his mother screaming when he turned the doorknob. Logan brushed past his brother and dashed to the sitting room, where he heard the voices coming from. Yvonne was beating her fists against Simon's chest.

"Of all the women in Atlanta, you slept with that whore! You made a baby with that bitch and lied."

Simon grabbed her wrists. "I didn't lie. I just didn't tell you."

Yvonne brought her knee up to his groin. Simon doubled over as Logan rushed over to his mother.

"What in the hell is going on here?" he demanded, looking from his mother to his father.

Yvonne pointed her finger at Simon. "Y'all better get this motherfucker out of my house."

"Your house?" Simon panted as he stood up. "You don't own shit around here. This is my house, and thanks to that Judas, I can't go one hundred yards away from this house."

"Why didn't you go live with that bitch?!" Yvonne spat. "How could you do this to me?"

Erik held his hand up. "What's going on here?"

Simon rolled his eyes at his son. "Nothing you need to concern yourself with. This is grown-people business and you need to mind yours."

"No!" Logan snapped. "This goddamn family has been built on secrets, lies, and unrealistic expectations. What is this all about?"

Simon snorted. "The day I answer to you two is—"

"Your father fucked Helen Graham, that knock-off wannabe model who he replaced me with, and made a baby with her. A child who is grown now. A child he's been supporting all of these years without telling me about it. Oh, and let's not forget that he was taking care of that rancid bitch since she left the company. Is there anything that I'm missing?"

"Where is the child?" Erik asked.

Simon walked over to the bar in the corner and poured himself a glass of scotch. He took a big sip and looked over at his sons. "Where all of my children should be. She works for the company and has shown me more loyalty than either of you!" Simon slammed his glass on the wooden bar, cracking the bottom of it.

"You have humiliated me for the last time, Simon Jordan. You are going to pay for your crimes one way or another. I don't want to be in this house. I'm leaving." Yvonne started for the door, then she stopped and crossed over to

Simon. She picked up the glass and tossed the contents in his face. "Bastard." Yvonne stormed out of the house.

Simon grabbed another glass and filled it with more scotch. "Why don't the two of you follow your mama and get the hell out of my face."

Erik gave his father a slow once-over. "So, that's why you did it? You were stealing to take care of your other family? You spent all these years lying to us about what it takes to be a real man and you were nothing but a sack of shit."

"Don't you stand there in judgment of me! Your mother isn't perfect and being married to her was just one step below hell. But I took care of my family."

"Yeah. If lying and stealing is what you call taking care of your family, then you did a great job, *Simon*." Logan sneered at his father, then dashed out of the house.

Simon sipped his drink and looked at Erik over the rim of his glass. "What?"

"Who is your child?"

"Guess I should tell you since you have a hard time keeping your pants zipped around pretty women. Ingrid is your sister."

"Does she know?"

Simon shrugged and took another sip of his drink. "I don't know what her mother told her. But I wasn't going to let my child suffer. Think what you want about me, but I took care of all of you. Even your crazy mother. See, y'all think she is some kind of saint. But that woman abandoned me long before Helen and I—"

Erik held up his hand. "I don't care to hear your story, Dad. That's my mother and I'm always going to have her back. Especially now." Erik started for the door, ignoring his father's ranting. Now he had to wonder if he should be the one to tell Ingrid the truth.

It made sense, his father hiring her when she had very little experience. Granted, she was good at her job, but looking at her résumé, she shouldn't have been running the PR department for Jordan Industries.

Was he supposed to keep her on staff? Would his mother see it as another betrayal if he did? But he couldn't hold Ingrid accountable for what his father did, and letting her go now would be the dumbest move of his short tenure as CEO. But he had to do right by his mother, because it was clear that Simon hadn't.

"Erik!" Logan called out when he spotted his brother on the porch.

"Yeah?"

"What did you and that son of a bitch talk about?"

Erik rubbed his hand across his face. "Dad has a daughter. And it's Ingrid."

"Damn. Didn't you—"

"Hell no! This puts me in a tough spot. Am I supposed to fire her because of an accident of birth? Maybe I should just walk away from all of this drama."

"And do what? You have always loved this company and what it stands for. You like making the products and seeing the reaction of women finding makeup that matches their skin tone and makes them feel beautiful."

"Why did you hate it so much?"

Logan shrugged. "Because it made Ma so sad. She'd act like everything was all right, but when she saw the commercials or the ads in magazines, she'd cry. I'd ask her what was wrong and she would always say *nothing*. That's why I started drawing pretty pictures of her. Simon knew what he was doing when he slept with Ma's replacement. I guess he didn't want to divorce Ma because of the bad publicity and the fact that this was supposed to be a family company."

Erik rubbed the back of his neck. "How did I miss Ma's pain?"

"Because she did a good job of hiding it from everyone. I was just around more. Not saying you did anything wrong. Dad took you under his wing for a reason."

"Where did Ma go?"

Logan shrugged. "Called her and she won't answer the phone."

"We need to find her." Erik pulled out his phone and sent Sylvie a text.

Rain check on dinner, please. Logan and I have to find my mother.

Tucking his phone in his pocket, he told Logan to get in the car.

Sylvie was about to pop her second bottle of champagne when her phone vibrated. "Ooh," she muttered as she read the text.

"Is it time for me to leave because Mr. Lover Man is coming over?" Olivia quipped.

"Erik said he's out looking for his mother."

Olivia stroked her forehead and reached for her phone. "I haven't gotten anything from Logan."

Sylvie set the bottle in the middle of the bar. "Do you think he's lying?"

Olivia grabbed the bottle of champagne and popped the cork. "Yeah, because his brother's girlfriend, who happens to be his girlfriend's best friend, wouldn't tell her."

"Well, why hasn't Logan texted you yet?"

"We didn't have plans. I mean, he'll get home when he gets home. But that's our relationship. What I need you to stop doing is judging Erik by the mistakes of others."

Sylvie sighed. "You're right. I hope they find their mother. I wonder what's going on."

"That's a good question. One thing I know for sure is that Logan is highly protective of his mother. If this has something to do with their father, then I hope that man has some security to keep Logan's hands from around his throat."

Sylvie watched as Olivia poured the golden

liquid in her flute, and silently prayed that Erik and Logan would be all right.

"So, what do we do next?" Sylvie asked as she fingered the rim of her glass.

"Wait and see what happens next."

Sylvie pushed her flute to the side. "Shouldn't we be sober?"

Olivia took a swig of her champagne and shrugged. "This is my first family trauma. We're in this together, sis."

Are you sure this is what you want to deal with? a voice inside Sylvie's head asked. She was going to put the champagne aside for sure.

It wasn't until Sylvie heard a banging at the door that she realized that they'd fallen asleep on the sofa in the den while listening to Whitney Houston's greatest hits.

Sylvie rubbed her forehead and slowly rose from the sofa. Looking out of the front door, she was initially confused when she saw Logan standing there. Seconds later, she saw Erik and opened the door.

"Hey. Is everything all right?" she asked as she ushered the men inside.

Logan laughed. "Are you drunk, and does that mean Olivia is as well?"

"I'm not drunk, and Olivia is in the den. But are you guys all right?"

Erik crossed over to Sylvie and pulled her into his arms. "This has been one hell of a night.

Whatever you and Olivia have been drinking, I hope you have some to share."

"Somehow, I don't think champagne seems appropriate, but I have some vodka or some rum."

Logan headed for the den, where Olivia had been snoozing. "Water. That's all we need."

Alone in the living room, Erik and Sylvie stood there looking at each other in silence. She felt as if she could feel the pain flowing though his body. "Babe, what happened?"

"My father is an even bigger fraud than I ever knew. My mother took off and we don't know where she is. Given her current condition, I don't want her out there roaming around, emotional and sick."

Sylvie took his hands in hers. "I wish I knew what to say."

He pulled her closer to his chest. "I wish I knew where my mother was." Erik kissed her forehead.

"Want some coffee or something?"

"Coffee would be nice. If Ma does decide to call back, I want to be able to meet her wherever she is."

Sylvie nodded. "We all could use some coffee," she said.

"So, tell me about this job that has you all excited." They walked into the kitchen and Erik took a seat at the breakfast nook while Sylvie crossed over to the coffeemaker.

"Are you sure you want to hear about that?"

"Yes, make me smile," he said.

She filled the coffeemaker with the Dancing Goats coffee grounds. "Well, if you really want to smile, then let me share some of these pastries with you." She pulled a pink box from the top of the refrigerator and set it in front of Erik. He opened the box and smiled at the fritters.

"Smells good."

"There's apple, peach, and pecan."

"What's your favorite?"

She shrugged. "All of them. The Sweet Spot is one of the best bakeries in America and soon the world."

"Oh really?"

Sylvie nodded, then told him how this was the first business she'd done interior design for and how the owner credited her for a turnaround in her business. "She sends me a care package every month."

Erik picked up a pecan fritter and took a bite. "This is delicious."

"Now they're opening a location in London, and I'm going to design the place for them."

Erik set his treat on a napkin Sylvie had sitting by the box. "So, that means you're going to London?"

"Not until I finish things at JI, but yes."

He nodded but kept silent. Sylvie wondered if this was the part where she was supposed to ask him if he wanted her to stay. But would she be prepared for the answer? Suppose he said yes?

She rounded the counter and sat beside him. "The timing sucks, doesn't it."

He patted her knee as he finished his fritter. "No, you go ahead and do your thing. You have a business to run, and if you didn't go you'd be missing out on a huge opportunity."

"Oh." She couldn't think of anything else to say. Sylvie did want him to at least have some sort of reaction to her leaving. He made it seem as if he didn't care at all.

Erik wanted to tell Sylvie to stay. But he also didn't want Sylvie caught up in the family drama that he was dealing with. He hadn't even told her the whole story, and he didn't know how. It still didn't make sense to him.

"Well," Sylvie began, breaking the silence that had engulfed them, "I'd better get this coffee."

"I'm really happy for you," he said as she crossed over to the coffeemaker.

"Thanks. And just because I'm finishing up the project at JI early, it doesn't mean that I rushed it."

"I know. You and your crew have been working ahead of schedule, and that's a good thing. Don't want to monopolize all of your time, you know."

She sighed, then grabbed two coffee mugs and filled them. Erik knew it was time to shut up.

"Cream or sugar?" Her voice was cold and he knew why. He even offended himself by his last statement.

"I'll take it black." He could've sworn that she

rolled her eyes at him as she slid the mug over to him.

"I'm going to check on Logan and Olivia." As she walked out of the kitchen, Erik could've sworn that he felt the temperature drop forty degrees. He sipped his coffee and pulled out his cell phone, hoping that his mother would answer when he called her this time.

Voicemail again.

Sticking his phone in his pocket, Erik headed into the den, where all conversation stopped and Sylvie rose to her feet.

"I'll be back with the coffee." She brushed by Erik without giving him a glance. Olivia pointed at him.

"What did you do to her?" Olivia asked through a series of hiccups.

Erik shrugged.

Logan shook his head. "Yeah, I was afraid this would happen. Olivia, let them handle it, all right?"

"You're just saying that because he's your brother. But Olivia, I mean, Sylvia, uh, Sylvie is my best friend and closer to me than my own sister."

Logan patted her knee. "You're an only child, babe."

"Oh yeah," she said, then laid her head on Logan's shoulder. She pointed her finger at Erik. "But she was happy before you got here. What did you do?"

"Opened my mouth and inserted my foot."

Erik looked toward the kitchen, and just as he was about to follow Sylvie, his phone rang. Looking at the screen, he released a sigh of relief. "It's Ma."

Logan slid Olivia off his shoulder and crossed over to his brother.

"Where are you, Ma?" Erik asked, forgoing a hello.

"I'm at the W. And I'm fine."

"No, you're not. Why don't you come home with me or Logan?"

"Not going to bring my issues to either of your doorsteps. I always thought your father had been with that cow, but to have a child with her and . . ." Erik could hear his mother crying. "I just wish he'd die. I gave him so much and this is how I get repaid?"

"This isn't your fault and you can't blame . . . I don't think Ingrid knows that he's her father."

"Oh, how do you know?"

Erik's mind drifted back to all the flirting that had gone on between them. There's no way she would've done that knowing they were brother and sister. After all, this wasn't a V. C. Andrews novel.

"There's no way she knows, Ma. We've all been left in the dark, here."

"Bullshit! Helen knew. What kind of mother does this?"

Maybe one who used her child for a big payday.

"Ma, you can't change the past, and I don't feel comfortable with you being alone tonight."

"And neither do I," Logan exclaimed.

"You boys are sweet, but I'm not going to crawl to either of my sons' houses with my tail between my legs."

Erik didn't want to say it out loud, but he wondered if his mother might consider hurting herself. The look that he and Logan exchanged told him that his brother was thinking the same thing.

"Please, Ma," Erik said. "Let me come pick you up and you can relax at my place."

Yvonne sighed. "I'm only doing this to make you feel better. I'd really like to be by myself tonight."

"Glad you're taking my feelings into consideration right now."

"I'll be at the bar."

After ending the call, Erik dashed into the kitchen and touched Sylvie on the shoulder while she set the coffee mugs and a carafe on a silver platter. "I found my mother."

"Great," she said, offering him a genuine smile.

"Yeah. She had me worried, so I hope—"

She waved her hand, cutting him off. "Don't even worry about it. Go to your mother."

He leaned in and kissed her. "Thank you for understanding. She's going to stay with me tonight. I was just worried about her being alone."

Sylvie nodded. "You're a good son."

He kissed her again. "I lo— thank you."

She waved to him as he headed for the front door. Standing on the porch, Erik chided himself for not telling her how he felt. He loved Sylvie and he should've told her. What the hell was stopping him?

Chapter 22

Sylvie walked into the den and tried to pretend she wasn't smarting from Erik's comments earlier or the fact that he stopped himself from saying he loved her. Maybe she was tripping. He could've been saying that he was leaving or he loved his mother. How could she assume that he was in love with her?

Just because you love him, it doesn't mean he loves you back. Wait? When did you fall in love with Erik Jordan?

"Sylvie, you all right or you just like holding on to that tray?" Olivia asked.

Sylvie rolled her eyes and set the tray in the middle of the table. "Sorry, I was just thinking about something."

"Erik?" Logan asked. "Where is he, anyway?"

"He went to pick up your mother."

Logan pulled his phone out of his pocket and fired off a text to his brother. "Ooh," Olivia said as she read Logan's text to Erik. "That wasn't nice."

"Neither was him leaving me. You mind if I

take your car and head over to his place to make sure Ma gets settled in?"

"Yeah. Go right ahead. But you're going to come and get me when she's settled?"

"Yes. And don't have another drink, all right?"

Olivia blew him a kiss and waved goodbye to her man. Sylvie sat on the sofa beside Olivia and shook her head. "You are such a lightweight," Sylvie said.

"I really am, but that champagne was so good." Olivia reached for a coffee mug. "So, what happened in the kitchen with you and Erik? You guys went in smiling and came out looking as if you'd gone fifteen rounds."

"I really don't get what happened. Maybe I'm overreacting, but he was all nonchalant about me leaving. I mean, I'm going to another country and I thought we had something . . ."

Olivia rubbed her friend's shoulder. "Aww, you love him. But if he asked you to stay, would you?"

"No."

"So, why are you upset that he didn't beg you to stay or get upset that he didn't burst into tears?"

Sylvie folded her arms across her chest. "Because I need to know that he's feeling the same thing I do."

Olivia smiled. "And what is it that you're feeling?"

Sylvie narrowed her eyes at her friend. "Shut up."

"You don't have to lie to me, just admit to yourself that you are in love with Erik."

"You know what will go good with this coffee, some of those fritters from Brooklyn." Sylvie rose to her feet and headed to the kitchen.

"Eating sweets won't cause you to love him less, I'm just saying."

"Shut up!"

Erik was over drunken women tonight. Now, he had to deal with his mother, who was holding court at the bar, talking to a group of business-men about her recent woes. All Erik could do was hope that none of these white men worked in the cosmetics industry.

He walked up behind his mother and placed his hand on her shoulder. "Ma."

Yvonne turned around and offered her son a runway-model smile. "Ah, my son. You know, he learned a lot of good things from his father. But when he put those qualities to use, you know what his father did?"

"What?" one of the men asked.

"Turned on him and tried to get me to fall in line. Because I blindly followed that man like he was the pied piper." Yvonne reached for her glass, but Erik reached across her and pushed it out of the way.

"Ma, it's time to go, all right."

"Hey!" another man said. "The lady is just having a good time."

Yvonne pointed her finger at the man. "What you're not going to do is speak to my son that way." She attempted to stand up, but was a bit wobbly. Erik grasped her elbow to keep her steady.

"Tell your little friends good night."

"Good night, boys, and remember, be nice to your wives. Women outlive men and y'all don't seem as if you're aging very well. Someone is going to have to change your diapers and your kids are probably not going to do it."

Erik hid his laughter and led his mother to the exit. "Remind me to lock my liquor cabinet."

"Oh, boy, shut up. You wanted me to come home with you, remember?"

"That's right. And I'm glad I got here when I did." Erik led his mother to his car and helped her get inside. He hadn't been driving for five minutes before Yvonne was sleeping. He glanced over at his beautiful mother and wondered what could've been, had she not given up her dreams for Simon. He remembered when she'd been offered roles in movies, on TV shows, and national stage plays. Simon always told her she could do it. Once the offers started drying up, that had been when Simon replaced her with Helen.

Then she tried to open a modeling school, with Jordan Industries funding it. Simon dangled the carrot in her face for years, but it never happened. And he'd misjudged his mother for years, listening to his father talk about how Yvonne was a pampered housewife. It wasn't until he'd gone off to college and started spending more alone time with his mother that he'd seen the real truth.

Part of him always felt guilty that it took him so long to see his mother as a human and not just the character that his father had made her out to be.

Did he have time left to show her that she was appreciated? Pulling into his driveway, Erik promised that he'd do whatever it took to keep his mother safe and happy. Erik wasn't surprised to see Logan standing on the front porch pacing back and forth.

"Wake up, Ma," Erik said.

Yvonne's eyes fluttered open and she looked around for a minute as if she was trying to get her bearings. "Oh, was I sleeping that long?"

"And I drove slowly. Have you been resting lately?"

"No. I've been thinking about everything that's been going on lately and what I should do about my health. Then your father drops this bomb."

"This isn't about him. I need you to start taking your health seriously. I need more time with you. And I know it sounds selfish, but—"

A knock at the window stopped him from finishing. Erik looked up at his brother's angry scowl.

"Y'all just going to sit in the car all night?"

"Both of y'all are here. This is so sweet." Logan opened his mother's door and helped her out of the car. Yvonne patted her son's cheek. "You know, I want to meet these women in your lives. I can't believe I'm going to have two daughters-in-law really soon."

Logan snorted. "Don't bet on that. Somebody royally messed up tonight. What did you do to that girl?"

Erik rolled his eyes. "I'll deal with her later."

Yvonne sucked her teeth. "You better not wait too long. Good women are hard to find."

Logan led Yvonne up the stairs and shot Erik a *don't fuck this up* look. He decided that after he got his mother settled into the guest room, he was going to go talk to Sylvie.

If Erik thought his mother was going to crawl into bed once she got in the house, he was wrong. She and Logan had found his stash of Kona coffee and were sitting around the table sipping coffee and laughing.

"So, you mean to tell me, she wrote a note on the mirror in red lipstick?" Yvonne giggled. "I like her already."

"Really," Erik said as he looked at his brother. "This is how we're doing things now?"

Yvonne patted Erik's hand as he passed her. "You know your brother always told me your business, right?"

He shook his head as he reached for his favorite mug. "I'm not surprised."

Yvonne shrugged. "And you should've introduced us when I was in your office. The poor girl must think I'm some rude, stuck-up bitch."

"I'm sure she doesn't."

"And your fiancée," Yvonne said as she turned

to Logan. "She must think we are the most dysfunctional family ever."

"She's understanding, and I'd love for you two to meet. But not tonight. She and Sylvie were celebrating and they overdid it on the champagne."

"Sounds like my kind of girls." Yvonne winked at Erik. "Boys, tonight showed me that it's time for me to take my life back."

Erik wanted to break into his happy dance. "So, you're going to get treatment?"

"Among other things. It isn't too late for me to do some of the things that I've always wanted to do. You know, when I was retired from being the spokesmodel at Jordan Industries, I had big plans, and now I think I should go through with those plans."

Logan nodded in agreement. "And since you have an in with the CEO, I'm sure whatever you want to do, he'll support you."

"Anything you want, Ma." Erik kissed her on the forehead.

They stayed up for the rest of the night talking about the old days and laughing.

It was after eleven when Olivia and Sylvie figured out that they weren't going to see their men anytime soon.

"We need pizza," Olivia said after they'd polished off the Sweet Spot treats. "Or at least I need pizza."

"You need a nap." Sylvie brought her knees to her chest and rocked back and forth.

"Seems like we're having a sleepover. Now, tell me, when does this London job start?"

"Guess I'll find out tomorrow when I accept it. I think I'm going to let my crew finish things up at Jordan Industries. They have my plans and can follow directions without me."

"But why would you do that? Are you seriously running away from that man because of a misunderstanding?"

"I'm not running from anything, but I'm focusing on my business."

"Which is code for *I'm running away from emotions*. Don't do this with Erik. Make peace with whatever is going on between the two of you, then go to London and shine like the diamond you are. Then when you come home, you'll have something to look forward to."

"And suppose I don't?"

"If you can see into the future like that, please tell me what the winning lottery numbers are. Sylvie, do you think you don't deserve happiness? Your mom lost the love of her life and found love again. You let an asshole go and you act like—"

"Not the same."

"Exactly. Erik could be the one who gives you all the love that your heart and soul need."

"Or he could break my heart," she muttered, then unfurled her legs. "What kind of pizza are we eating?"

"Depends on if you're pretending to be a vegetarian today or not."

"No, I want sausage."

"Bet you do, but they can't put Erik on the crust. Please call that new joint down the street. I keep hearing so many things about it."

"You've probably eaten there already."

Olivia shrugged. "Logan and I are thinking about starting a family and I so don't want to do this alone."

"Logan is going to be right there with you."

Olivia rolled her eyes. "You know what I mean. I need you to be there every step of the way with me. So you can't mess things up with future baby Jordan's uncle."

"What does this have to do with pizza?"

"Nothing, but I just don't want you to mess things up with Erik and you feel like you have to stay away."

Sylvie rolled her eyes. "Whatever. Maybe he shouldn't mess it up with me." She pulled her phone out and looked up the restaurant's phone number. She crossed her fingers and prayed they delivered to her address. Olivia was right, she would've enjoyed a pizza with Erik as the delicious topping.

Stop it. He's clearly handling business with his family and you're just another distraction.

Chapter 23

Sylvie woke up with a start, wondering why her eyes were puffy and her stomach aching. The pizza. The champagne, followed by the coffee and then the whisky and the sweets. That was too much. It was a good thing she'd already made the decision not to head into work today. She sent a quick text to her staff and told them to follow the diagrams and send her pictures if there were any questions.

Sylvie was about to roll over and go back to sleep when Olivia bounded into her bedroom as if she'd spent the night drinking water and eating kale salads.

"Wake up, sleepyhead. Have you called Myra yet?"

"How is it that I have a hangover and heartburn, but you're looking like you're ready to take on the day?"

"Because I drank water before bed and not Crown Royal? Y'all can call me a lightweight, but you won't call me Hangover Hannah."

"Oh, my headache is making you cornier than ever."

Olivia took Sylvie's phone from the nightstand and tossed it at her. "Call Myra. Get the details on your gig and let's have some coffee and oatmeal."

"Umm, that would be nice. Except I only have coffee."

Olivia shook her head. "I need you to buy some groceries because you can't live on takeout alone."

Sylvie shrugged. "You're right. But for now, we're drinking coffee and eating pizza for breakfast."

"About that pizza. I may have woken up in the middle of the night and ate it."

She gave Olivia a slow once-over. "Are you sure that family hasn't been started already, greedy?"

"Shut up. You do realize that when I'm traveling all over the world with LJ, we eat some of the nastiest food in the name of gourmet. These past few weeks here have been so good. That's why I'm eating everything."

Sylvie shook her head, then burst out laughing. "Well, when you explain it that way, I guess I can forgive you for eating my pizza."

"Thank you, because I'm not sorry that I ate it." Olivia clasped her hands together. "Now, let's get moving. Take a shower and put some clothes on. And maybe grab a big pair of shades. What's with the puffy eyes?"

Sylvie rubbed her hand across her face. "I guess I did one of those drunk cries last night. But let's not even talk about it. Today is a—" The doorbell's ringing interrupted her.

"I'm going to get the door because you look like trash and no one should see you looking like this."

Sylvie tossed a pillow at Olivia's retreating figure. Then she climbed out of bed and headed to the bathroom. After catching a glimpse of herself in the mirror, Sylvie realized that her friend was right. She looked like warmed-over death.

"Shit!"

Erik walked into Sylvie's place behind Logan. "Glad to see you're up and about, babe," Logan said, while Erik looked around for a Sylvie sighting. He knew she was still at home because the truck was still in the driveway. He knew her car wasn't running and she was somewhere in the house.

"Yeah, Sylvie and I were getting ready to get some breakfast, but look at y'all coming in with food."

Logan held up the two white bags. "Omelets and pancakes made by our mother."

She stroked Logan's shoulder. "How is she?"

"Better than she was last night."

"Where's Sylvie?" Erik asked.

Olivia pointed toward the bathroom. "In the shower. You probably shouldn't go up there right now. The food is a good touch." She led the Jordan brothers into the kitchen and helped unpack the food.

"Erik, you know you messed up, right?" Olivia said as she reached into the cabinet for plates.

"What do you mean?"

"Olivia, mind your business," Logan chided. "Whatever stupid thing my big brother did, he's going to have to clean it up on his own."

Before Erik could reply, Sylvie walked into the kitchen looking fresh-faced and relaxed. "Good morning," she said, seemingly looking past Erik. "What's all of this?"

"Breakfast," Erik said as he crossed over to her. "Ma spent the night with us last night and woke up in a cooking mood this morning."

Finally, she looked at him and Erik noticed her eyes. Was he the cause of those tears? But why? Granted, pausing on telling a woman you loved her was enough to piss a woman off, but crying?

"Are you all right?" he asked.

"Yes. Thanks for bringing breakfast."

"If you look in that bag, you'll see I brought something else too," he said with a wink.

Sylvie crossed over to the counter and reached into the bag. She pulled out a container of coffee beans. "Kona?" she asked with a half smile.

He nodded. "I saw you had a coffee grinder, so I figured you'd want to grind them yourself." He took another step closer to her. "Whatever I did, I'm sorry."

"Who said you did anything?"

"This cold shoulder that you're giving me says I must have done something."

She shrugged. "I'm just getting ready for this project in London. Sorry if I'm not giving you the attention you obviously need."

Everyone focused on Sylvie as she walked over to the coffeemaker. Looking over her shoulder as she placed the beans in the grinder, Sylvie shrugged. "What?"

"Why don't we give you two the room," Olivia said as she picked up her plate and nodded for Logan to do the same.

Once they were alone in the kitchen, Erik folded his arms and glared at Sylvie.

"You want to tell me what's going on with you?"

She pressed the button on the coffee grinder again, then turned around and faced him. "Why would you think something is going on, Erik? You have things going on in your life and so do I. Maybe we just jumped into this thing too fast and—"

"What are you saying?"

She dumped the ground coffee in the filter basket. "We should just slow down, take a break."

"Is that what you want?"

"It's what we both need. Let's be honest, your family needs you a lot more than I do right now."

Erik chewed his bottom lip and nodded. "All right."

She blinked and then turned back to the coffeemaker. "You want cream?"

"Nah. I'm going to head back to the office. Enjoy breakfast." Erik stalked out of the kitchen and ignored Logan as he called his name. He hopped into his car and banged his hand against the steering wheel. *She did it again.*

Erik was the king of ending things before it got too serious or emotional. But he wanted all of that with Sylvie. He wanted to hold her when she cried, listen to her issues, whether they were rational or irrational, and tell her everything was going to be all right.

That ain't what she wants and I'm going to respect that. Erik sped out of the driveway and told himself that he'd never look back.

Sylvie cried as she listened to the door slam and Logan call after his brother. What had she done? Why had she told him that she thought they needed to take a break when it was the biggest lie she'd ever told?

It didn't take long for Olivia to come rushing into the kitchen. "What the hell, Sylvie?"

Wiping her eyes, she turned around and faced her friend. "I don't need this right now."

"Did you just break up with Erik?"

"Leave me alone. I did what I needed to do and I don't have to explain myself to you or anyone else."

Olivia shrugged her shoulders. "Fine, if that's how you feel. But I saw a devastated man slam out of your house."

Sylvie folded her arms and gave Olivia an icy glare. "If he was so . . . I did what was best. I've never been to London. I need to focus on the trip, the project, and establishing my footprint in the industry. Tell me where a relationship is supposed to fit into this?"

"You know what, Logan told me to mind my business and that's what I'm going to do. But seriously, Sylvie, you're on some self-sabotaging bullshit that I don't understand at all."

"Well, I never understood why you flew around the world to be with Logan when you had a thriving business right here."

Olivia's mouth dropped open. "All of us aren't afraid to live. Maybe you ought to stop wrapping your self-worth in your company and go after that man who obviously loves your crazy ass. I'm going to head home, otherwise we're going to say things that we don't mean and that will be another friend that you'll lose today."

Sylvie rolled her eyes and threw her hands up. "All I'm saying is, I didn't question your choice and I'd like the same respect."

Olivia shrugged. "You're a grown-up and I'm always going to have your back."

Logan walked into the kitchen with their empty plates. "You guys good in here?"

Sylvie smiled. "We're fine, and since we've eaten and you brought Olivia's car back, you guys can go."

"Ouch," Logan said. "I came in here to wash the dishes, but that's always been the one thing

I hate to do, so we're going to go." He placed the dishes in the sink and crossed over to Olivia. "Let's go before this gets really ugly."

Olivia gave Sylvie a tender look. "Tell me what London neighborhood Myra is going to put you in and I'll make sure you're in a good place."

Sylvie smiled at her friend, then walked over to her and gave her a sisterly hug. "I'm going to call you later. You and Logan need some alone time. And do me a favor, don't spend any of your time together talking about me."

Logan and Olivia shared a knowing look, then left without saying a word. After Sylvie heard the door close, she pulled out her cell phone and called Myra.

"Sylvie," she said when the phone stopped ringing. "You're going to live a long time. I was just about to call you."

"Glad I called you, then."

"We finally have the space for the London Sweet Spot, and it looks as if we can get started next week. I know you're working on the project with Jordan Industries, but I'm really excited about going across the pond."

"I know you are. Do you have any pictures of the space, so that I can come up with some design ideas?"

"Yes, I can send you some. But I was wondering if you could come to the UK a little early. I understand if you can't. But I'd love to steal you away from Jordan Industries."

Sylvie closed her eyes and sighed. "That's not

going to be a problem. I'm going to leave the conclusion of that project in the capable hands of my assistant. I cannot wait to head to London."

"I'll email you the photos, and let me know when I should book your flight."

"Will do. I'm excited about this."

"Me too."

After hanging up with Myra, Sylvie cleaned the kitchen, then headed to her office. Maybe she should get her car fixed before she headed to London. She could spend all the time she wanted today looking for all of the parts she needed to get the Jag running again.

Erik slammed into his office and paged his assistant. "I'm not taking any calls this morning."

"But sir."

"Was I clear or not?"

"Erik, I'm coming into your office whether you like it or not," Ingrid said. Seconds later, she walked through the door. "What's going on with you today?"

Erik looked at his sister and wondered if he should tell her everything about his mood. Who was he kidding? He was pissed off about Sylvie. He wanted to ask Ingrid if she'd had a conversation with her mother about Simon, and why her mother and Yvonne had gotten into a fight.

"Ingrid, sit down. We need to talk."

She reached into her jacket pocket and pulled

out an envelope. "I'm going to resign at the end of the month."

"Why?"

She smiled sardonically. "You know why. My mother always told me her name was Violet and that she was going to be a star using that name. I remember seeing her on a Jordan Industries promo back in the day. When I asked her about it, she was dismissive. Called it a chip in the yellow brick road. I never asked her about it again. Then she got into a fight with your mother for what seemed like no reason."

"What did she tell you?" Erik was curious to hear the other side of this twisted tale.

"She said my father was a selfish bastard and though he took care of us financially, he didn't want anything to do with me. Later, after she found my vodka and woke me up in the middle of the night, she told me the truth. She wanted him to leave Yvonne and move her into that big house. When he told her that the only person who would live in that house would be me, she balked. She said Simon wanted to cut her out of the picture altogether. Pass me off as Yvonne's daughter and continue the Jordan family legacy."

Erik listened in disbelief. At what point did Simon think his mother would've ever gone along with that shit?

Ingrid shook her head. "I can't work here knowing that this is all going to come out at some point and bring more issues to the company and cause another controversy. I have a list of people who can—"

Erik shook his head. "You can't leave a company that is just as much your legacy as it is mine." He rose to his feet and crossed over to her. "We didn't ask for or create this shit show. Why should you suffer and Logan and I get to reap the benefits?"

Ingrid smirked. "We didn't suffer. Mom made sure of that. I think it's safe to say that the money Simon stole went to Los Angeles."

"You grew up in LA? No wonder you're so good at spinning stories."

"Must be in my DNA. So, what are we going to do when this story breaks?"

"I'm not worried about the story breaking. I think we need to talk to Simon. All of us deserve answers. And since he's on house arrest, he can't run away from us. Let's go now."

They headed out of the office and down the stairs that led directly to the parking lot. Erik ushered her to his car and opened the passenger door for her. As she slid into the car, Erik saw Sylvie's truck rolling into the parking lot. She was the last person he'd expected to see today. But when the door opened, he was disappointed to see a man hop out and wave at him. There was no sign of Sylvie.

Erik slammed into the driver's seat and peeled out of the parking lot. Part of him thought about calling her and telling her that she had a contract and he expected her to finish it, not one of her workers.

But that was a power play out of Simon's book, and he wasn't going to do that. If she wanted a break, he'd give her one.

"Do you always drive this fast?" Ingrid gripped her seat belt.

"Sorry," he said as he eased off the accelerator. "I'm going to call Logan and see if he can meet us over at the house."

"As long as you slow down before you do that."

Chapter 24

Sylvie spent the rest of the day creating designs for the Sweet Spot UK. It wasn't until her stomach started rumbling that she realized that she hadn't eaten all day. Throwing out the breakfast Erik brought over hadn't been the best idea. Now she had nothing in the house but coffee.

"Good job," she groaned. She rose from her desk and stretched her arms above her head. She started to order takeout, but decided that it was too beautiful a day to stay in the house. Part of her had hoped to hear from Erik, but she wasn't going to call him. No. Way.

If she wanted him to take this break seriously, then she couldn't be calling and texting him as if they were on the best of terms. Reaching for her favorite sneakers, Sylvie heard the doorbell ring. Since she wasn't expecting anyone, she ignored it. After she put her shoes on and her favorite black hat, she headed out the door and nearly tripped on a package. Picking it up, she was surprised to see that it was from a classic-auto-parts store. *What is this?* she thought as she opened the box. Tears welled up in her eyes when saw what was in the box. The part for her Jag that she'd been looking for.

Erik did this, I know it. She wiped her eyes and took the box inside. It was time to stop acting foolish and tell this man she was wrong and how much he meant to her. Forget lunch, she was going to head over to his office. In her mind, she imagined a reunion and maybe Erik telling her that he'd come out to London with her for a week or so. They'd leave together and make love for the rest of the night. Maybe they'd have a midnight snack from the pizza shop around the corner and they'd definitely have Kona coffee in the morning.

By the time she pulled into the parking lot of Jordan Industries, Sylvie had made up an entire apology speech and a dance to go along with it. But when she reached the executive suite, all of her hopes of a reunion were dashed.

"Hey, Sylvie," Erik's assistant said. "If you're looking for the boss, you just missed him."

"Oh, do you know where he went?"

"He and Ingrid left together, no idea where they went."

"Oh. Okay," Sylvie said, her voice filled with disappointment.

"Want me to tell him that you stopped by?"

She shook her head. "I'll call him tomorrow. Thanks." As she turned to leave, Sylvie pulled out her phone and called Myra.

"Hey, girl. I was hoping to hear from you again today."

"Well, I wanted to call you and tell you the pictures that you sent me of the new space put me in such a creative mood. I'm ready to get started."

"Yes! I'm so excited."

"Well, check your email in about an hour. I have some ideas to show you." She forced herself to sound excited, but inside she wanted to cry. Erik left with Ingrid? *That was fast. Maybe he is the playboy the Internet says he is.*

Before she left, Sylvie headed down the hall to check on her crew. And just like she thought, they were doing an amazing job. After waving to her foreman, she slipped out of the building and went home.

She'd gotten the answers she needed and now she was going to London without any regrets.

Erik and Ingrid sat in the driveway of the Jordan mansion waiting for Logan to arrive. She turned to Erik and smiled nervously. "This is weird, and I guess it is a good thing that we kept it professional."

"Yeah. This is a cluster."

"We've been lied to our whole lives."

Erik stroked her shoulder. "That's why we're going to get some answers."

Seconds later, Logan pulled in the driveway behind her. The three of them exited their cars and Logan crossed over to Ingrid. "Anybody else feel like they're standing in the middle of a Greek tragedy?"

"It could've been a lot worse," Ingrid said as she extended her hand to Logan.

He pulled her in for a hug. "We're family, forget a handshake."

They walked up the steps and opened the door. Erik noticed that the house was quiet.

"Where is everybody?" Logan questioned. "I can't believe Dad is in here without the staff."

Ingrid looked around the house as they headed for the living room. She saw pictures of what looked like a happy family. Erik glanced at his sister. "Don't be fooled by those pictures."

"Yeah, we were trained to always smile for a camera," Logan said.

They entered the living room and found Simon napping on a chaise lounge. Erik shook his head, knowing Yvonne would be livid if she saw him on her favorite ivory-colored piece of furniture. Part of him wanted to push the old man to the floor to wake him up. Instead, he just shook his foot.

"Wha-what the hell?" Simon muttered as he

opened his eyes and glanced up at his children. "Why are you all here?"

"Because you owe us answers, especially Ingrid." Logan rolled his eyes, not trying to hide his contempt for his father.

"I don't owe y'all a damned thing. I mean, all of you are grown. I made sure you had everything you needed and I regret nothing." Simon hopped up and shook his head.

"But I needed a father in my life," Ingrid said, her voice barely above a whisper. "I should've known who my family was."

"Your gripe is with your mama, not me. She used you like a credit card to make me pay for her lifestyle because she was jealous of my wife."

"A wife you didn't love, obviously," Erik bellowed. "How could you do this to us?"

Simon looked his oldest son up and down. "You're going to stand there and act like you have some moral high ground, when you started all of this. Had you just gotten the board to sign off on the sale of the company, none of this would've happened. I was finally done with sending Helen money, we could've covered the losses and been just fine. But you." He pointed his finger in Erik's face. "You wanted to do what you thought was the right thing, and look at things now."

"I don't even know why we deal with this son of a bitch!" Logan snapped. "You never take responsibility for anything you do. Have you ever wondered why I wanted to be far away from you and this company?"

"I don't give a damn, little boy. Your mama made you soft."

"And what did Grandma do to you to make you such a heartless bastard?" Logan asked. He turned to his brother and sister. "You two can stay here and try to make heads or tails about whatever lie he's going to tell. But I'm out."

Simon laughed. "Just like your mama. Hear something you don't like and you're gone."

Logan started toward the door, then stopped and turned around. "I'd rather be just like my mother than to have anything like you in my soul. I hope you rot in prison and that the world knows this family-man image you've cultivated over the years has been nothing but a lie." Looking at Ingrid, Logan smiled. "Consider yourself lucky that he was only a check and didn't try to run your life."

"Why don't you get out of here!" Simon yelled. "Poor Logan, grew up in the lap of luxury and complains about it to everyone he meets. You think you'd be an artist if it wasn't for me? You had a trust fund that funded your little artist bullshit." Simon nodded at Ingrid. "Who do you think put you through college? I did everything I could for you ungrateful kids and this is the thanks I get. To hell with all of y'all."

Erik nodded toward the door. "Let's go."

"No," Ingrid said. She crossed over to Simon.

"Did you ever love me or my mother? Or was I just another pawn for your chessboard?"

"Little girl, I've given you everything you're ever going to get from me. I don't owe you anything."

Tears welled up in Ingrid's eyes and then she tore off down the hall. Logan and Erik followed her, realizing that Simon wasn't going to give them any answers and they would just have to make peace with that.

Two Months Later

Much to the delight of the Jordan Industries board and Erik, Simon took a plea deal in his case, which saved the company from additional scandals. The remodel of the company went off without a hitch, or Sylvie.

Erik had tried to reach out to her several times over the last two months, with no response. Since Olivia and Logan had left for New Orleans, he couldn't reach out to his future sister-in-law to find out what was going on with Sylvie.

Sitting at his desk, he wondered what had gone so wrong between them. Logging on to his computer, Erik pulled up his social media and headed straight for Sylvie's Facebook page.

At least he knew she was having a good time putting the Sweet Spot together. He smiled as he thought about Sylvie's sweet spot and how he missed spending hours there.

"She made the decision to cut me off. Just like

she did on New Year's Eve. Maybe it just isn't meant to be," he muttered as he scrolled through her pictures. At least she wasn't posing with some English dude.

One picture stood out to him. She'd taken a flat in London? Just how long was she going to stay there?

London, England

Sylvie wiped sweat from her forehead as she stood outside the Sweet Spot admiring the design on the plate-glass window. She had fashioned it with classic Brooklyn landmarks and some of the highlights of the Marylebone neighborhood, like the reptiles from the London Zoo and a rendering of some of the most popular mannequins at Madame Tussauds—including the royal family.

Though there was an American flag in the corner, near the Brooklyn section of the window, Sylvie was debating if she should put a Union Jack in the background.

"That might make this window too busy." Sylvie pulled out her phone and snapped a picture of the window. Then she uploaded it to Facebook with the caption: *A little Brooklyn in London. #SweetSpotUK*.

She sighed, realizing that she was missing Atlanta. Particularly, Erik Jordan. But every time she thought about calling him, she remembered that he'd left with Ingrid. She knew Ingrid had designs on him, and obviously he was feeling her more than he'd been willing to admit.

If that's what he wants, then good for him. I can do anything I want, even start over in London.

Sylvie had been keeping her conversations with Olivia really short because she didn't want to ask about Erik or hear Olivia slip up and tell her that he and Ingrid were so in love now. Nope, she'd rather live in ignorance. But her friend did send her the magazine that featured the redesigned interior of Jordan Industries.

She loved how the article focused on Erik stepping up to lead the company that so many women loved, and that he was focusing on black beauty across the world. Sylvie was impressed with the new project he and his mother had started called Beautiful Soul.

When she'd seen the picture of Erik and his mother standing in his office, she had put the magazine down. Seeing him made her heart skip a beat.

She'd thought about calling him, but pride and disappointment got in the way.

"Sylvie!" Myra exclaimed, breaking into her thoughts. "This window is amazing! I just love it."

"Thanks."

"Not that I'm complaining, but you've been working nonstop since you got here. I need you to take a break."

"What? But I'm almost done and—"

"We have a month before we open, and you need a break. Not taking no for any answer. I have a ticket to a show at the Royal Festival Hall tonight and you're going."

"Myra, I appreciate the offer, but—"

"No buts! You said it yourself, this is your first time in London. Do you want all your memories to revolve around work?"

Sylvie shrugged. "At least I have a nice flat."

"And now you're going to a nice show. Go home, change, and have a good time."

She sighed and nodded. "Fine. I'm going. But, before I leave, what do you think about a Union Jack as a transparent background on the window?"

"Mmm, I think that's a question I can answer tomorrow," Myra quipped. "Get out of here."

Sylvie gave her a mock salute and started toward her rented Fiat. She really liked her Notting Hill flat, even if it was smaller than her place in Atlanta. But it had a lot of style. Myra knew exactly what she was doing when she chose that place for her. Every day, Sylvie got to see the creativity of the future fashion designers when she rode pass the London College of Fashion. The other day must have been wedding collection day. Sylvie couldn't help but think of the amazing brides who wore those avant-garde dresses. She'd snapped some photos of the models crossing the street in the dresses, but didn't post them online. She wasn't sure if the designers were ready to share or not. But Sylvie knew she wanted one of those dresses. Or at least she could show them to Olivia, since there wasn't going to be a wedding in Sylvie's future anytime soon. *Or ever.*

Sylvie tried to turn her thoughts away from Erik and love. Her heart hadn't healed from the fact that Erik chose Ingrid over her. When she arrived at her flat, Sylvie went into her closet and pulled out a slinky red dress. She'd packed it on a whim, though she figured she'd never wear it. But, she was going out on the town in London and she might as well make the best of it.

She showered, blew out her Afro, and started to put on some makeup. When she reached in the bottom of her makeup kit, she found the tube of red lipstick Erik had given her. She started to toss it in the trash, but then she remembered how soft it felt against her lips. She decided to wear it anyway.

After her face was flawlessly painted and her lips colored a bright red, she slipped into her dress and liked what she saw in the mirror. She snapped a selfie and posted it to her social media sites. *#HotLondonNights.*

Chapter 25

Erik was ready for a quiet evening by the pool with a thick steak and some whisky. A lot of whisky. Part of his dinner tonight was a celebration; Jordan Industries' stocks had rebounded and the company was making a turnaround. The magazine article, which highlighted the new direction of the company and showed off Sylvie's remodel, did a lot to lift the morale around the company. The board had been happy that Simon's plea deal and the announcement of Yvonne's women's empowerment program put the company in the media for all the right reasons.

And Erik was happy to introduce the new and improved Yvonne lipstick, which had four shades of red for every mood and every skin tone. He felt some kind of way when he didn't hear from Sylvie after he announced that her favorite lipstick was coming back. As much as he'd done it for his mother, he couldn't deny that Sylvie had been on his mind when he created all four of those colors.

Just thinking about her made him wonder what she was doing. Since he had no luck reaching her on the phone, he went back to social media. When he saw her latest post, he knew it was time to stop sitting in Atlanta, cyberstalking her. He was going to London to win his woman back. Or at least find out how he lost her in the first place, especially since Olivia was sticking to the I-don't-know-what-happened story line. She had even told Logan the same thing, at least that's what his brother said.

Erik was on his phone, about to book a flight, when it rang. When it was Logan and not Sylvie, he was beyond disappointed. Though he should've been used to not hearing from her, it didn't mean he didn't still yearn to hear her voice.

"What's up, Logan?"

"Why do you sound like you're about to take a flying leap off the side of Spaghetti Junction?"

"Because I was about to do something important before you interrupted me. What do you want?"

"Well, I wanted to let you know that my trip to London was canceled and I have an open ticket . . ."

"I didn't even know you were going to London."

"Yeah, I was supposed to do an installation at a museum, but I pushed it back two months. I really want to spend some more time with Ma while she's going through chemo. She and Olivia have become fast friends."

"I've noticed," he said with a chuckle. "Nice to see them get along, going to mean a lot fewer problems when you two get married."

"And we're not going to be able to have the most amazing wedding in the world if my best man and her maid of honor don't get their shit together."

"You've saved me a headache. I was about to book a flight when you called."

"Really? Why now?"

Erik snorted. "Because I love that woman and it's time that she knows it. She can accept it or tell me to fuck off."

"Let's hope it's the former and not the latter. I'm going to text you my information. My flight was scheduled for tomorrow at six."

"In the morning."

"Yep. Need a ride to the airport?"

"I do. But I need a favor from Olivia."

"What kind of favor?"

Erik chuckled again. "I'm sure she has keys to Sylvie's place. I have a mechanic who can fix her Jag, and he's mobile, so if she can let him in her garage so that he can fix her car, I'd be grateful."

"Hold on."

Seconds later, Olivia was telling him hello. "So, you're going to get my girl and you want to fix her car?"

"Yes and yes. Do you think she'll be upset if I do that?"

"No! Erik, make sure she knows that you're in this for the long haul."

"I will, because I am. Do you know where Sylvie is staying?"

"I don't, but my friend hasn't learned to turn her location off on social media. But you didn't hear that from me."

Erik walked inside, forgetting that he was about to drown his sorrows in whisky, and grabbed his laptop. He pulled up his Internet browser and logged on to Facebook. "She's going to have to adjust her privacy settings," he said. Erik had been so taken by her pictures that he didn't notice the geo-tags.

"I've been telling her that for years. But you see her apartment is in Notting Hill. The bakery she's designing is—"

"In the Marylebone neighborhood. Now, I just have to figure out how to get to all of these places."

"And don't forget the time change, okay."

"Got it."

"What time is the mechanic coming and . . . Wow!"

"What's going on?" Erik asked, his voice peppered with concern.

"Just saw this picture of Sylvie in that red dress. Oh my goodness, she looks amazing. You better bring your A game, Erik! She is out there looking like a whole snack."

"Thanks, Olivia."

"Why don't you like the picture and let her know you see her out there in those London streets."

"Umm, I'm not doing that. I don't want to look like a stalker."

Olivia burst out laughing. "Yeah, because flying to London and showing up at her work or her house isn't stalker-like at all."

Erik clicked *like* on the picture. "All right," he said. "I'm going to eat my steak, then go to bed. I got an early flight."

"Good luck. And, oh! What time do I need to meet the mechanic?"

"At two."

"Awesome. Your mother said don't mess this up."

In the background he heard Yvonne yell, "I said in the words of RuPaul, don't fuck it up."

"I'm hanging up now," Erik said. Looking up, he saw his chef standing in the doorway of his home office.

"Are you eating and working tonight, Mr. Jordan?"

"Yeah. I have an early flight in the morning. Thanks for dinner," he said as he stood up and took the tray filled with a bone-in rib eye steak and a loaded baked potato. He ate the food while he continued to scroll through Sylvie's social media. He saw that she had posted another picture in her red dress with the London Philharmonic Orchestra behind her. Some guy had photo bombed her. Then in the next picture, they took a selfie. Erik felt jealousy flowing through his veins when he couldn't see the stranger's hand and assumed it was resting on Sylvie's wonderful ass. Slamming his laptop shut, he realized that six a.m. couldn't get here fast enough.

London, England

Sylvie was glad that she had attended the concert, but sorry that she'd taken a picture with Kurt Reynolds. Now this man wanted to go out for coffee, and she just wanted to go home and take her shoes off.

"Come on, beautiful," he said. "Let me take you out on the town. The night is still young."

"Sorry," she replied as she patted his shoulder. "I have an early morning."

He nodded and frowned. "Ah, the beautiful ones always turn me down."

Sylvie gave him a slow once-over. Any other time, she would've said yes to coffee with the tall, dark, and handsome man. He looked like Idris Elba with an Afro and glasses. His big hands reminded her of Erik. His swagger wasn't as powerful as Erik's. His smile didn't make her heart flutter like Erik's did. Wait. Why was she comparing this man to the one who had broken her heart?

Didn't Erik tell her there was nothing going on with him and Ingrid? But the words of his assistant still rang in her head.

He left with Ingrid.

"I'm sorry, Kurt," she said. "In another time I'd love to have coffee with you, but I just want to be alone tonight."

"I get it. Hope he's worth the sadness you're feeling right now."

"What are you talking about?"

He tilted his head to the side. "I can tell when a woman is carrying a torch. Don't let your arm get tired." He took her hand in his and brought it to his lips. When he kissed her hand, Sylvie felt nothing. But she was sure he wouldn't be leaving the music hall alone. She, on the other hand, was happy to do so. As she waited for a taxi, she realized how much she missed her Jag, even if she was going to have to shell out a gang of money to get it repaired when she returned home.

Maybe it was time to make it a weekend car. But she knew one thing for sure, she was not going to buy a Fiat.

Arriving home, she kicked her gold heels off at the door and pulled her dress off. Walking around in the flat in just her underwear, Sylvie sighed and turned on some John Coltrane. Immediately, she regretted that decision. Her mind returned to that night in Atlanta, Erik's arms around her on the sofa as they swayed to John's sax. Maybe it was time for her to grow up and call him. Looking at the clock, she realized how late it was across the pond and promised that she'd call tomorrow. Tonight, she was going to drown her feelings in a bottle of merlot.

* * *

Back in Atlanta, Erik couldn't stop looking at the picture of Sylvie and fake-ass Idris Elba. What if she'd gone back to his place or if this guy was some member of the royal family and he wooed her away with a sparkling tiara?

Now you're just being stupid. There aren't any black British princes.

Erik rolled over on his back and looked up at the ceiling. First, she was going to have to explain her disappearing act. What had he done to cause her to do this? Then he'd tell her that she is the only woman who could make him leave the country to find her. Erik didn't have a problem with Sylvie finishing her work in London. But he needed to know that she would come back to him, because he couldn't spend the rest of his life without her. And he didn't plan to leave England until he knew for sure that Sylvia Elaine Gates was going to be his forever.

Chapter 26

Erik felt like a child on Christmas Eve. He woke up three times during the night, just to check the clock. It was only two forty-five. If he had his way, he would've been at the airport at three. But Erik wasn't the kind of man who could comfortably sit around an airport waiting.

About twenty minutes later, Erik got out of bed and checked his bag. He'd packed light because he wasn't sure if Sylvie would want him to stay. But if she did, he had three days to devote to his woman.

She was still his woman, right? Had she let him go, for the man at the concert? What if she was planning to start over in London and he didn't fit in her life anymore?

He zipped his carry-on bag and sat on the edge of the bed. That was an option he hadn't wanted to consider, but suppose Sylvie had moved on. For a split second, he thought about canceling the trip and accepting her decision.

And live in a world of what-ifs? Nah, it's not going down like that.

Erik took a quick shower, brewed some coffee, and pulled up Sylvie's social media while he drank it. At least he didn't see another picture of her and that guy. That was a good sign.

He tucked his phone in his pocket. The cyber-stalking was getting a little out of control. Erik was tired of the pictures; he wanted to see, feel, and kiss Sylvie.

London, England—

Sylvie couldn't believe that she was into tea. Or that she's missed out on these flavors over the years. Peppermint tea was her new thing, though she wasn't giving up coffee completely. And as soon as she started thinking about coffee, her mind went back to Erik. Why was it so hard for her to realize that he'd moved on and forgotten all about her? It wasn't as if he'd reached out to her in the past two months. She was about to take a picture of her tea for social media when she noticed that Erik had liked her picture from the music hall.

She scoffed and tossed her phone on the futon. Oh, he could look at her on social media, but he couldn't send her a message and explain himself. She laughed. He probably just liked the fact that she was wearing his lipstick.

"Wonder if he was with her when he was all up and down my Facebook page," she muttered.

Ever think that they aren't together and you're overreacting?

Sylvie looked around because she could've sworn she'd heard her dad's voice saying those words. "I'm losing my mind, I need to get out of here."

She headed for the bathroom and took a quick shower. She started to call Myra and see if she could go to the Sweet Spot this morning, but she decided to explore the neighborhood. She dressed in a white romper and her favorite walking shoes. The weather in London was crisp and warm and no humidity, and Sylvie was in love and hungry. Since she hadn't tried some of the restaurants in the neighborhood, Sylvie dipped into a corner café for breakfast. The place was half full, but she had been lucky enough to snag a table near the window, which looked out over the street.

"Good morning, what can I start you off with today?" the waiter asked.

"This is my first morning having a real English breakfast. What would you suggest?"

"Aww, I would be remiss if I didn't offer you a fry-up."

"What's that?"

"A traditional breakfast that will keep you energized all day: bacon, eggs, grilled tomatoes, beans, fried mushrooms, and bangers. Then you have your choice of fried bread or buttery toast."

Sylvie raised her right eyebrow. "That sounds like a lot of food, but I'll try it."

"And to drink? We have freshly squeezed orange juice and a wonderful pineapple and cranberry mix. Of course there's tea and coffee if you'd like."

"I'm going to go with the orange juice and coffee, a flat white actually."

"Good choice. I'll put your order in and be back with your drinks."

Alone at the table, Sylvie regretted not bringing a book. But when she reached down in her bag, she was happy to find a sketchpad. A little bit of work wouldn't hurt. When she opened the book and saw the layout she'd drawn of Erik's house, she closed it and decided to scroll through social media. She got bored after a few minutes and pulled the pad out again.

Wonder what Ingrid is going to come up with for his place? Stop it. What that man does is no longer your concern.

Erik hated waiting in airports. But today's wait was even more annoying because he wanted to be in London sooner rather than later. And honestly, he wanted to make sure that every man passing his Sylvie knew that she was spoken for, that her American man had come to take her heart back across the pond where it belonged. Granted, he'd love to be taking her back with him, but he knew she had to handle her business.

"Ladies and gentlemen, thank you for your patience. We will begin boarding flight 4532 to London in twenty minutes. Our plane was delayed because we had a sick flyer and we needed to disinfect the plane for your safety. We apologize for any inconvenience this delay has caused."

Erik shook his head. This delay was testing his patience like the SATs. But he wasn't going to turn back. Not until he had Sylvie in his arms again. Thanks to her geotags on social media, he'd drawn a map of her movements. It wasn't lost on him how easy it was to find her. In the back of his mind, he wanted to believe that she was dropping digital breadcrumbs for him to follow. But when she'd left Atlanta, she hadn't said two words to him, so it was just wishful thinking.

Once the plane started boarding, Erik said a silent prayer of thanks for his brother having priority seating. He took a window seat and leaned his head against the window, hoping to catch a nap on the eight-hour flight. He knew when he touched down in London it was going to be late evening and he hadn't even found a hotel yet. Sitting up, he pulled his carry-on bag from underneath the front seat and pulled out his iPad. He googled Marylebone hotels. Landmark London popped up immediately and Erik quickly booked a room before the flight crew told everyone to place their electronics in airplane mode. Leaning on the window, Erik closed his eyes and counted down the hours to when he'd land in London.

He knew he needed to find roses. As cliché as it seemed, he had to give her flowers because roses always meant love to him. That's why he'd never wanted to give them to any other woman. But Sylvie wasn't like any other woman. From their first encounter to the last time he felt her lips against his, he couldn't get her off his mind, out of his system or his heart. Erik just didn't understand what had happened to make her disappear. Two months was a long time to be away from the woman who stole his heart.

"Ladies and gentlemen, we are preparing for takeoff. Please shut off all electronic devices or place them in airplane mode. Make sure your seats are in the upright position and your seat belt is securely fastened. We expect to land at Heathrow in eight hours."

Erik took a deep breath and closed his eyes. Part of him wondered what he would find when the plane landed.

London, England

Sylvie's feet were aching by the time she made it home. She'd hit all of the tourist attractions, including Madame Tussauds, where she took pictures with some of the famous wax statues—especially the new duchess. She texted the picture to Olivia, then posted it on Facebook: *#HangingwithRoyalty*.

Then she took the Tube for the first time and headed to Westminster for a tour on a vintage London bus. As she took more pictures and uploaded them to social media, Sylvie noticed that she had been sharing her location with her pictures. She shivered, then thanked God that she didn't have any stalkers. Still, she'd turned her location settings off and then headed home. She stopped at the corner café again for a dinner of Yorkshire pudding, peas and chips. Sylvie promised herself that when she returned to Atlanta she was going to give the vegan thing another go.

Kicking her shoes off at the door, she crossed over to her futon and plopped down. Tomorrow, she'd be able to tell Myra that she spent her day soaking up London, and now she could work without interruptions. Tonight, she was going to veg out, listen to some jazz, and try not to think about Erik Jordan.

Leaning back on the futon with the music blasting, she was about to close her eyes when her phone rang.

"Hello," she said with a faux British accent.

"Don't do that," Olivia said. "Don't be Madonna up in here."

"Whatever. How much is this call going to cost us? Well, you, actually." Sylvie had gotten a new number while she was in London because the international plan on her stateside phone was beyond expensive.

"Logan reminded me that he has an international plan on his phone. I could've been harassing you for months."

"Gee, thanks. How are you, though?"

"Great. And you?"

"Umm, tired. Spent the day playing tourist. You got my picture from Madame Tussauds, right?"

"It was cute. Glad you're having fun and finally turned off those geotags on social media."

"New phone, forgot about those settings."

"You look like you're having a good time over there. Really loved that red dress and your Pam Grier Afro. You know who else was impressed . . ."

"If this is where you start talking about Erik, I'm going to hang up on you."

"Fine, hang up if you want to, but at least let me tell you some great news."

"What's that?"

"I saved a lot of money when I switched my car insurance to GEICO."

Sylvie sighed. "I really hate you right now."

"Seriously, I think I'm pregnant."

"I'm so happy for you and Logan."

"And that means we're going to have to move the wedding up, so I hope that you and Erik can get your shit together and not ruin my big day."

Sylvie rolled her eyes. "There you go. I don't

want to talk about that man. Have you seen him and his new woman?"

"New woman? What are you talking about?"

She expelled another frustrated breath. "Olivia, you don't have to try and spare my feelings. I know he and Ingrid are seeing each other."

"Wow. Where did you get such an idea?"

Sylvie told her friend about her encounter with Erik's assistant and how she'd told her that Erik and Ingrid had left together.

"I'd gone to his office to apologize for allowing my issues to get in our way and I was proven right. So, I know you're about to marry his brother and we're—"

"Sylvia Elaine Gates, you have never been more wrong about anything in your life. I mean, just wrong like two left shoes."

"What are you talking about?"

"Erik and Ingrid are not together. Not at all."

"Whatever," Sylvie snapped. "He left his office in the middle of the day with her. I know what that means."

"She's his sister."

Sylvie's mouth dropped open and she nearly let the phone slip from her hands. "How—What?"

"So, you mean to tell me that you've been loud and wrong for two months because you thought he was with Ingrid? You need to call him."

She heard Logan tell Olivia to mind her business. "And he's the reason why I never told you. But you should call him."

"I would, but I'm guessing it's too late. The

only thing he's done since I've been here is like my picture."

Olivia laughed. "At least he listens to me. I've got to go. Miss Yvonne and I are going to have breakfast."

"This time difference is still taking a lot to get used to. Make sure you get some bangers."

"Some what?"

"Sausage."

"Umm, let me find out you've given up on this vegan lifestyle."

"When in Rome . . ."

"Chick, you're in London and you're just not about that plant-based lifestyle."

"Once I return home, I'm all about it." Sylvie yawned. "But right now, I'm getting in this bed for a mid-day nap."

"All right. We'll talk soon."

After hanging up with her friend, Sylvie turned the music up and lay back on the futon, thinking about how she was going to be able to fix this thing with Erik. Was it too late? Or did she have a chance?

Jet-lagged didn't describe how Erik felt. He felt as if he'd dragged the jet by his teeth with his eyes closed. Standing at the front desk, all Erik wanted was to go to sleep. His body needed to adjust to the time change and get his game plan together.

"Good evening, Mr. Jordan," the front-desk clerk said after he gave her his reservation number. "We'll have someone take your luggage up to your room."

Erik tapped his backpack. "This is all I have. Just point me in the direction of the bed."

The woman smiled at him and gave him directions to his room. Once he got on the elevator, he closed his eyes and nearly went to sleep standing up. The doors to the elevator opened and he was happy to see that he had a short walk to his room.

Erik didn't take in the grandeur of the room. He just dropped his bag on the end of the bed and fell down on top of it. As he slept, he dreamed of seeing Sylvie walking down the road and calling her name. She'd turn around and run into his arms. Their lips would meet in a hot kiss as raindrops fell gently on them. The thought of kissing Sylvie made him sit straight up in the bed.

Was it really going to be that easy to win his woman back?

Chapter 27

Morning came too soon for Erik. His body needed another day to sleep. But his mind was ready to find Sylvie. He pulled himself out of bed and headed for the bathroom. As he stood underneath the warm spray, Erik thought about what he was going to say when he found her. Didn't he deserve an explanation for her actions? Erik knew he hadn't done anything to make her think what he felt wasn't real. If he'd left any doubt in her mind about how he felt for her, he was going to fix that now. Well, as soon as he found her.

As he dressed, the in-room phone rang. Crossing over to the nightstand, he picked up the handset. "Hello?"

"Mr. Jordan, this is the front desk. Would you like breakfast delivered to you?"

"No thank you. But I do have a question. Where can I rent a car from?"

"I can take care of that for you. Do you want a luxury or an economy vehicle?"

"If you can find me a red Jaguar, I'd be forever grateful."

The woman laughed. "Living a James Bond fantasy?"

"Only if I get the girl in the end."

"I'll call you when everything is arranged. It could take a half hour. Are you sure you don't want breakfast sent up?"

"Sure, why not. Just send me your most popular dish and some black coffee."

"Yes sir," she said.

Erik ended the call and dressed in a pair of black slacks and a formfitting long sleeve red T-shirt. He was ready to find his woman.

Sylvie woke up around six and decided to take a jog. Then she checked the weather and decided that it was too cold for this Southern belle to pretend she liked running. She pulled the covers back around her and went back to sleep.

When her alarm blared at her, she got up and showered. Sylvie spent a little too much time underneath the warm spray and ended up rushing to dry off and dress because she was about to be running late.

As she left the building, she noticed a new doorman working. "Good morning," she said as she headed out the door.

"Good morning, and this is the last time you touch the door handle, all right?" He smiled as he followed her and grabbed the door to hold it open for her.

"Thanks. You're such a gentleman."

He tipped his hat with his free hand. "Just doing my job, madame."

Sylvie fought the urge to bow to him. Talk about being an American feeding on stereotypes. So she just smiled and left. As she walked out to her Fiat, she caught a glimpse of a red Jaguar circling the block. The car made her smile and miss her classic car. The first thing she was going to do when she got home was get it repaired and take a long drive to Charleston, South Carolina. She owed her mother a visit, and it would be nice to see some of the sights and get ideas for new projects.

Okay, maybe she was thinking about going to Charleston to avoid Erik and having to face up to her huge mistake. She couldn't deny that it would serve her right if he didn't want to see her again.

Ingrid was his sister, not his lover. She'd been the biggest fool for not even giving him a chance to explain why they'd left the office together.

It's true what they say about assuming. Sylvie slid into the car and started it up. As she pulled away from the curb, she saw that Jag again. *Must be a popular car,* she thought.

Once again, she slowed down near the fashion academy and watched the different creations from the students at the school. Today must have been a business-wear day. But when she saw a woman dressed in a formfitting floral pantsuit, Sylvie knew she needed to meet the designer. A horn blew behind her and Sylvie pulled into one of the lots and chased the girl in the floral.

Erik walked up to the entrance of what he assumed was Sylvie's building. Before he could touch the doorknob, a bulky doorman opened the door. "Good morning, sir, are you a resident?"

Erik smiled. "No, I'm not. Actually, I'm looking for one of your residents."

"Are you a bobby?"

"A what?"

"My bad, you're an American. Are you a police officer or the FBI?"

Erik sighed. "No, I'm looking for the love of my life."

The doorman took a step back. "This isn't a brothel. And we don't hand over our residents' information to strangers."

"Listen, her name is Sylvie—Sylvia Gates."

"You don't even know her name. Sir, I'm going to have to ask you to leave."

The last thing Erik wanted to do was leave or cause a scene. However, he couldn't do both. He'd leave and go to the next stop he had on his cobbled-together map.

"Sir," the doorman called out. "I have my eye on you. Don't come back here starting trouble."

"Wouldn't dream of it. Thanks for keeping my lady safe." Erik gave him a mock salute, then jogged over to his rented Jag.

The restaurant where Sylvie had posted most of her pictures from was about four miles from the building that he assumed she lived in. All he could do was hope that she was at the building and he wouldn't have to go back to her apartment, because it was clear he wouldn't be getting in.

He parked his vehicle across from the building that would be the Sweet Spot UK. He could already see Sylvie's hand in the design of the window. She made art and he loved it. She'd done the same thing with his business and his heart. Now, he just needed to know if he could make this thing last forever. Sitting in the car, he wondered if he did have the look of a stalker right now while he waited for her. Not wanting to deal with a real bobby, Erik got out of the car and started walking to drink in some of the scenery of the area. It seemed fitting that Sylvie settled here. He imagined her hanging out in the park, sipping tea and fighting the English fellows off with a stick. What if the guy in her Facebook picture had captured her heart with that damned accent?

Erik stopped walking and realized that he hadn't gotten the roses yet. He saw a Marylebone flower shop and decided that fate had led him to this place. As he walked up to the counter, he wondered, did Sylvie even like roses?

* * *

Sylvie smiled as she adjusted her floral pants and was happy that her red shoes matched the roses in the suit. The young designer had been wearing her own suit and was thrilled that someone wanted to buy the suit that her instructor had called an abomination. Sylvie hadn't even questioned the exchange rate for US cash when she handed the girl three one-hundred-dollar bills.

This suit made her feel powerful, and she resolved to call Erik today and tell him how wrong she was about everything, and hope that he would forgive her. But right now, she was going to walk into the Sweet Spot and make some magic. Heading for her car, she sped down the road and made it to the building and was surprised to see the red Jaguar parked across the street.

Things were starting to get scary. Was the driver of this car following her? There weren't this many coincidences in the world. She definitely needed to tell Myra what was going on. Sylvie grabbed the door handle when she heard, "Sylvie."

Now she was losing her mind, because she could've sworn that was Erik's voice. Turning around, she knew she'd lost her mind because that wasn't Erik Jordan walking toward her with a bouquet of roses. He didn't know where she was. He was also in Atlanta.

She blinked and there he was, inches away from her.

"Erik?"

"Hey."

"What are you doing here?"

"I missed you and I needed to see you. Thank you for not turning off your geo tags on social media." His smile made her knees go weak. "You're going to have to do better. I wouldn't want the wrong person finding us." Erik held the roses out to her. "You look amazing."

Sylvie took the bouquet and sniffed it. "I'm speechless."

"Good. That gives me a chance to say what I need to say. Sylvia Elaine Gates, I love you. These last two months have been hell. And I'd like to know why you have avoided me."

"Because I'm an idiot."

Erik leaned in to her and stroked her cheek. "No, you're not."

"I left without saying anything to you because I thought you'd left your office with Ingrid because you two were going to be together."

"You know Ingrid is my sister."

She nodded. "Olivia told me, and I've been trying to figure out how to stop feeling like the biggest fool in the universe."

"So, that's what it was. I thought I'd done something really wrong for you to come all the way to London and forget about me."

Tears sprang to her eyes. "I've been hurt before, and I wanted to protect myself from getting my heart broken again."

"I'm never going to break your heart. Sylvie, I love you."

She blinked twice before the tears spilled down her cheeks. "Erik, I-I love you too."

"And that night when I should've told you, I'm going to always regret that. You made me feel things that I'd never wanted to feel. Sylvie, I need you to be mine, forever."

"What are you saying?"

Erik dropped down to one knee and pulled a black velvet box from his pocket. "I'm saying, I want you to marry me."

"Yes." She nodded. "Yes."

He opened the box and Sylvie was surprised to see a sparkling sapphire solitaire. "Erik, how did you know?"

"Olivia tries to mind her business, but after she saw that picture of you and fake-ass Idris Elba, she put me up on my A game."

"Game well played," she said with a smile as he slid the ring on her finger.

DON'T MISS

Strategic Seduction

Alicia Michaels needs a major career reboot,
so she's got no time for romance. But starting
over in Atlanta is an uphill battle for the
cautious marketing consultant—especially
after she teams up with wealthy Richmond
Crawford on a make-or-break project.
For one thing, the risk-taking entrepreneur is
nothing like the staid businessman he used to
be. For another, she and Richmond can't see
eye-to-eye on *anything*—except that the
reckless attraction between them is sizzling,
off-the-charts trouble . . .

Available wherever books are sold

Enjoy the following excerpt from
Strategic Seduction . . .

Chapter 1

Alicia Michaels walked across the campus of Clark Atlanta University with a smile on her face. Being back on the yard made her think about the carefree days of an undergrad. Even though she was having a good time with her girls, she was tired of hearing the *Alicia, girl, you're next* refrain as soon as someone noticed Serena Billups's wedding ring or when Jade Goings showed off her pictures of Jaden or her growing baby bump.

"I figured I'd find you out here," Kandace Crawford, one of her best friends and business partners, said as she and Richmond Crawford approached the library. "Still hiding from people?"

"I'm not hiding from anyone. Well, not really." Alicia locked eyes with Richmond Crawford, Kandace's brother-in-law. This was not the man she'd met a few years ago in New York with the glasses and pudgy belly. And was he smiling? She'd never seen this man smile before. *Why am*

I paying attention now? Alicia thought as she turned away from him briefly.

"Hi, Alicia," he said, once again blinding her with his warm smile.

"Hi. What are you doing here?" She didn't even try to keep the shock out of her voice.

"Looking to start a new business venture down here in Atlanta, and Kandace was nice enough to show me some of the city," he said.

"And Solomon figured I needed a bodyguard, since he had to stay in New York for a meeting." Kandace nudged Richmond in the side.

"I'm not a bodyguard," he quipped. "Solomon knows that you can't wait to get back to him."

Kandace blushed. "True. So, Alicia, why are you hiding out at the library?"

"Just tired of the same questions. Richmond, what kind of business venture are you working on out here? I'm actually in the process of moving back to Atlanta."

"Laying the ground work for some new hotels. I hear Atlanta is the place to be."

She nodded. "I can't wait to make it home again. I've been hanging out in Old Fourth Ward and I think I'm in love."

Kandace folded her arms across her chest. "Your girl Jade is not happy about that. She even tried to enlist me in helping her talk you into staying in Charlotte." Shaking her head, she added, "I'm staying out of it. But, Richmond, if you're looking for someone to help you with marketing, you're looking at a genius right here."

Alicia stood up and smiled. Moving to Atlanta meant that she would be starting over. She'd been laying the foundation for her marketing firm by visiting the city and reconnecting with old friends who were in powerful positions. Atlanta had changed a lot since Alicia had moved to Charlotte to start Hometown Delights with her friends. Neighborhoods had been gentrified and new businesses had popped up all over the place.

A few of Alicia's college friends were launching businesses or were looking to expand what they had going on. She'd made some important contacts already and couldn't wait to hit the ground running. She'd even signed two small clients and would be meeting with them next week.

"She'll get over it. What time is the awards ceremony? I can't believe we're getting honored after all the hell we went through in school for being forward-thinking women," Alicia said.

"Maybe they had no idea that you ladies would grow up to be this fine and successful," Richmond said. Alicia felt her cheeks heat up as Richmond looked at her and winked.

Weird, so weird, she thought as she turned her head. *Isn't he married?*

"Want to head to the Busy Bee Café?" Kandace asked. "Richmond needs to experience some real soul food. Especially if he's going to be meeting with folks around here about those hotels and doesn't know the difference between collard greens and kale."

"Oh yeah. Where's Jade and Serena?" Alicia tore her eyes away from Richmond, deciding that he was being extra flirty because his wife wasn't around or maybe he'd been drinking.

"They headed to Miss Maryann's bakery." Kandace winked at her. "You know how Jade is about that woman's icing."

Alicia shook her head, thinking that Jade was just going to get icing to use with her husband later. She was sure that Maryann, Jade's mother-in-law, had no idea that Jade and her husband, James, used that icing on each other and not cinnamon buns. "All right, let's go." When Richmond extended his hand to Alicia, she took it without a second thought. She didn't miss the side eye that Kandace shot her way.

"We'd better get a move on if we want to get a seat this century," Kandace said.

Alicia dropped Richmond's hand and smiled. "This place is small, but the food is amazing."

"That means a lot coming from you guys, since you have your own restaurant."

Kandace laughed. "This place is historic to us and was the reason—"

"One of the reasons," Alicia interjected.

"That we started our restaurant."

"What were the other reasons that you guys went into the restaurant business?" Richmond asked, then focused on Alicia. "Kandace said you have a background in marketing, right?"

Alicia nodded. "I handle the marketing for the restaurant and I'm starting my own firm here in Atlanta."

"And Alicia would definitely be a great asset for the boutique hotels project," Kandace said. "Everybody in the Southeast will be making reservations."

"I am that good," Alicia quipped.

"So that's why you ladies started your restaurant, just because you were good at it?" Richmond asked.

Kandace and Alicia exchanged a knowing look. "Revenge," Alicia replied. "Jade had been involved with a loser who tried to open a restaurant in Charlotte, and we bought the spot from underneath him."

Richmond looked toward Kandace, who nodded in confirmation. "We're not that way anymore, but people know better than to cross us."

"I hope Solomon knows that too," Richmond quipped.

"Pretty sure he figured that out when she stabbed that crazy . . ." Alicia glanced at Kandace, then let her statement die. Though years had passed since the death of Carmen De La Croix at the restaurant, Kandace was still uncomfortable talking about it. The woman had been obsessed with Solomon and followed the couple to Charlotte. She'd attacked Solomon with a meat cleaver and Kandace saved their lives when she'd stabbed Carmen in the chest.

That had been one of the morbid headlines that made their restaurant, Hometown Delights, one of Charlotte's most popular dining destinations. Then, there was the time when disgraced movie director Emerson Bradford tried to kill Serena in the restaurant.

The notoriety had died down since then and the restaurant was finally known for its award-winning menu and great service.

Alicia worked hard behind the scenes to make that happen. The community involvement and donations the restaurant made to major events changed the narrative about the place and turned it into one of Charlotte's premier eateries. She wasn't too egotistical to realize that part of the successful restaurant had to do with Jade's relationship with James Goings, the brother of Carolina Panthers wide receiver Mo Goings.

Then there was Marie Charles, the former socialite who married chef Devon Harris. Marie's influence also helped the restaurant because she mentioned it in her popular Mocha Girl in Paris blog all the time.

Alicia wanted a challenge and Atlanta was it. Things had changed since Alicia and her girls ran their business in Georgia. Many of the power players they'd known were gone and the landscape had changed a lot. Alicia knew things were going to be different, but at least she didn't have to worry about blind dates every week.

She glanced over at Richmond and wondered if Kandace would try to do that setup trick that their other friends were becoming famous for. Though, she'd be interested in bouncing some business ideas off him, maybe even help Richmond get his footing in Atlanta. There was no way she was attracted to this married man. But there was something under the surface that had piqued her interest.

Richmond noticed Alicia's glances as they walked to the café. Maybe he was just imagining things because he was looking at the ebony enchantress with new eyes. When he was married, he'd ignored Kandace and her friends. But over the years, his admiration for Kandace and her crew grew when he saw how they handled their business and turned every controversy at their restaurant into gold.

He could've used some of that magic after the scandals that happened in his life over the last few years.

When they arrived at the café, the line was wrapped around the block and the smell of fried chicken perfumed the air.

"If the food tastes as great as it smells out here, then I'm going to love it," Richmond said.

"Oh, you're going to love it," Alicia said, then nudged Kandace. "Remember how many times we ended up here, eating away our blues?"

"That was you and Jade. I just came for the

biscuits. Remember, I was in love." Kandace twirled around. "Foolish, but in love. And Devon could cook anything I wanted."

Richmond laughed, wondering what fool would've broken Alicia's heart. He could only imagine what a knockout she was in college, because like fine wine, she'd gotten better with time. Her body reminded him of the classic Coca-Cola bottle—curves for days. And she was smart. That didn't happen overnight. Remembering the vapid women he'd attended NYU with, Richmond wondered what it would've been like to be around women who were focused like Alicia and her friends.

At the awards luncheon, he'd been impressed when he heard about their investment group and the after-hours café they'd opened during their freshman year. Of course, it had been an illegal setup, but the school administration had been so dazzled by their business plan that they had given the group a permit to run the café for a year.

"Are we going to wait in this wave of humanity?" Richmond asked as he glanced at the line.

"It's worth it, Mr. No Patience," Kandace said. "This food will melt in your mouth. You'll be here every day, once you move to Atlanta."

Alicia turned to Richmond. "You're moving to Atlanta?"

He nodded. "We're looking at expanding the Crawford Hotels franchise further south. I'm going to be heading the project. Can't do that without being a part of the city."

Alicia rubbed her throat. "Atlanta can be hard for a newcomer. Or someone who's been away for a while."

"I've been in tougher situations," he said as the line inched forward. "As they say, if you can make it New York, you can make it anywhere."

"Good luck with that," she said with a smile.

"When you have talent, you don't need luck. I've researched this city and I'm ready to take it by storm. And I'm going to have a great team to help me out."

Alicia smiled brightly at him. "That confidence is awesome. You're going to need it."

"Maybe you can be a part of my team." He winked at her and Alicia's knees went weak.

Kandace rolled her eyes. "It looks as if there is an open table. Praise the Lord. Let's move, and quickly."

Following her lead, Richmond and Alicia got to the table before a couple who were moving a lot slower.

"Savage," Alicia said as they sat down. "You know those two were waiting for this table."

"If you're slow, you blow," Kandace said. "Besides, when is the next time we will be together here?"

Richmond glanced at the couple as they shot them an evil look. Turning away, he laughed. "Real estate in this place comes at a premium, huh?"

Kandace nodded as Alicia picked up a menu.

"How are things in New York?" Alicia asked as she glanced at Richmond over the greasy menu.

Snorting, he shrugged. "So great that I'm moving to Atlanta. You'd think our family was the Kardashians or something."

"Tell me about it," Kandace muttered. "Kiana shouldn't know what the paparazzi are, but she does. Thank God her dad taught me creative ways to hide her face."

"That's why you should let her take a giraffe every time you go out."

Alicia raised her right eyebrow. "A giraffe?"

Kandace shook her head. "This man is obsessed with stuffed giraffes and has turned Kiana's room into an African safari. And she loves it."

"Guessing that you don't," Alicia said.

"Overkill." Kandace pulled out her phone and showed it to Alicia. "See what I mean?"

"Come on," Richmond said. "Those stuffed animals are beautiful. Even Solomon agrees with me."

Alicia shrugged because she did think the room looked amazing. And it wasn't the typical princess design that most little girls had.

"Whatever. I'm ready to toss all of those damned things, but she's going make her own choice soon enough. I can't wait until she gets into Barbie dolls."

"I'm hoping that never happens," Alicia said. "Those dolls are self-esteem killers."

Kandace waved her hand at her friend. "Says a woman who looks like a damned doll."

Richmond definitely agreed that Alicia looked like a doll, only with more realistic curves. And those thighs. Richmond had always been a leg man, and he couldn't help but wonder what they would feel like wrapped around his waist.

Their eyes met and she smiled, then pulled her skirt down over her thick thighs. "I know what I want," Richmond said as he looked down at the menu. But what he wanted was not on that greasy paper.

Alicia turned away from Richmond. Was he really staring at her legs like he wanted to dive between them? And why was she shivering with want? Had it been that long since a man showed her attention, that she found herself wanting Richmond Crawford? Now, she couldn't deny that he was looking a lot different than he did when she'd met him years ago. He was chiseled, his face slimmer, and those eyes. Hypnotic brown orbs that seemed to penetrate her soul.

She pulled a napkin from the dispenser and dabbed her top lip. "It's a little warm in here," Alicia said as she looked toward the counter. "We'd better order and get out of here before someone snatches this table from us."

It wasn't long before the trio was chowing

down on crisp fried chicken, fresh cabbage, and cornbread.

After finishing his plate and Kandace's cornbread, Richmond patted his stomach. "I'm going to have to spend about three hours in the gym tonight to work this off. Maybe if my ex could cook like this, I wouldn't be divorced now."

Alicia inhaled sharply as she thought about sweat dripping down his chest. Did he wear compression pants or gray sweatpants? And he said he was divorced. Was the universe giving her a green light?

What in the hell is wrong with me? Alicia turned away from Richmond and rose to her feet. "We'd better give up this table before we get thrown out."

"Wouldn't be the first time," Kandace muttered as she and Richmond stood up.

"Don't tell me you ladies were rowdy college students," he said with a smirk.

My God, this man has dimples. Why have I never noticed this before? Oh, he never smiled before. Who knew Richmond Crawford was human? Alicia thought as they headed for the exit and Kandace recounted the time that Serena had cursed out a waiter at the café because he'd had the nerve to ask her for her phone number.

"And Alicia didn't help the matter," Kandace said, breaking into her friend's thoughts. "She tried to help Serena assault the man with chicken bones. We were so young and silly."

"That's not what happened!"

"Don't try to rewrite history now."

"So, you're forgetting that you were tossing cornbread?"

Richmond laughed. "Is that why you didn't have a problem with me eating yours today?"

Kandace shrugged. "All right, whatever. You messed with one of us, you messed with all of us." Then she looked from Richmond to Alicia. "And that hasn't changed."

Connect with Us

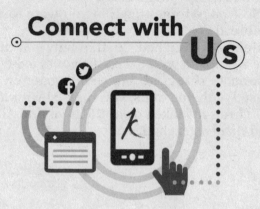

Visit us online at
KensingtonBooks.com
to read more from your favorite authors, see books
by series, view reading group guides, and more.

for sneak peeks, chances to win books and prize packs,
and to share your thoughts with other readers.

facebook.com/kensingtonpublishing
twitter.com/kensingtonbooks

Tell us what you think!

To share your thoughts, submit a review,
or sign up for our eNewsletters, please visit:
KensingtonBooks.com/TellUs.